THE UNREDEEMED

BY

LUKE WALKER

A HellBound Books LLC Publication

Also by Luke Walker –

Dead Sun (paperback and ebook fantasy)

Hometown (paperback and ebook horror)

Die Laughing (paperback and ebook short story collection)

Creepy Campfire Quarterly 4 contains short story *All The Time In The World.*

9Tales At The World's End contains short story *Rapture*

Wicked Words Quarterly 2 contains short story *6/13.*

Coming Soon:

2018/19: Novels *–The Dead Room. Ascent. The Day Of The New Gods.* Novella*: The Mirror Of The Nameless.*

Acknowledgements:

Thank you to James and the rest of the HellBound team for their work, advice, passion and expertise. Ditto to anybody who's read and reviewed my books. Once again (for her critiques as well as her unwavering support), thank you to my wife Rebecca. Lastly, cheers to the bad guys.

Dedication:

This is for the monsters...

The Unredeemed

Luke Walker

THE UNREDEEMED

8

Chapter One

I could say this began back in the old days when I committed my first murder. I could say it began more than fifty years ago when I started spending my time in the park close to Azalea Drive. I could even say it began when I died. But I think saying any of that would be a lie.

This began when I met Hayley.

The woman entered the park at half past five that evening, exactly as I'd known she would. For the last three days, she'd approached from the entrance on Bedford Avenue at around the same time and jogged through the green in four complete circuits. Dennis and I watched her from a wide cluster of oak trees in the centre, sitting up there on the high branches to study her speed, her grace. She was no older than thirty, tall, thin and had the look of a woman who didn't take much pleasure in exercise. She wore those dangling wires in her ears, the ones that connect to a device playing music. After watching her complete her jog that first night, I'd wondered about speaking through the wires in her ears, whispering right into her head.

That wasn't my style, though. I'm not a fan of modern technology. Instead, the situation called for something a little more old-fashioned.

On the third night, a Wednesday, Dennis and I watched and waited until she drew closer before asking Dennis to keep an eye out. While he wasn't particularly happy with my plan (a cautious fellow, Dennis), he agreed to keep watch.

The woman passed our trees on her second circuit and I swooped down, letting her see me from the corner of her eye.

She turned but all she made out was her long shadow, trailing off into the bushes and gravel that formed a curving trail around the pathways. There was no reason she should think anyone was in those bushes; if someone had been behind her, they couldn't possibly have made it out of sight so quickly. She jogged on; I followed, keeping to the spiky leaves, slipping through them and ignoring their stupid mutterings that I should leave, that I wasn't welcome there. What little intelligence living in the greenery and trees had never cared for me, and had spent much of the previous fifty plus years moaning on the wind for me to leave.

The woman and I went around the park for another moment, passing a group of teenage boys who shouted unpleasant comments to the woman, then level with a sleeping man who gripped a bottle of cider while spittle soaked into his matted beard, before we hit an empty section of path. It was perfect.

I shot from the bushes, streaked behind her and crashed into half a dozen weeping willows directly level with her.

She heard nothing, but did see the tremors in the long branches several feet above, despite the lack of wind. She came to a jerking halt, panting hard and staring at the nearest tree. By this time, I'd moved to float right behind her. Her thoughts sped in a blur of images: a bird hitting the tree trunk, a falling branch, conkers (which made no sense since it was late May and the willows were obviously the wrong type of tree), or an animal in the bushes.

For a second, her mind froze. I leaned in closer and caught a thought that wasn't much more than a flashing image.

Snake.

She wiped her mouth while perspiration on her forehead and neck cooled rapidly and her thinking kicked back into life. Snakes. Stupid idea. No snakes in the park. Even if there were, they'd be grass snakes. Small. Frightened of human noise. Stupid idea.

Interesting, I mused, although it wasn't with much surprise. Homing in on someone's weak spot has always been a strength of mine.

The woman took a final look in all directions and resumed jogging. Dennis had followed and waved at me from the willows, his little face pinched and strained.

Are we alone? I called to him and he nodded, still clearly not happy with my minor haunting. To be honest, I knew it was risky. I hadn't remained on Earth for so long by causing trouble or giving myself away, but sometimes, old habits do indeed die hard.

I waved back to Dennis and followed the woman. She'd barely covered any distance before I brushed against her shin.

She let out a frightened shout and fell, tripping over her own feet. Hitting the ground hard, she rolled to the earthy flowerbeds and held her knees, panting and struggling not to weep. Blood ran in thin streams from cuts on both her knees, and her mouth trembled more in shock than pain. Her eyes rested on the spot I occupied on the other side of the path; she squinted and in the shadows cast by the trees and bushes, she saw the suggestion of my shape. Despite it being only for a moment, it was long enough. She gave a tiny squeak and one hand blocked her mouth as if wanting to keep any noise inside.

I remained still, letting my energy return. Gliding and floating took a fair bit of effort. Walking was easier but not quite as effective when it came to this sort of thing.

Enjoying yourself? Dennis asked and while the woman couldn't hear his exact words, she caught something in the breeze, something she instinctively recognised as unpleasant – like a bad smell from miles away, blown in by a gust of wind. Still, her eyes didn't move from the area I filled. She was sure something was there, sure of it but unable to see it.

As always, I replied and Dennis's worry travelled through the trees.

Don't get carried away, he warned.

The woman stood, still watching for me. Wincing she took her hand from her wounded knee; dirt and earth spread over the grazes, turning the white of her skin into a grubby red. She glanced down the pathway to the brighter area not overhung by the old branches. Her feelings were clear: she didn't want to be here. Not right here on this section of path, but in the park at all. She wanted to be at home with the television on loud and the curtains closed against the approaching night.

"Snakes," I said to her.

She froze. Her eyes were stuck to the flowerbeds opposite. I flapped at the greenery; it shook slightly, creating a whisper in the stillness.

"Snakes."

She couldn't hear my word as Dennis would have and that didn't make a bit of difference. She sensed it and there may even have been a bit of her mind, some part she no longer needed to use, that knew what had spoken to her.

The breeze freshened abruptly which was superb timing for me. The fine hairs on her forearms rose; she hugged her arms across her breasts and limped a few steps away. As soon as her eyes were off me, I breathed to her ears.

Snakes.

Her focus flew back to the bushes across the path. She saw them shake, and saw the first snake slither from the earth. It didn't matter that there was nothing there. She saw it.

The snake moved faster than it should have. Within a few seconds, it had cleared the bushes and reached the path. It halted; its tongue flicked out, tasting her scent, tasting sweat and blood.

The woman couldn't move. Her fear was here, just a few steps from her frozen feet: a snake, dark-green, thin, all scales and lifeless eyes. It gazed at her and tasted the air again. She heard the hiss of its tongue and let out a noise like a hurt kitten.

At the flowerbed, two more snakes appeared. One was as black as the mud below it; the other an ugly yellow. They slid across the path and stopped beside their brother. Each one gazed at the woman and each one tasted the scent of her blood.

At that point, she could have run faster than she ever had before, but more rustling whispered in the bushes and she saw four, five, six more snakes appear. Two slid to the middle of the path at her right; two went to her left and the last two joined the three directly in front.

She was trapped.

Benjamin, Dennis said. *You've got a man walking his dog coming your way. Two minutes, tops.*

Thank you, Dennis.

The approaching dog walker was an inconvenience but inevitable. The park was a popular area and I'd been lucky to have so long alone with the woman. Time for the final move.

Her eyes were still stuck to the path and the snakes which weren't there. I breathed to her and she saw one raise its head to stare at her with its ghastly eyes. Its tail shook and she let out the same hurt kitten noise, understanding.

It was going to jump to her, going to jump at her face.

I readied my energies to make the woman see what I wanted to and sunlight fell, reflected sunlight, bouncing through the leaves beside me, come from Park Road.

My attention flicked that way, shooting through the green, leaping over the railings, hitting the pavement as the car drove by.

A woman, a man, a teenage girl and beside her, a boy no older than a year.

Confusion and an odd panic spun through my head, a dizzying haze knocking my concentration into nothing as if I stood atop one of the giant buildings in London or New York and the level ground was hundreds of feet below. My vision took a lazy tumble, sending the sky into the parkland floor for a moment, and making the evening light as grey as my hair instead of a healthy shine. Sound wavered; my head and ears could have been under water – all a muffle, all slowed down to spread its details to the muddle of my thinking. The car, clean and shining and the drawn-out growl of its engine an animal's song; the man driving it a handsome fellow with only a few lines beside his eyes, despite being in his forties, while his wife was trim and healthy. The girl in the back, in the few months between child and adult, curious about their journey and destination, tempering that wonder with a youth's natural suspicion. And the babe asleep, his immediate needs taken care of while any future demands didn't exist because there was no future. There was *now* for him and it was all he understood or needed.

The car turned into Prince's Gardens which ran alongside the park. The sunlight bounced through the trees and bushes, shooting straight towards me as if eager to do so, as if furious and shouting to get my attention, and I slammed back to myself with sight and sound clicking into their rightful places.

The woman I'd terrified with her snakes broke into a sprint. Her survival instincts had leaped into life the moment my concentration snapped. Logic and rationality ordered her legs and feet to move. She ran to her right, shaking mouth wide open, and jumped. Momentarily, I saw through her eyes: the snakes vanished. There one second, nothing the next. She sprinted from me and the hallucination I'd put into her head and her eyes.

I let her go, no longer at all concerned about the small entertainment provided by the jogging woman.

Something much more interesting was close by.

Chapter Two

Dennis joined me on the long path where I stood motionless after the few minutes with the woman. He approached hesitantly, as always checking every direction for trouble.

"Benjamin? What happened?"

Gathering myself as well I could (the impact from the sense of dislocation a moment before had not yet fully faded), I faced him and offered a reassuring smile.

"I'm not sure. Something with. . .potential, Dennis. Potential."

"What?"

Now he was *really* worried. He knew what *potential* meant to me. While we'd kept our hauntings low key for a few hundred years, I have to admit to occasionally wanting more. There isn't a great deal of entertainment to be found when you're dead, after all. The living, as much of a waste of time as they can be, were the closest I had to finding any joy in my death. And haunting them to various levels was the nearest I could get to carrying on my life's work. Not that I could kill them, of course. Doing so would be akin to bellowing into the wind where I was and *who* I was. Do that and I'd be dragged down to Hell within moments. Dennis was well aware of our situation and had often acted as my caution. That day was no exception.

"This is not a good idea, Benjamin. Staying here *is*. You may not want to admit that, but you know it's true. You've always known it. That's why we're here, after all."

He attempted a winning smile. Instead, it just made him look slightly untrustworthy. I took a moment to appear to be considering his words while I listened to the evening approach the park and the stream of traffic heading along Thorpe Road a quarter of a mile away. Early summer warmth caressed the green on every side; the voices and shouts from the teenage boys were a grating noise as they crossed the grass to the exit. And somewhere close by, potential waited for me.

"Dennis." My pause was deliberate. He needed to believe I was debating my words. "You can trust me. This is simply to look. There'll be no trouble. We're just looking."

He gazed at me, eyes resigned. "If you say so, Benjamin."

"Wonderful."

We crossed the road, followed it for a few moments and reached the turning for Azalea Drive. The houses there were all expensive buildings, four bedrooms, at least one garage on each along with well-tended gardens. The road was very much a family area as were most of the streets around there. Perhaps that's why I liked it so. And perhaps that was the attraction for the couple in the car.

That same car was about halfway down the Drive, parked outside a house with a *For Sale* sign attached to its hedges. The house was instantly familiar. Number twenty. It had been on the market for a few months; an elderly lady lived there alone. Her husband had died the year before, her children had long since left to begin their own lives and their own families, and there was no reason for her to live in such a large family home.

We crossed the road, side by side, and halted close to number twenty. The husband and wife were on the paving slabs set out over the front lawn, studying the home while the elderly lady stood a respectful distance away. They were talking about the area, about schools and such. At this, the daughter walked from the front door, holding her baby brother. He was asleep, head comfortable against his sister's shoulder. Dennis let me study her in silence, for which I was grateful.

There was a familiarity about the girl, something vague. I'd never seen her or her parents before, and yet, the line of her jaw and the slight curl of her hair weren't unknown to me. For a moment, I flashed back to another teenage girl, one who I'd haunted during the autumn of 1971. She'd been a dull thing, but I hadn't been able to leave her alone. Haunting her was a drug for some reason, and I raged at myself for bothering with her. For weeks, I'd watched the child fill her diary with scribblings about a boy who didn't deserve such attention and had no idea the girl thought of him as she did. Finally tiring of her childish prattling and my own need to be in her life, I'd led her one day after school to a park where I knew the boy would be with another girl. She'd seen the two of them together and run home to her tears and her diary. Three weeks later, I'd learned her father was sleeping with his secretary (such a tired cliché even back in those days). So once again, I led her to a scene she didn't want to witness, a shared moment between her father and the other woman on a bench in a park not unlike the one Dennis and I had left moments before. Two days after that little scene, she'd jumped from a bridge to railway lines and I was glad to be done with her. A weak, boring thing she'd been. This girl, however, this child with her brother was different. There was strength in her face. She was no older than fifteen and yet, there was something solid in her, something adult. I liked her immediately.

"Hayley," the father said and waved at his daughter. She joined them on the grass; the mother took the baby, and the owner led them inside. Dennis and I exchanged a look and followed without a word.

Once inside, the woman took the family to the spacious kitchen and the dazzling sunlight pouring through a wide window to make the surfaces and appliances sparkle. She set about making coffee while they talked. The family lived several miles away in a house they'd inherited from his parents and were searching for a larger home in which to settle, somewhere with decent schools and places for the baby to one day play when he was few years older. A home of their own rather than one filled with decades old memories. I tuned them out and beckoned Dennis to follow me when the girl headed to the stairs.

We remained behind her; she entered the bedroom that might be hers and gazed at it with a teenager's critical eye, attempting to see it full of her possessions and not those belonging to an old woman. Her bed there beside the radiator with her computer no doubt resting on the covers, a wall mirror mounted over here, the wardrobe door open wide and her clothes fully visible, and shelves crammed with her possessions.

The girl smiled at the images and right then, she became Hayley to me instead of just being *the girl.*

The adults ascended the stairs and stood in the hallway, talking. Hayley's father crossed to the bedroom door and poked his head in while his wife and the owner entered another room.

"How's it look?" he asked.

Hayley shrugged but couldn't hide her smile

"Yeah, I thought you'd like it. Come on. There's more to see," the father said.

She stepped towards him and I moved at the same time.

I streaked to right beside the man, slid a formless arm around his head and whispered. My action took less than a second but that was long enough – his gaze dropped to his daughter's chest, to the outline of her small breasts.

At once, his face flamed, he turned fast and strode towards the sound of his wife's voice coming from the main bedroom. Hayley watched him go, frowning in a pretty way. After a moment, she followed.

"That probably wasn't a good plan," Dennis muttered. "You know we have to stay quiet. Why did you do it?"

"No idea, to be honest." I smiled. "But I never argue with my instincts. You know that, Dennis."

He stared at me. For the first time in all the long years we'd known one another, a small flame of anger burned in his eyes.

"No trouble, Benjamin? Just looking?"

"Trust me." I pointed to the door. "After you."

Chapter Three

The family viewed the house for another half an hour. Sunset was still some way off by then, although the shadows were lengthening and the sky was edging towards a fantastic shade of red.

We'd learned their names in that half an hour. Mark, Tracy and baby Chris. And Hayley, of course. Hayley, fifteen years old and full of more potential than anyone I'd met in years – even if I couldn't say exactly why.

They grouped in the hallway close to the front door, the owner still wittering on about her years in the house and her dead husband while Hayley shuffled on the spot and Chris let out tired moans. Eventually, the woman ran out of words and Mark took the opportunity to open the door. The family exited with promises to be in touch; Dennis and I watched them from the front garden, and when Tracy drove them towards Prince's Gardens, we gave them a wave they of course couldn't see.

Behind us, the elderly lady closed the door and Dennis studied me.

"You think they're going to buy, don't you?"

"No, Dennis." I smiled, truly happy. "I *know* they will."

He snorted, not amused. "I've always admired your confidence, Benjamin."

We drifted to the pavement and as soon as we left the grass, a change took hold of the evening light. The approaching red of sunset shifted to an unpleasant creamy shade, the colour of old bruises.

Both of us froze, and then gazed at the sky. Clouds had come from nowhere, although some sunlight still shone above, falling in thin streaks. Something in the clouds wasn't right; the yellow light all around was the colour of sickness and fevers.

I heard—or thought I heard—a name. If it was there, it whispered in the low mutter of traffic on Prince's Gardens and in the distant roar of a lawnmower. A word. A name.

My name.

"Everything all right?" Dennis asked.

"Yes."

My reply was immediate, without any internal denial. The ugly yellow faded, normality returned. Sunset was not far away, night would be right behind it.

For the first time in centuries, the idea of night was uncomfortable. I wanted to be back in the trees long before dark descended.

Dennis turned in a full circle to study our surroundings. Without making a move, I also appraised them. The pavement, houses and pleasant gardens were all utterly normal. Even so, disquiet pricked me. I hadn't cared for the bruised light or for the suggestion of my name whispered from miles away. The only ones who could possibly know where Dennis and I spent our time were dead. What's more, they were my allies. The ones I needed to worry about – one – were far below.

My unease faded. I gave the street a final once over. Then, content all was well, I departed from the house and Dennis followed, two ghosts floating over the road while the living gave us no thought.

23

Chapter Four

Food isn't necessary when you're dead, of course. Neither is sleep when it comes to recharging or resting, but we still do it. Call it an old habit.

Dennis and I had our own trees, our places where we slept. Much like the bushes below, the dim intelligence in the wood had long since attempted to get us to leave the park. As much as it hated our stain on its bark and wood, there was nothing to be done to make us leave.

We returned to the park that night as we always did and hid in the high branches. At some point, I slept and woke to dawn light and Dennis' screams.

He was in an oak a short way from my own. I flew to him, instantly awake and checking the area for threat. There was nothing but the dawn light growing to real morning and the air full of Dennis' terror.

He lay on a thick branch, fingers like claws, mouth wide open and all his noise battering at the morning peace. I shook him and he woke. Thankfully, his wailing ceased and he gazed at me with naked fear.

"Benjamin?" he whispered.

"Yes. Now, what the hell are you making all this noise for?" I managed a smile. "Nightmares, Dennis?"

He bolted upright, shivering.

"Teeth," he said.

"Teeth?"

For the first time in long centuries, I felt fear and it made no difference that it possessed gentle fingers instead of a battering fist. Fear was almost an alien concept after so long. I shook it off at once, convinced there was no possible way my trepidation could be justified. Dennis was two hundred years dead, all that time spent free from Hell because he knew how to hide. I was double his two centuries, and while I also knew how to hide, I more importantly knew how to make a deal. There was no need for any other party to renege on their side of a deal. And no need for fear.

Dennis stared at me. "I saw teeth. They were coming for me, coming through the trees."

He jumped to his feet and whirled, trying to stare in all directions. Around us, leaves waved a little and the park was as it had been for years. It was our place, our home.

"There's nothing here, Dennis. Now tell me what's going on."

He settled as much as he could although his arms still trembled and his eyes wouldn't rest on any one object for more than a moment.

"I don't know what it was," he said, eventually. "Just teeth. Dozens in one mouth, coming to tear me apart." He was quiet, frowning. "The light changed, too. It was daylight but wrong, different." He gazed to the north, towards the heart of the city. "It was like yesterday. Remember the light?"

I remembered. The change in the daylight, the clouds come from nowhere and the suggestion of my name whispered as if from somewhere far away.

"Something's wrong," Dennis said. "And it's here, right here."

I snorted, attempting to diffuse his nerves with scorn. "Where? There isn't a living soul anywhere near us." I gestured to the empty path and wide spaces of grass all around us. The park was free from dog walkers or joggers; the morning lived almost silently. All we had for life were a few birds overhead. "See? No people and no ghosts for miles."

"It's not people." He met my gaze fully. "And I don't think it's ghosts, exactly. There's something off. We should go."

"To where?"

He didn't hesitate at all in his reply. "Thistlemoor Wood."

Unable to stay silent, I laughed. "We haven't been there in years, Dennis. Decades. The last thing I'm going to do when we aren't in any danger is go to Thistlemoor."

"I think we *are* in danger."

As always, I took control of the situation. "You think what you want, Dennis. Just bear in mind one nightmare isn't reason to panic. And it's definitely no reason to run."

I dropped to the grass below and inhaled deeply as if I could take refreshing breaths of the morning. So what if it had been best part of four hundred years since I'd been able to do so?

A new morning had come and Dalry was as it always was.

Mine.

Chapter Five

I arrived at the house an hour before the removal men left, and I came alone. While weeks had passed since his vision of teeth, Dennis had been unable to let go of his odd panic and insistence we flee to Thistlemoor, the ancient woodland several miles away. That morning, we'd had a conversation while still in the park, our words edging ever closer to a full argument as time passed. Something was wrong, he said and while he admitted to being unable to name the cause of his fear, it changed little for him. There was a danger around the family. Best if we let them alone, he said. Best we stay in the park or simply run for shelter in the woods. I was having none of that and told him to wait for me in the trees while I got to know the adults and the girl. Not appearing at all happy with this, Dennis faded into the bushes and greenery, his whisper to me fading at the same time: *be careful, Benjamin.*

That was fine for Dennis. *Careful* mattered to me as much as to my companion, but so did the chance of being with new life. That chance mattered more than anything, it seemed.

I floated throughout the house, tasting each room and letting the bricks get a feel of me as the trees in the park had for all those years. The dumb stone of the building possessed less intelligence than the trees, but even so, it knew enough to know it didn't want me there. With the creaks of its floorboards, the house muttered its displeasure. With the odd draught, it whispered for me to leave. I ignored it all, of course, and explored each room and the rear garden at my leisure.

Lunch and the afternoon came and went. There was no urge to return to the park and Dennis. Let him have his shelter. Let him hide in the trees. I was with a new family, a new home. For the first time in years, I wanted to indulge myself. Petty hauntings in the park were all well and good, but there was nothing like this. Nothing like *flesh* ready for me. There was life here and I would be a part of it, no matter what Dennis thought, and no matter what scared him.

Shortly after six, Mark and Tracy were in the kitchen, unpacking with next to no enthusiasm. Mark placed a final box on the side and turned on the kettle.

"Let's leave it for tonight," he said. Tracy looked ready to protest but only on the surface. While she was the same pretty woman I'd first seen in the car and could have passed for ten years younger, the stress of the move had put bags below her eyes and turned her pale with tiredness.

"Take your pick," Mark said and pulled two menus from his back pocket. "Chinese or Indian?"

They bought a Chinese takeaway for dinner; Mark put the baby in his cot in the main bedroom, squeezing past boxes to do so, and they sat in their living room with the television on. Unsorted boxes, a sofa and an armchair placed at awkward angles to each other filled the room. Earlier, Mark said they'd taken care of the essentials and they could start work on sorting everything properly in the morning.

I joined the family for an hour, making no movement. If any of them had an idea they weren't alone, it lay buried far below their aching limbs and strained muscles from days of lumbering with their packed possessions.

They only talked a little which was obviously down to their long day. None of them seemed to be paying much attention to the film on the television. Tracy was nodding off. Mark hadn't noticed and Hayley was playing with her phone, presumably in conversation with one of her friends. Shortly after nine, Tracy's eyes closed and didn't open. I drifted across the room, brought my strength together and turned the television off. Hayley jumped as if the volume had suddenly risen and not vanished.

"Did you do that?" Mark asked.

"I haven't got the remote," Hayley replied.

Mark found it beside his feet, almost buried under a small box. He turned the television back on and rested against his sleeping wife. A few moments passed, father and daughter got comfortable. The lights were off as twilight hadn't yet passed. Even so, the containers on the kitchen floor and paper plates dirty with the remnants of the family's dinner were perfectly visible to me.

My next action took a great deal more energy than turning off the television which was fine. There'd been plenty of time in my death to practice.

The plates fell to the floor, not making the satisfying crash they would have if they'd been dinner plates. The ruckus was enough to carry to the living room, though. Tracy mumbled, asking what was going on. The heavy weight of sleep almost buried her words.

After a moment, Mark entered the kitchen, hand flapping at the light switch and the other holding his head.

"The plates fell off the side," he called. And then in a mutter, "Although I have no idea how."

He checked the kitchen window, found it closed, and cleaned the mess on the floor. I stood away from him, content for the moment. My actions may have been small but they were enough to plant suggestions in their minds. Even if they didn't yet feel those suggestions, they were still aware of the idea of something not quite right in their new home.

I let them get ready for bed and did nothing to disturb their peace. Half an hour after the lights went off upstairs, I left the kitchen and went to Mark and Tracy's bedroom. They were deeply asleep as was the baby. Mark slept with one arm around his wife, the bedcovers around his waist. His ear was exposed.

The situation was ideal. I leaned towards the man of the house and whispered in his ear.

His dreams came.

Bad dreams.

Chapter Six

Dennis had gone.

I stood before our trees, gazing at the glorious spread of leaves and buds and intertwining branches, then turned to study the deserted park while the rustling on all sides whispered and hissed.

"Dennis."

Nothing replied, not even the breeze which was much fresher than usual.

He'd left me no sign, nothing to say where he'd gone. I knew, though. He'd gone to Thistlemoor Wood as he'd said we should. He'd gone to one of the few refuges he could for ghosts such as he and I. While I stood beside our trees, he was in a woodland free from people, surrounded by old branches and those who'd been dead for years, decades, centuries.

"What was it, Dennis? What did we see?"

Despite believing the moment after our first visit to the house hadn't meant much, sticking to that idea just then was harder. Certainly, whatever caused the clouds and change in sunlight had been enough to send Dennis from me for the first time.

I played back those moments. The diseased light shone again in my head, the clouds massed, a stain coloured the June evening. And my name whispered from far away. My name said in a way nobody had before. A *secret* way.

Movement flickered off to my left. It raced low over the ground and vanished into a wide patch of flowers. Immediately, I followed, shooting to the flowers and dropping to the ground. There was nothing out of the ordinary there, only the flowers and earth. Its rich life and the nutrients in the thick soil didn't care for my presence so close which was of no concern. I crouched and felt for movement in the land. There was nothing. But I'd seen something, though, something shifting at exactly the right time.

That wasn't an accident.

I knew I was correct. Whatever the thing had been, it moved at exactly the right time for me to see it.

"Show yourself or be damned," I shouted. Nothing moved. "Damn you, then. Have the park. Have Dennis' fear. You'll have nothing of mine."

The only life in the park was two drunk men propped up by an elm, their bottles of vodka resting on their legs. Both slept the sleep of the addicted, restless and full of regret and bad dreams. Sadly, I knew that sleep. Four hundred years since my killings; four centuries since my work was interrupted by death, and four centuries of having to be content with meaningless disturbances of anyone who drew too close to the few trees I'd chosen as my home.

Enough was enough. There was no way I could still be on anyone's radar after so much time had passed. Decision made, I allowed a smile.

Work to do. Best get started.

Below, the earth continued with its constant breaths. I left it to its business and went about mine.

Chapter Seven

Number twenty, Azalea Drive became my new home. The family's bedrooms, their shared meals, their bathing: it was all mine as much as it was theirs.

For that first week, I brought small troubles to their house, made life inconvenient in little ways. I did everything from hiding keys to tapping on the bathroom door when one of them was in the shower to jamming the garage door shut. None of these actions required much strength which was half the reason for keeping my meddling small. Affecting the living in physical ways can take a lot of energy. Despite all my practice, working on the living is still often more effective when it's something small.

After two weeks, I made myself known a little more. That day was a Saturday. Mark had gone to get a few things from the local shop, Hayley was still in her room (she was awake. I'd watched her doze in her bed) and Tracy was in the kitchen, brewing fresh coffee. The baby was in his cot and it was to him I decided to begin the introductions.

I stood in the main bedroom and gathered my energy. Despite the fresh sunlight pooling on the carpet in front of the window, the temperature in the room dropped fast. The light dimmed, shadows lived and breathed. From below me, the house argued against my presence; the floorboards, the bricks, the glass in the windows— none of them wanted me there, which of course changed nothing.

I floated past the mirror, casting a thin shade over the glass, and stood beside the baby's cot. He stirred, snorted but didn't wake.

Grinning, I leaned down to the child, my face only a few inches from his. He snorted again and woke.

Such a scream, such power. The child's cries battered at my face; I remained where I was, staring at him, opening my mouth to show sharp teeth and blowing my stink into his mouth. He coughed, got his breath back and screamed again. Tracy's running feet pounded from the kitchen to the hallway and stairs. On the other side of the stairs, Hayley's bedroom door opened and she thudded over the carpet.

I blew the baby a kiss and vanished. Hayley ran into the bedroom and stared where my form had been. She couldn't see me but she felt something. I'm sure of that. Shaking off my image, the girl ran to her brother and pulled him from the cot. He was still screaming and again I thought of his power held inside his breath.

Beside me, Hayley shivered as she registered the cold. She crossed to the window and comforted her brother in the daylight with nonsense. Tracy dashed from the stairs and ran into the room, reaching for her children.

"What happened?" she shouted. "Is he hurt?"

"I don't think so. I heard him crying and ran in here."

Hayley handed the child to her mother who cradled him against her breasts and softly breathed against his cheek until his cries faded to tearful mutters. I stood behind Tracy and resisted the temptation to let the baby and Hayley see me if only for a second. Instinct said the time wasn't right.

"Come on," Tracy said. "He'll be happier downstairs."

"I need to get dressed," Hayley said as if only then realising she was wearing her underwear and a large shirt which hung almost to her knees.

"Breakfast in five minutes," Tracy said as she walked to the stairs.

Hayley followed; she reached her bedroom door and I swooped down the stairs to shove hard against Tracy's back. Hayley turned as her mother yelled, feet catching one another.

"Mum." Hayley was already running down the stairs. Quick, I was impressed to see. Not quick enough, though.

Tracy spun, back to the bottom of the stairs, arms around her son probably tighter than she had held him since his birth.

She dropped down the last five steps and crashed against the wall. Her head thudded on the wall, the baby still wailing.

"Mum!" Hayley screamed again and ran the stairs. I flew upwards before she passed through me and hovered above them.

Tracy attempted to speak and the words emerged too soft to make sense, forcing Hayley to put her ear to her mother's mouth to hear over the baby's racket.

"Take him," Tracy croaked.

Hayley eased the baby from her mother's grip and checked him over. Satisfied he wasn't injured, she quickly took him to the living room and placed him in his playpen before running back to her mother. Tracy attempted to rise but her legs wouldn't work. A thin line of blood ran from a cut in her forehead and her eyes were dazed almost to the point of blindness.

"I'll call an ambulance." Hayley didn't say her next words, they stayed in her heart. She was praying for her father to return from the shop.

For that time, though, there was only her with her terrified brother, her bleeding mother and her own savage terror.

And there was me, of course, me, floating above them and laughing.

Chapter Eight

The meaty roar of a lawnmower, the discordant jangle of an ice cream van, a few children playing in a garden somewhere close by; those sounds were all around with the house at my back and the sun directly overhead.

"Are you there, Dennis?"

He heard my question, there was no doubt of it. No reply came my way and there was need for one, to be honest. Dennis made his choice by leaving for Thistlemoor Wood and I was alone with my haunting.

The thought was depressing, especially given how well things went with my first act. Tracy was home from the hospital, had been so for the last half an hour. She was lucky not to have concussion. What she did have was a steady whine of fear and utter terror at what could have come if she'd been facing front when she fell down the stairs.

The experience was a definite achievement, as were Hayley's unspoken imaginings. She knew something was wrong in her home, but to even think of it in real terms would be ridiculous for her. Less than a hundred years before, people in the family's situation would have been much quicker to name their troubles for what they were. Times change, though.

I shook off my melancholy and returned to the house. Mark and Hayley were in the living room, Hayley watching television while Mark worked on the small computer on his lap. A moment's mental searching told me Tracy was asleep upstairs, Chris dozing in his cot beside the bed. Her sleep was restless, her dreams rich and vivid. Chris, on the other hand, slept the sleep of the blameless. He saw only the rich, warm colours of parental love and heard his name, a meaningless but still comforting word, said over and over again.

"How long are you going to let Mum sleep?" Hayley said.

Mark checked the time. "No more than a couple of hours. She told me to wake her by five but I think she could do with longer than that."

"Dad?"

"Yeah?"

He glanced at his daughter, frozen in the act of typing on the computer. Briefly, I considered directing his vision to her legs, framed by her shorts, but decided against it. I hadn't worked on him in that way since the first day. Knowing the idea was there, though, that was enough. There and festering.

"Do you think this house is okay?"

Hayley said this as quickly as she could which was strangely pleasing. Despite her obvious maturity and strength, she was still a teenage girl, still reliant on her parents to make sense of much of the world.

"Sure. Why?"

"I don't know. It just seems weird. Stuff goes missing, it's cold sometimes for no reason – Mum falls down the stairs."

Mark gave a laugh which was almost convincing. "You make it sound like she does it all the time."

"Well—"

"This place is fine. It's got an atmosphere, that's all. Loads of houses do. We make it our home and it'll be *our* atmosphere, all right?"

"Is that right?" I said and if they heard me, my voice was a tiny burst of static on the television.

Shortly after five, Mark went to the kitchen to make their dinner. Soon after, Hayley walked to the computer her father had left on the sofa and reached for her mobile. Except the phone was not where she'd left it on the little table beside the sofa. I'd moved it earlier. Not far, I should say. My actions that morning had taken a fair bit of effort. I'd only possessed the strength to knock her phone to the floor and nudge it to the shadows beside the computer table.

"Dad, you seen my phone?" she called and Mark appeared at the kitchen door.

"No. Why? Have you lost it?"

"I thought it was here," she said and it took me a moment to understand the panic in her voice. Without her phone, she was cut off from her friends and without her friends, she was alone with the house and the something wrong with it, something unpleasant, something that lurked in the privacy of her dreams.

Her foot nudged the device. She crouched and retrieved it from the floor.

"Must have fallen off," Mark said and returned to his cooking.

Hayley turned her phone the right way around. Behind her, I shifted a fraction and my dim reflection bounced off the screen of her phone.

Hayley whirled, a tiny squeak coming from her mouth. I'd already moved away from her and so all she saw was the wall. She stared at it and its framed photos, trying to look at all of the pictures at once. I floated to her side, unable to hold back my laughter. A moment passed and she decided she'd seen nothing. She returned to her chair and sat. I brushed my fingertips over her bare legs as gently as possible.

By that point, she was tapping on her phone and didn't look from it. Although she did rub at her knees as if something unpleasant—a spiderweb, perhaps—had slid over her skin.

"Hayley," I said.

She tapped on her phone. In the kitchen, Mark prepared chicken for dinner. On the television, a newsreader repeated the day's stories. I extended my fingers to within an inch of Hayley's hair. She tapped on her phone. Deep inside, a murmur breathed to me. A warning.

I listened. The warning flowed in and out as if brought to me on a wave striking a shoreline, a simple command to stop what I was doing. As much as heeding my instincts had served me for such a long time, I wasn't about to let a strange self-doubt stop my work then. However, with some small regret, I withdrew my fingers.

There was work to do and it wasn't with the girl.

It was with the baby upstairs.

Chapter Nine

After the weeks of constant sunshine and contentment, the time came for the final act, the time for the end of my haunting.

Work began first thing that morning. Causing waste in the toilet to remain no matter how many times Mark flushed, rapidly increasing the water temperature in the shower a second before Tracy turned it off, hiding Hayley's underwear—this was all the start of that Sunday. After weeks of not affecting the family at all, sending their confusion and annoyance edging ever closer to panic was most satisfying. None of them had said the word *haunted*, but it was there all the same. As that morning drew towards afternoon, it breathed in their minds and in their hearts stronger than ever before.

After lunch, Mark took the baby outside and gave him to Tracy who was sunbathing. Mother and son cuddled in the garden, wonderful sunshine caressing their bodies while the smells of summer—freshly mowed grass nearby and blooming flowers—spoke of good days. Back inside, Mark went to their bedroom and stripped off his clothes to change into his gardening shorts and a tatty t-shirt. Hayley was in her bedroom. Mark heard her music and with my influence close to him, he pictured his daughter at her desk, books open around her and pen in hand. I whispered to him and he crossed the hallway to stand outside Hayley's door, swaying. He appeared drunk. He was not in the least. My whispers were having the desired effect. He placed a hand on the wall to keep steady, not aware of the sweat dripping from his head, trickling to his neck and staining his t-shirt, or his damp fingertips marking the wall with his prints. The temperature wasn't overly hot in the house which made no difference. Mark sweated like a man ready to collapse.

I readied myself. My next move would take a lot of effort, but I could do it. I'd done it before.

See her, I whispered to Mark and gave him an image of Hayley, Hayley in the bed he and his wife shared, Hayley smiling at him, Hayley ready.

Mark let out a weak groan. His spirit argued with mine. It shrieked horror at what festered in his mind. It made no difference. My will and strength had spent centuries growing and could bury Mark's in a heartbeat.

He saw his daughter in ways no father should and despite his spirit's outrage, his body responded.

See her.

His efforts to ignore my will changed. He searched desperately for anything to fight me and mentally screamed that nothing had been in his head about this since the day they'd viewed the house and that was how it should be. He hadn't thought of it since that first night and that was right while this was wrong, this was an abomination against everything natural.

See her.

I left him; he swayed again, too sickened by the images I'd given him to do anything but keep his eyes closed and dig his fingernails into the wall. Moving fast, I faced the window that overlooked the garden. Sunlight slid through the glass, pretty sunlight. That light and the house itself bellowed their outrage. They knew what was coming; they knew my next move and could do nothing but protest.

See him, I said to the window and let my words drop to Tracy in the garden. There was nothing at first. In my mind, the vision was clear; she looked from her book to her son on the grass.

She saw.

His face, his lovely face, so fat and smiling, now a monstrous skull, the flesh peeling to expose the muscle and sinew, to turn it into the face of a corpse, dead for weeks, mouldering every single second since, rotting further into terrible decay with each second his little heart no longer beat.

She saw the sickness in his blood, saw the infection I'd breathed into him night after night all through the hot summer.

Her screams were locked in her throat. Her arms and legs were like lead. All she could do was stare at her dying son.

Back to the father, I thought and whispered to Mark. His argument was nothing. He took a few lurching steps forward, reaching for Hayley's bedroom door and his mind full of images I'd given him. His fingers rested on the handle and his mind hollered for the last time.

No, I won't, leave me alone, leave me alone, leave me—

The door flew open, crashing against the wall, and Tracy's screams flew upwards from the garden.

Perched on a chair near the bed and tapping at her handheld computer device, Hayley whirled around, already rising. She saw her father, saw his sweaty and strained face and her attention tried to focus on the sight of one parent and the sound of the other.

"Dad?" she said.

Tracy screeched again and Mark lurched forward as if his legs were on stilts. Hayley saw her father's shorts and cried out, one hand flying to her mouth.

He lurched again and the curtains behind Hayley flapped. A dull light filled the room. There was time to take my attention from Hayley's terrified face but no time to move.

A man flew from the curtains, arms outstretched.

"You bastard!" he bellowed and flew through Mark, who collapsed, all ugly and terrible images of his daughter shoved out of his mind. The man from the curtains crashed into me, knocked me to the stairs and down. At the bottom, he yanked my head up and howled into my face.

"You evil bastard!"

His hands fell on my throat.

Chapter Ten

The best part of four hundred years had gone by since anyone touched me in such a way. That thought filled my head with wonder as the man's hands clamped around my throat. Then survival kicked in, powered by anger.

I smacked the man on the side of his head and shoved him away. Both upright, we stared at one another. He panted like a dog on a hot day and in the few seconds before he spoke, I took time to study him, to store his features in my memory.

He was a large man, easily my height, in his mid-sixties with a full head of healthy hair, each strand gloriously white. A small beard spread across his chin; he bared his teeth. They were strong and even.

"You're a monster," he told me.

"Very possibly."

Tracy continued to wail in the garden. Mark remained upstairs, sobbing in his daughter's bedroom. Hayley raced down the stairs and almost passed through me on her way to her mother. I ignored her and focused my attention on the man.

"Who are you?" I asked.

At first, it seemed he wouldn't reply. Then he spoke and his few words possessed a strength I hadn't heard in a long time. "Richard Cooke. I'm dead and so are you."

"True."

"I heard about you," he said, and let out a small laugh of disbelief. "It was a lot to take in, I tell you. Discovering I was dead, wandering the streets until I found others. They told me about you and the things you do."

He shouted the last few words and shook. Anger wasn't a new emotion for me to witness. This was something more, though. Cooke was nearly all rage, despite his surface calm.

"My reputation precedes me," I said.

He grinned. It wasn't friendly.

"You're strong," I said. "I've found it takes people in our position many months to relearn the things we leave behind. Touch, movement." I rubbed my neck. "Not you. Impressive."

Tracy's din stopped and Cooke glanced over my shoulder, then back my way. He was no longer grinning but continued to tremble. A brief mental picture came to mind: a cat, its eyes narrowed, its tail perfectly still and its hindquarters ready for the pounce a second before it landed on an unsuspecting mouse. I didn't react to the sudden stop of Tracy's noise, despite knowing what it meant.

Cooke had undone my work. Without my presence being close by, baby Chris would beat my sickness. The image I'd given to Tracy had already faded, leaving the baby's face healthy. While he wasn't totally free from my touch, he was on his way back to normal health and at a deep, maternal level, Tracy knew that.

"This family. That poor girl. The baby." Cooke's words were oddly flat, but still he shook, his wrath pulsing off him.

I shrugged and tensed the muscles in my legs at the same time.

"I like to keep busy," I said.

He roared and flew at me. I moved at the same time, and we crashed into one another in the centre of the room. My legs bashed into a dining chair. Cooke's rage and my own developing irritation gave us a type of physicality that only comes in such times of extreme emotion; as my legs hit the chair, it split in two with a fierce snap. The wood fell to the carpet, I booted a piece towards Cooke. It passed through him and splintered against the wall; the movement made him turn his head and bought me a second of advantage.

Crashing my fists into his face, I knocked him backwards and down. He kicked out as I advanced, striking me in the stomach and I fell on to him. We crashed to the hallway and somehow managed to both stand. He grabbed my shoulders and propelled me to the front door. We passed through it, both blind for the moment it took us to slide through the wood before we hit the driveway and lurched in an odd staggering run to the pavement. He was cursing at me the entire time, while I concentrated on keeping my feet moving.

Our momentum took us to the middle of the road and I managed to push him away. We were both gasping for breath (not that we needed oxygen, but old habits are terribly hard to break, even after such a long-time dead). My shirt was untucked and Cooke's trousers were ripped. With a hand still clenched into a fist, he wiped his mouth and stared at his fingers in dumb shock. I knew what he felt. He expected his hand to come away bloody or at least damp with sweat. We don't bleed. Nor do we perspire. Just because we're dead doesn't change a thing, though. For us, especially those new to our state, we *feel* that we should bleed. After all, we can hurt. And more importantly, we can be destroyed.

This jumble went through my mind in flashes and I'd hazard a guess some of the same ideas hit Cooke's thinking at the same time.

He took a few deep breaths and pointed at me, aim steady. The rage was still there, though, but now tempered by a forced calm.

"I have met a lot of bastards in my time," he said. "But you, Harwood." He dropped his hand and gazed at me with a mix of pity and anger. "You're the worst. Leave the people alone. Everything you've done, it ends now."

From a distance and closing in, sirens; an ambulance coming for the baby now no longer dying, now no longer with the face of a monster. A few people left their houses as the sirens drew closer. They'd heard the awful noise coming from number twenty but none had come outside until now. I wanted to point out their lack of interest to Cooke, wanted to show him what the people were like, but the words weren't with me. All I could say was:

"Who are you?"

He took slow, mannered steps forward and stopped when he was arm's reach away. "I'm Richard Cooke and I—"

That was as far as he got. I grabbed his arm.

We went back to his life.

I saw.

Chapter Eleven

There is an empty building across the road, white stone and glass forming its front, steps leading to the entrance, a reception area beyond, a foyer. It's a theatre, I realise, but no plays are here, no audience or actors. It's dead, as dead as me. I drift on the wind, powerless to stop my movement. The pavements are thick with people hurrying through an area I now see is the centre of Dalry; all the bodies crossing Bishop's Gate. Most carry bags and all are wrapped up against the wind and specks of snow. They pass through me and not a one reacts. I'm not here for them. I'm nothing and for the first time in decades or maybe even centuries, I want to scream.

The theatre is as lifeless as a cemetery. For the Christmas shoppers, it is a building long since forgotten or overlooked.

Everything shakes, as if my surroundings are a painting jerked from side to side and my vision flickers. The theatre remains, but abruptly bright now, open now. People fill the steps; the jostling crowd is massive. Nobody wears hats and scarves. There is no snow, only the sun bouncing off the expansive sheets of glass and racing along the steps and pavements. Someone walks from the building and it is not my will that sends me higher, shoves me above the peoples' heads to see. Whatever has brought me to this scene is in charge of my form and will send me wherever it likes.

The figure the people have come to see is someone famous, I know that much. An actor, maybe. More likely a singer. He waves to the crowd and they wave back, some calling his name. The sounds are audible but could be moving through a layer of water. The whims of the wind toss me about, pulling my form back and forth as if I am made of nothing more than motes of dust.

A second person comes and although he's younger, although he is healthy and although he is alive, I know him.

Richard Cooke stands beside the celebrity and waves at the people. If it is possible, they are even happier to see him than they are the man by his side. Cooke shakes the man's hand and laughs when he speaks. Cooke's laugh floats to me as if through water. It is a well-practiced, self-deprecating laugh of a modest man and all at once, I understand.

Cooke brought this man to the people. More than that, he brought the theatre to them. He brought it back from the dead.

There is another shake of the painting, another flick and the picture changes again. The theatre, the people and the road are gone. I am outside a restaurant half a mile from the theatre; the side facing the street is one giant window exposing a pristine interior of gleaming floor and spacious tables, and beautiful paintings on the walls. Cooke is at the entrance, moving forward with a heavy pair of scissors, ready to cut the ribbon blocking the doors. Around him, people in smart suits watch and applaud and a photographer takes pictures. Cooke smiles because it is another building given to the people, another achievement.

Flick.

A playground in one of Dalry's older suburbs, the equipment renovated and clean and shining. Cooke with one large hand on the slide, a middle-aged gentleman in a child's world, smiling his handsome smile while local people applaud the man who brought a small piece of happiness to their estate.

Flick.

The local football team. A trophy cup. Cooke beside the footballers and all the men smile their honest and unforced happiness.

Flick.

A bus depot and two new buses, drivers gathered with the managers and Cooke, the staff in fresh uniforms and the afternoon pleasant with the warmth of early summer.

Flick.

The mayor and Cooke shaking hands at a dinner for dignitaries, investors, the great and the good.

Flick.

A standing ovation in the Town Hall, Christmas decorations and lights festooned all around, the winter night kept at bay by good food and cheeks reddened from good Scotch.

Flick.

A cheque handed to a woman surrounded by dozens of children, all blind, all cheering for Cooke in the community centre, and their joy floats to me like the scent of a feast.

Flick.

Cooke.

Signing. Smiling. Waving.

Cooke.

A wedding, Cooke the proud father, his daughter the beautiful bride, giving her away and wiping his eyes while the vicar speaks and the stained-glass windows usher in the fierce sun and heat of mid-summer.

A baby grandson on his knee, unwrapped birthday presents in messy piles all around, the child playing with grandfather's beard and Cooke laughs hard and healthily.

The grandson walked to school on a warm morning, a stroll home alone, a slowing down, a pain in his arm, a pain snarling through his body, a rest on a low wall while traffic passes, a woman dashing from her house to him and asking if he's all right, an explosion like a bomb inside his chest and all the light he has ever known closing in from miles and miles above.

Chapter Twelve

Cooke threw my hold off his arm, which was easier than it might have appeared. Whether we'd travelled in time or simply experienced a shared vision, nothing like that had happened to me before. Nearly all my strength was lost, my feet didn't want to offer any support, and it took a moment of blinking to register the change in sunlight. Once again, the air became murky, an oddly horrible bruised tinge that made me want to flee from Azalea Drive as quickly as possible.

"Quite a life," I said and cursed the way my voice fell into a croak on the last word.

"Yes," he said, unblinking as he gazed at me.

"So am I right in thinking that the good man is here to beat the evil man? That you've come to vanquish me?"

Cooke's face flamed a fraction at that as if my words made him uncomfortable.

He smoothed his shirt and cleared his throat. It gave everything away. His violence against me was utterly out of character and had been brought on by simple ire.

All the same, my instincts warned that underestimating this man at any point would be a tremendously bad idea.

"Close enough," he replied.

I smiled and extended my hand. He eyed it as if it was a bag of filth rather than a seemingly friendly move.

"I've seen your life," I said. "Would you like to see mine?"

"No need. I know what you are. Plenty of people have told me."

The ambulance sped to the junction of Azalea Drive and Magnolia Avenue and bore down on us, slowing only at the last second. It pulled over as people pointed to number twenty and Hayley and Tracy ran from the door, Chris in Tracy's arms. Presumably, Mark was still in his daughter's bedroom, cursing himself.

The men jumped from the ambulance and rushed to the weeping mother. Cooke turned away before he had chance to see the baby's face. The tremble returned to his hands. My strength was still lacking so I could do little but hope his trembling wouldn't grow to the same strength of feeling that brought us to the street.

"What people?" I asked.

Surprise brought colour to his face. "This city is full of ghosts. They know you. They know the things you've done and none of them will stand for it. That's why I've been looking for you."

I laughed hard at that. "If none of them will stand for what I've done, why are you here alone?" I dropped my hand and took a few steps towards him. He held his ground. Despite his actions, I was warming to the man in a strange way. Certainly, I didn't like him. Not in the least, but I thought I might respect him.

"I'll tell you why you're alone." I moved closer to Cooke. "Because people are cowards. Because they're worthless. Because I am better than them. *We* are better than them. We always have been. Why else do you think we're still here and still able to affect them? It's our strength, Cooke. Our control." I waved to the gawping crowd. "These people, they're pointless just like the spirits you've met. Those people know what I do is wrong and they still don't face me. What does that make them if not cowards?"

He started to reply. I lifted my hand and grabbed his index finger. "I saw you, Cooke. Now you see me."

He couldn't fight back. I barely possessed the strength to hold his hand and yet he couldn't fight me. Perhaps he didn't want to.

We left the street and the people with their ambulance and their tears and we went back.

Chapter Thirteen

Cooke drops my hand and spins in a circle. When he faces me again, his mouth is open and dismay is stamped on his features. Around us, Dalry breathes. The seventeenth century breathes and we are ghosts swallowed by my past.

"Where are we?" he asks and even though he must know the answer.

"Listen," I tell him. "I'll show you."

Listen.

The first.

The young man is a homosexual. He comes to my pub once or twice a week for two months, sits alone and does not speak a great deal while he takes his drink. Several of the prostitutes attempt to start conversations with him but give up quickly when they realise they have no chance of making any money from him. He is a handsome man, well-spoken to the few with whom he does converse and always offers to buy me a drink. One of the few comments he makes is that it is useful to befriend a landlord. I think he wants to put the image across of a roguish lad, a man about town. I do not believe it for a second. He does not drink with other men or flirt with the ladies, he does not start fights. He spends a few coins, speaks a little to me and leaves at least an hour before I close for the night.

I'm going to kill him.

I'll do it because I can. Because he will be the first. Because I need the experience.

But mostly because I can.

The last night, his last night, I make sure I am not working. It is a Friday so the pub is full of men singing, drinking, some already making use of the ladies in the quiet corners, money changing hands before fluids are exchanged in the quiet. I cross the pub, walking from table to table, drinking with each group of men but making sure I am not even close to inebriated. My young man sits close to the doors as if wanting to ensure he is free to leave quickly. He drinks three ales. I watch him swallow, watch his hand hold the tankard and watch him study the men. If he is after that certain kind of companionship, he is in the wrong pub. My locals consider any homosexual to be utterly degenerate and while one or two of them might be interested should he make his feelings clear, I know none of them will really spend any private time with him. He will be lucky to make it out of the pub alive should anyone know his secret business.

He finishes his last beer, rises to leave, already pulling his cloak and hat into place. I position myself directly in his line of sight and meet his eyes as he steps away from the table.

I smile. It is all that is needed.

He gives me a wave, the sort that simply bids goodnight to a host, before he turns to the door. As he reaches it, he glances back, unsmiling. He is a fine looking young man. The doors open and he slips outside as a few men enter.

I count to ten and follow.

Catching sight of him in the massing bodies filling the street is a struggle. Thankfully, he has considered that and waits close to a group of prostitutes offering their services without any attempts at subtlety. As my young man is the only male not paying the whores any attention, he stands out.

Pushing my way through the crowd, I cross to him, unconcerned with subterfuge. So what if anyone should see us together? The man will not be missed.

"Leaving my pub so early?" I ask as if it is still daylight and not gone ten. The night is warm. This early May is a fine time.

He replies in a deliberately low voice. "I apologise, sir. I am rising early on the morrow and need my wits."

"I understand. You must be a conscientious young man. Your wife or sweetheart expects you?"

He averts his gaze and any doubts about his preferences are squashed.

"No, not this night," he replies.

"Then let us walk. It is warm and it will do an older soul such as I good to see the sights and hear the sounds of our town after dark."

My words are ridiculous. After all, I am no more than ten years his senior. However, offering up the pretence of a friendly uncle is exactly what I need to do. It is exactly what he wants to hear.

We walk from the women and the drunks, not talking, following the river. Our route leads across grass and towards trees. It will be many years before the town expands this far south and develops the riverside. As it is now, we will be witnessed only by the stars within no more than another hundred steps. Even so, soft sighs along with vigorous grunting emerges from the bushes.

"This is not the most private of places," I remark.

"No."

"Would you care to stroll in the woods?"

"Yes."

He will not or cannot look at me. That is fine. Let him see what he wants to, I think. Let his eyes land where they will for the last time.

Moments later, we enter the woodland, I walk in front and twigs snap below our boots for a few moments. Upon reaching a tiny clearing, luck is with me; slivers of moonlight slip between the leaves, the silver faint but still pretty. While the illumination does not dispel the gloom to the point of revealing the details of his face, his shape becomes clearer and that is enough.

"Do you like my pub?" I ask him.

"It is fine."

"Thank you."

We move closer together and his lips part. There is a gentle intake of breath. As our lips meet, I slide my knife into his back.

He slams against my chest as if a mighty wind has blown behind him. I take his weight and work the knife further inside, penetrating bone and long lines of muscle. He gurgles and the sound is less of a word than a formless entreaty. I kiss him. Blood lives in his mouth, the liquid hot, viscous.

He falls from my grip, his blood on my knife and hand. I am quite proud of myself. I breathe normally and have not broken a sweat. His hand brushes my shin. There is still too little in the way of moonlight to illuminate his face so I lean in close and whisper to him.

"Thank you for this opportunity, young man."

I crouch behind his head, lift his hair and pull his head back as far as I can. He makes another sound that wants to be a word. I thank him again and open a wide line in the tender meat of his throat.

Chapter Fourteen

"You bastard."

Cooke does not raise his voice, this despite looking very much as if he wants to. He turns in another circle but there is nothing to see. We are in an infinite void of soft and silent white and there is nobody here but us. No up or down. No sound but Cooke's two words. It is equally wonderful and horrible.

Cooke completes his turn and his eyes are brighter now. Hate burns from them. This good man who has done wonders for our city and is loved by all, now looks at me with murder on his face. It crosses my mind to tell him we are not particularly different but I do not. There is something else to show him.

"Do you want to see more?" I ask and continue before he has chance to answer. "Do you want to know why I did what I did or is it enough to know I did those things? Do you want to know my reasons or have you judged me already?"

Emptiness presses in on us.

"Do you, Cooke?"

"I don't care about your reasons. Who would? You're a murderer. You're—"

"At first," I say, overriding him. "Yes, I was. And I won't lie to you. There were many times I was only that, but there were plenty of other times I was much more."

"It doesn't matter what you were, Harwood."

"Of course it does. And it matters why I did it. Think about it, Cooke. Putting a knife to flesh. The blood. The end of a life. Do that and you have a power that's different to anything else. What I did changed the world."

He does not want to answer me but can't help himself. "What are you talking about?"

"It's simple. If I killed a man who provided for his family, then the family had no income. They starved, maybe to death. Perhaps the children would have become thieves or worse. Anything to survive, after all. Perhaps they would have become great writers and thinkers. And if they *did* survive, they grew up in a family without a father. They were marked by that. It affected their friendships and relationships. They might have had their own children and been a worse parent for it. If they died young, they wouldn't have been there to change life in their own tiny ways. The people they would have influenced, the mark they would have left on the world, however small, it's all gone. Just by killing one person, the knock-on effect is huge. You can't measure it. And it's all because of *my* actions. It's all down to me. That's power."

"You're. . ."

Cooke's voice dries up and raises his fists. I raise a hand to pacify him.

"What I did wasn't just random acts of violence. I chose my kills carefully. I decided whose death would have the utmost impact on the world. Businessmen;

prostitutes who serviced the clergy; farmers who made the food the people ate. When I took them out of the world, then there was no way of knowing how far the effects would go. Even now, four hundred years after my death, who's to say the effects aren't still being felt? I kill a man all those years ago, his family are left without a husband and a father. His children, they have their families, and those families have their children. All the way down to now. And all those descendants in some way touched by my actions four centuries ago. So many years between now and then. More time than the human mind can understand because it dwarfs the average life. More time than the living have any chance of understanding, and it's mine. That gives me a tiny bit of forever, Cooke. Think about that. I perform one action, one little murder, and that takes a single person out of the world." I hold up my index finger. "A solitary person; a knife in the throat as quick as you like or a rock right here." I tap my forehead. "No work at all. Not really. But the effect. . .well, that's beyond reckoning. It's beyond time. I killed for that time, you see. I killed to last in time. My own little piece of forever." My pause spins out between us. "Of course, others I killed just because I could."

Cooke shakes his head, mouth open. No words come out. He does not appear to be able to perform any action but the idiot animal shaking of his head.

"Listen, Cooke."

Listen.

Chapter Fifteen

I watch the scene unfold, struck dumb with wonder. This is my past come to life. It is as solid as it was back then and there is a brief but powerful urge to run from what is happening ahead, to run to my pub and see all the old faces now dead for hundreds of years. Movement is impossible, though. I can no more leave than I can stop what is coming.

Cooke is beside me and he screams. It makes no difference and he swings his fists. They pass through me. Cursing, he shoots towards the other me and flies through him. There's not a thing he can do to change this because it is already happened. He realises this and drops to the ground, mouth opening, closing, opening. I drift closer to him and do not say a word.

We watch.

###

It is like seeing pictures come to life. A collection of fine drawings and paintings in the world's greatest gallery become flesh, become breath. Ink and parchment crumble, and in their place, a warm breeze and unbroken sunlight. Coming behind the moving air, a jumble of raised voices, all good-natured; barking dogs, the animals excited by the proximity of so many bodies with their wonderful mix of smells. With the voices and the noise of the dogs, squealing pigs and grunting cows from the farmer's market further along the road; yells of the men there offering their animals for the dinner table, cries of children as excited as the dogs. And the disagreeable aroma of the farm animals' waste barely masked by the women selling their flowers from a dozen stalls nearer the river.

Today is the nineteenth of June, 1657, and all is right with Harwood's world. The world is everything he wants it to be. With summer sunshine, with the streets and faces all familiar, life does not come any better. What is more, today is his day. He whispers this as he walks and he does not fear anyone will hear him. The streets are full and his whisper is lost far below the heavy thud of feet on stone and traders' happy shouts.

Harwood passes along the middle of the street, a tall fellow, dressed impeccably and out for a stroll in the early afternoon. He is a well to do gentlemen enjoying the sights and smells of a fine town. On all sides, people walk and talk. There are market traders, shoppers, children, a few stray dogs. Harwood stops at a stall selling fresh pies to chat to three men he knows from the pub and smiling faces greet him. All around is flesh and blood. Beneath a bright sun, people go about their business and live their lives. The tall man is right in the middle of it.

Harwood bids good day to the three chaps and greets other customers now working and they return his greetings. Not a one sees what he sees. They pay no attention to the two children ahead of him.

The two children he will kill in broad daylight.

He closes in on the tots when instinct tells him it is the right moment. There are people on all sides and he does not care at all. Nothing stops him when it comes to this.

He crouches and has his arms around them before they can do so much as turn.

"Good afternoon, lovely children," he says.

"Good afternoon, sir," the boy replies. The girl—his sister, Harwood assumes—simply gives him a shy smile. She is two or three years younger than the boy. Five, perhaps. They are as well dressed a poor family can manage – hand-me-downs for the boy with patches on his knees, and a faded dress, slightly frayed for the girl – and appear to be in reasonable health if somewhat under nourished. An issue for which they and their parents will soon have no concern.

"Would you two fine children care to earn a penny?" Harwood asks and the boy's eyes shine like stars. He is almost as beautiful as his sister. Given time and perhaps an easier life in a family with either fewer children or more money, they might achieve a comfortable adulthood.

Alas.

"Yes, please," the boy answers while his younger sister beams and Harwood loves the siblings for what they are, their innocence, and for what they shall give him in the next few seconds.

Harwood reaches for his pocket and the movement robs all worries from the boy's mind of any warnings his mother might have given, warnings to stay away from strangers, to not dawdle on the way home. He thinks of the penny in Harwood's pocket, of the penny and nothing else in the entire world.

Harwood's smile grows big enough to feel as if it is going to split his face in two and he withdraws his knife. The handle is small enough to be lost in his hand while the small, small and curved at its tip, is freshly sharpened. Two inches of cool metal. Something so small but so very final.

There comes a moment he will remember forever, a moment where the sibling's smiles remain strong and shining and that makes him happy. Their last act, this beautiful brother and sister, is to smile.

His knife slides deep and fast into the boy's stomach, is withdrawn and slips into the girl's stomach, the knife's serrated tip slicing skin, flesh and abdomen with no trouble. Harwood twists the blade with both withdrawals, cutting nerves and innards as easily as the farmers in the market will slice the throats of their stock upon a successful sale.

The girl lets out a tiny grunt, the same sound she would make had he given her a playful punch. There is no blood in this frozen second. The girl continues to offer her sweet smile while the boy is stilled in the movement of his hands to the hole in his tiny body.

Harwood rises and strides into the flow of traders and shoppers, knife deep in his trouser pocket. As he walks without rushing and without freeing his hand from his trousers, he wipes the blade and his finger tips on a thick handkerchief. It is a two-minute walk to the river where the water will swallow blade and handkerchief. His pub is another ten minutes away, and he thinks he will treat himself to a drink of the best whisky in the house.

He is one more figure in the crowd as a scream drifts high above feet on stone and the traders' shouts.

Beside me—the me watching the replayed memory—Cooke staggers upright. His face is a strained, white skull. His eyes bulge as he stares at me.

"You," he says.

"Quite."

He lunges for me and as it had during my vision of his life, the scene flips. We go from that day to one a few years later and Cooke tries to cry out.

The plague.

It is all around us.

The dead, the dying and the grieving fill the streets. Not an inch of stone is visible. All we see are bodies; all we hear are the moans of those still strong enough to be able to mixed with the wretched gasps of those close to death, and the sobs of those left behind to grieve and eventually sicken and die themselves. And perhaps some will welcome the disease. After all, it means they shall be reunited with their loved ones. This is their hurting hope, at least, and who am I to tell them of what comes after this life?

Cooke shields his nose but it is an instinctive movement. We have the sights of the dead and the sickness, but we don't have the smells. I remember them, though. It's been a long time since I walked the town's streets as her people fell, but I remember the stink of those days, weeks, months when it seemed the very world was ending and the Lord would usher all good souls into his Kingdom. The stink clung to my mouth and nostrils for a long, long time. Even now after so many centuries, it is impossible to forget.

"See this? This was my time," I tell Cooke.

He drops his hand.

"This is where you belong," he shouts.

Not a foot from him, a woman runs past. She collapses beside two bodies against the wall of a pub, holds them and weeps. From a long-gone memory, a name speaks. In turn, I speak it.

"Molly Doolan. That's her husband and eldest son."

Cooke turns away and I finish my words.

"She's the mother of the two children you just saw me kill."

Face heavy with disbelief, Cooke turns around and stares at me as if he's seen something not quite real.

"You brought me here for this?" he whispers.

"No. *You* brought us here."

I open my arms to him as I finish speaking. He makes another lunge and the scene flips again, and it is no more than a few weeks later. We are in a tiny bedroom of a slum, stained walls and uneven floor lit with one small candle as the me of the seventeenth century plunges a knife into Molly Doolan's gaping mouth, metal shredding tongue, gums and larynx with wonderful ease.

Flip.

And we are watching me tie two vagrants together in a pitch-black woodland at three in the morning, their pleas muffled by the bundle of rags stuffed into their mouths, watching me soak them with two bottles of the house Scotch and set them on fire before I stroll away and their screams are drowned by the merry crackle and roar of the flames.

Flip.

And I am nearing the end of my life. I'm still going, though, still having my fun. On this summer day, less than a year before I die, I'm dunking a child in the river at dawn, holding him under the water until the last of the bubbles stop breaking the surface and all is still save for my slightly panting breath.

Flip.

And there is a moment of nothing, a moment where Cooke's hand is not on mine and I am left in black, not oddly comfortable white. It is all the black in the universe, and I am in the middle of it, buried under a trillion tons of rock, not shouting Cooke's name but shouting my own. *Screaming* it.

Then everything is gone and—

Chapter Sixteen

We were back.

Barely any time had passed during our journeys; the ambulance was still parked outside number twenty and the crowd in the street had grown by a good dozen or more, eyes hungry for sight of scandal or pain or suffering while some recorded on their loathsome phones and some wept their mannered tears.

Cooke watched me, face without colour or expression. I could barely stand. Whether we'd really travelled in time or somehow been witness to gone days, I had no idea. All my energy had vanished and the odd light that still resembled old bruises was developing a distinct pulse. It was familiar. Discomfortingly so. If I'd been a praying man, I think I would have asked for divine assistance. For obvious reasons, that was not likely to be asked or answered.

"I think you should go," Cooke said.

I barked out a laugh, and it was an effort to do so. "Are you threatening me, Mr Cooke?"

The croak of my voice was horribly dismaying. It belonged to a weak, old man.

Instead of answering, Cooke turned away as if I was no longer important and watched the ambulance pull out to the road. People moved out of its way and the elderly couple from number eighteen stood outside twenty, holding one another. The afternoon was quiet as it grew closer to evening. Words would come; people would discuss what might have happened in the house and to the baby, but for now they couldn't get beyond the ambulance and the noise.

Cooke glanced at me and I itched to make him scream, to go for his eyes and turn their cool blue to the red of fresh blood.

I couldn't. Whatever had stolen my strength remained deep in my old bones. If I made a move on Cooke, there was no doubt he would beat me.

Call it pride or wilful ignorance, walking away was not an option.

"Tracy screamed like Molly Doolan screamed when they brought her dead children to her," I said.

Cooke bellowed. His fists crashed into my cheeks, knocking me to the ground. No blood flowed from my nose which made no difference to the beating or the knowledge he was much stronger than I.

He kicked me in the chest, the neck, the head. I tried to curl up but couldn't move. Swearing and spitting, Cooke pummelled my face. He cursed me; Hell was too good for me, I was an abomination, I was filth. Eventually, I couldn't hear him. There was nothing but his feet and his fists pounding me into the cool darkness.

Chapter Seventeen

When my surroundings returned, I was at the edge of the park. Night had landed on the world. Occasionally, cars passed by. Their headlights illuminated the bushes and trees and I was forced to squeeze my eyes closed each time the lights caught me.

Move.

I couldn't. I'd never been hurt so fully, so fundamentally. All I wanted to do was stay in the park and not think about Richard Cooke.

Time passed. An hour, maybe two. Maybe even three. There was nothing but my aches. The traffic grew less frequent and eventually ceased. A hedgehog crept out of the bushes closest to me and trotted past as if I was nothing. It disappeared into another hedge and my anger grew a focus. It formed into Cooke's face, mouth wide open, howling, damning me with his curses.

Formless things in the shadows moved below trees and around bushes, watching, waiting: the essences of the leaves and grass. All were interested to see if I would leave the park. They'd wanted me to for many years and there was never any intention of making them happy.

Creeping forward, I listened to the murmurs of disappointment come from the shadows.

"I am not leaving," I told them and they faded into proper darkness.

It took almost half an hour to crawl into the park, cross the grass and slump against an oak tree. In the silence, I let my anger live and breathe. It told me what to do.

###

Days passed.

A blurred jumble of dreams filled my head; Cooke beating me, howling curses down on my form, spinning lights coating me and the road below my face, then flying miles above it, looking down on the streets and fields—the country laid out like a meal. And through each scene, a suggestion, a whisper of something chasing me, something I couldn't quite hear, no matter how hard I tried.

Alongside those fevered imaginings, there were moments of no dreams, and those moments were blessedly silent. I existed in the same void Cooke and I been a part of during our visits to the old days of our lives. In those hours, I found it easy to think none of it had happened: Cooke, my beating, Hayley and her family, Dennis fleeing to Thistlemoor Wood, my years and decades spent haunting Dalry, my death, the murders and all the days beforehand when I'd been Benjamin Harwood, and not a ghost long since forgotten.

Easy to think that. Impossible to pretend it, even in that deep silence.

A week went by. I didn't leave the tree's side, even when the earth below pleaded for me to take my muck from it. Its tears helped me to recover. They meant I wasn't finished yet.

Gradually, the impact from Cooke's beating faded from my skin, but wouldn't fade from my mind. If I'd been alive, his beating would have given me physical scars by which to remember him. As it was, all I had was the memory. It filled me even when the discomfort faded and rage replaced it. With that rage, there was something more. I had a purpose.

To see Cooke again, to teach him who I was.

On the morning eight days after our confrontation on Azalea Drive, I left the park for the first time and I walked with my back straight and my hands ready.

I was going to hurt Cooke. And I was going to enjoy it.

Chapter Eighteen

Standing at the junction of Azalea Drive and Magnolia Avenue revealed what I'd suspected on the walk from the path: the place was deserted. Straight ahead, an uninterrupted view led all the way to the far end. Other than a few parked cars on driveways, there was no sign of human life. Of course, life was not where my interest lay. Not that morning.

"Cooke!" I bellowed and birds flew from trees, crying to each other. They flew to the roofs, rested on chimneys and gazed down with their stupid eyes, so black and unthinking.

"Cooke."

Somewhere, a dog barked in high-pitched yaps. I walked in the middle of the road, not looking at any particular house, not paying attention to the silent number twenty. By then, the Wilson family was miles from my mind.

Someone coughed politely behind me. I counted to three and turned, ready for him.

Cooke stood in the shadow of a tall bush. The living might have made him as the leaves wafting a little.

However, he was as solid to me as if he was flesh once again.

"I knew you'd be back," he called.

"Come a bit closer and we'll talk about it."

He let out a pleasantly warm chuckle. He sounded like someone's loved grandfather which, I realised, made perfect sense.

"I come any closer and you'll kill me." He laughed again. "Killing the dead. I never considered that when I was alive. But then, I didn't really consider dying."

"Few do," I said and he nodded.

"True."

He took a few steps from the pavement and stopped on top of a drain cover.

"May I ask you a question, Harwood?"

My surprise stayed locked far below. Polite curiosity was the last thing I'd expected from Cooke.

"Of course," I said.

"For the sake of argument, let's say *killing* each other is the correct term, despite us being dead already. . .if you should kill me or if you should be killed. . ." He smiled as if such an idea was ridiculous. "What would happen? Where would we go?"

I slowly lifted a hand and extended my index finger.

"You'd go that way." I pointed upwards. "I'd go the other. Simple, really."

"I thought you'd say that. It doesn't frighten you? Dying completely? No longer being stuck to the world?"

"No."

He took two more steps forward. The sunlight brightened his face. In life, he'd been a strong, capable man. Not much of that strength had faded in death. The first whisper of doubt spoke in a weak, frightened voice and I ignored it.

"Another question, if I may?" he said.

I stayed silent and he took my silence as agreement.

"How have you managed it? How have you stayed here for so long? Surely you should have gone that way the second you died." He pointed to the road below.

"I kept my head down. Laying low wasn't much fun, but it had to be done." As I spoke, I realised I should have listened to Dennis all those weeks ago. Indulging myself by taking my haunting of the Wilson family to such a level had led me to this point. Cooke would not have bothered me if I hadn't bothered the family.

That consideration was far too much to deal with just then. I had to focus.

"But what about when you died? What kept you here then?"

There was no harm in telling him, I decided. I still did not like Cooke. He had strength, though, and he stood his ground. Perhaps those two factors were enough to respect the man. Admittedly, we approached things in a different manner, but all the same, we were not dissimilar. We both believed in what we were doing, for one.

"I had a friend," I told him.

"A friend? And they helped you out? Kept you here?"

"Something like that." I floated closer to him, ready for our conversation to finish.

He smiled and the bitter joy sitting below his face didn't suit him at all. I recognised his overriding expression for what it was.

Triumph.

"Your friend is here," Cooke said.

There might have been time to flee if I hadn't been so desperate to wipe the smile from Cooke's face.

Daylight exploded in silence. Blinding sunshine hammered at my eyes, winked out and flashed again:

light like bruises, breathing in slow exhalations. The nauseating light coated each brick, each little piece of road and pavement.

A whisper spoke.

It was my name from somewhere so distant as to be lost and forgotten, come as a huge shout but withered down to a murmur by the time it reached me. Dennis' face filled my head.

Teeth.

All at once, I knew what was coming and what the horrible light meant.

Behind Cooke, the bushes shook and the air rippled as if extreme heat was rising from the ground. The shiver at Cooke's back remained formless although there was something inside it. Something that might have been a face.

Harwood.

It'd been centuries since my name had been spoken in such a way—breathed on the wind and suggesting a rumble of thunder closing in fast. I held my ground despite the threat of trembling that wanted to burst out of my legs and race up my body.

Behind Cooke, everything blazed briefly red That blaze brought back the past; the demon chasing a woman I'd brought for him, bringing her down to the damp ground beside the river as I watched him go to work on her.

But that was the past. This was now and Cooke could not be doing this. I would not allow it.

"Drude," I said. "It's been a long time."

Many years. Drude's reply rolled over the ground with a tremendous rumble. Had any of the living been on the street, they probably would have heard it as muted thunder.

How are you? There was another red flash. Brighter that time.

I didn't back up.

"Why do you come here? This is my business with Cooke."

And you are my business.

Silence played out between us. The breeze had gone and all that was left was the space between the demon and me.

"Did I not give you enough lives?" I asked.

The air shook. It took me a moment to realise the demon was laughing.

You gave plenty of lives, Harwood. And I'm grateful. But time has moved on. You haven't.

I gave up any pretence of polite conversation. We'd passed miles beyond it.

"You've come for me, is that right? You've come to do the bidding of this man who understands nothing about what we do, about life or death?"

Drude said nothing.

"The places I have been, the times I've known, these mean nothing to you, do they? They mean nothing while this man who only a week ago would have scoffed at the idea of your existence is fit to order you here?"

No. I came when I heard what had happened between you two. Cooke's the first man to challenge you in centuries. I've been looking for you for a long time. You've been clever until recently. Kept quiet. Didn't bother the living too much. The outline of a huge finger formed. It pointed at number twenty, silent in the early morning, before vanishing. *What drew you here? The girl? On the young side for you, wasn't she?*

Cooke grimaced. Ignoring the unpleasant insinuation in Drude's words, I took a moment to study Cooke. The slightly smug cast to his face vanished. He didn't want this; he didn't want anything to do with a demon, but the stronger desire was to vanquish me.

"I thought that sort of thing was below you, Drude. You know what I am and what I definitely am not," I said.

My apologies, Harwood. You're a lot of things but that sort of monster, no. He paused as if considering. *Although you* know *monsters, don't you?*

I smiled. "Who doesn't?"

Almost forgotten by the two of us, Cooke shifted forward. He jabbed a finger at me. "You should be in Hell, you son of a bitch."

Interestingly, the man's temper from our last conversation seemed to have deserted him. Perhaps bringing a demon into this was too much to deal with. Perhaps he felt out of his depth. Either way, much of his surety had vanished.

Knowing full well it would needle Cooke, I ignored him and faced Drude's vague shape as he spoke again.

I came back for you and you alone, Harwood.

I used the last weapon available. "You can't. Remember?" I bellowed my words as if hoping they'd carry down through the road and those higher than Drude would hear and understand.

"You know our arrangement. You can do nothing to me without ruining yourself. Those are the rules now just as they were back in the old days. You needed me, remember? Needed me to do your work. And you need me now to keep your cover. You'll expose yourself if you do anything to me. Understand?"

I understand. And I don't care.

For a terrible second, he allowed a glimpse of his true shape. It skittered over the road while Cooke tried to move away. He couldn't do it and there was a moment of joy that he should be obliged to witness my demise.

I dropped into the road and let my form spread over the surface. Drude overshot where I'd been standing before racing backwards. As he turned, I'd gone to the road in front of the drain to skim through the tarmac.

I hit the drain as Drude flew at me once more. My last sight of Cooke was his face caught between dismay at what he'd been forced to do to beat me and joy at seeing my shadow on the road drop into the stink of the drain.

There were pipes, bricks and filthy smells. I followed them all down, chased by Drude's howls. He didn't come after me and I knew why. His game had only just started and he wanted to take his time.

I struck dirty water and let it take me wherever it would.

Chapter Nineteen

For what may have been hours, all I knew were pipes and sewer and stink but those things were gone and I was in a new place with birdsong, sunlight and clean water.

The surface of the river closed in on my face. I let it, too weak to fight. The current took me east and birdsong followed towards a narrow bend.

I struggled to the tall weeds growing at the bank, swam through them, reached rocks and pebbles and hauled my way up to land.

The sun beat through my form.

I rested and tried not to think. That was impossible. Cooke's face wouldn't leave me, nor would the moments before Drude had made his move. And while I lay beside the water, the same question ran around and around my mind.

How could this have happened?

There were no answers. All there was in place of those answers was the knowledge that Cooke had won and that the demon would find me.

I lay there with that question and that knowledge until voices filled the air, one high and excited, the other calm, more mature.

Curious, despite my condition, I made my way through the high weeds to level ground and watched a father and young son set up their fishing equipment a short way further down the river. The father gave the son a rod and sat back to study the boy clumsily cast into the water. The boy's face wasn't visible but his concentration was clear, as was his need to impress his father.

Interesting.

I took a moment to study my location, a wide field which met a narrow line of trees. Beyond the trees, a path ran alongside another field and a manmade lake. A few people were visible around the lake, some walking dogs, some with pushchairs. The river had brought me to an area of Dalry known as the Meadows—a large expanse of fields, trails and trees that grew from the outskirts of the city centre right out to the suburbs. I'd spent a few years there a long time ago, back when it had been simple countryside beyond a growing town. It was pleasing to see that it still featured that wildness in certain places, in the overgrown trail that ran alongside the river for a good mile or more, in the shaded woodland that cut through in a meandering line and in fields largely untouched because of the wild nettles growing tall and proud around their perimeters.

Moving with fierce aches (and extremely dismayed at how strong they were), I crossed the grass to stand a short way behind the man. His love for the boy was like a scent flowing from his pores and that was good. It gave me something to work with.

I'm here. I'm still here. And it doesn't matter about Cooke. He failed. The demon failed. I'm still here.

Once closer to the man, I drew what little strength I had. The act of moving, of telling myself I could do so helped more than I would have expected.

The man watched his son and didn't see me skirt around him and lean close to the boy.

I yanked on the boy's line as hard as possible. He flew forward, hit the riverbank and lay partially submerged in the water. Coughing and crying, he tried to stand as his father jumped from his chair. I shoved the boy's face under the water, absorbing his choked gasps. At the last second before his father reached him, I let go and jumped away. The boy splashed out of the water, spluttering and calling for his father.

I left them with the father's words of comfort and the boy's cries, too exhausted to do much more.

I'm still here. I won't be stopped.

The words played around my head on my walk through the Meadows. They tried to stop me thinking of anything else. I had to, though. My survival depended on it.

I sat on a bench beside the rowing lake, a young couple walked hand in hand towards me. I barely had the strength to lift my head and still, the urge to follow them, to go with them on their walk and find the right time to pull the woman's legs from under her was huge.

Such wonderings were no good and no use. In my state, I was hardly a threat to the living or the dead.

So what to do? Sit here and wait for them to find you? Hide? Face them?

None of the options were appealing. I'd never been one for hiding, but facing them would be suicide. And that left one option.

Run.

I considered it. Leaving my city, skulking through the fields and woodlands surrounding the city, existing in the shadows wouldn't be much of a life. Or death, for that matter.

Cooke's face bloomed into life inside my head as did the picture of his dismay that he'd needed to associate with a demon and joy at having vanquished me.

I'm still here, Cooke.

"True, but that doesn't tell you what to do," I muttered and sighed. All at once, I felt like an old man, too tired to face the work of the day. The warmth and the sunlight on the water did nothing to raise my morale. And why would it? I'm centuries beyond appreciating such things. Sometimes, I can't remember if I ever did.

Cooke and Drude. Focus. What of them? What next?

Drude's mocking words about Hayley and what had drawn me to her replayed in my head. It wasn't the implication in what he'd said—he and I both knew there was no truth to that. What bothered me was knowing be that becoming involved in the family, and principally the girl, was what had brought to this place. It had brought Drude back to me; it had threatened everything I had, and all it would have taken to avoid the whole sorry business would have been avoiding the family.

But I had not. I *had* been drawn to them, especially Hayley, and there was no escaping that.

In my mind's eye, I saw my return to Azalea Drive, back to face Drude and Cooke, the demon rushing towards me—a demon who'd once been my ally—and Cooke behind him; the good man Cooke, the benevolent, decent man still playing the good guy in death.

Cooke and Drude against me. In my state, I was almost talking about an army against one man.

You know monsters, don't you?

An idea gleamed far below.

One idea.

"Interesting," I whispered and howls sounded from close by. Drude was perhaps two miles further along the river, following my scent like a hungry dog.

I stood and faced north.

Drude. After all I did for you. After all I gave you.

Rage began to trickle and grew closer to a flood with each passing second. I welcomed it. It made me feel like my old self.

"After all the lives I gave you, demon. All that killing for you."

It made no difference. Too much time had passed, and according to Drude, my time was up.

"Not if I have anything to do with it."

Drude howled from somewhere close again. The people around the rowing lake didn't hear those howls and they *did* hear them. The sounds might only have been a rumble of thunder or a car speeding dangerously on the parkway or even a dog barking in the seconds before it bit, but they heard the demon.

What they didn't hear was my name bayed across the grass and water. Knowing there was no choice, I ran to the only place I could.

Thistlemoor Wood.

Chapter Twenty

Thistlemoor Wood is for the dead and the dead alone.

The living still walk in the general area, but not as often as might be expected. Greenfield Wood is a couple of miles to the east and that is noticeably more popular with dog walkers and teenagers with their bottles of beer, even though it's a longer journey from Dalry's suburbs. People avoid Thistlemoor for the most part. Its old trails haven't been walked on in years. A tyre hangs from a particular tree close to the edge on the western side; as far as I know, no child has swung on that tyre in forty years. People throw sticks for their dogs and the dogs crash through the undergrowth at the edge of the trees. What people don't do is go too far into the gloom below the trees. Those that do have a habit of getting lost. Some get lost permanently. In any case, people definitely don't go into the centre of Thistlemoor or attempt to walk from end to the other. Nobody living has for years and not a soul could say why they avoid it.

They used to, back in the old days. That was when Thistlemoor Wood was different. Something lived there, something good in the mud and branches. It gave

Thistlemoor a strength and a healing power. I've come across a few of these places on my travels. Woodlands, hills, a scrap of a beach; they're all half-forgotten corners of the living world but still places of power that people like when they come across them, even if they don't know why.

That was Thistlemoor Wood in the old days. Then the power in the earth left it, abandoned it, and the dead came. It's our refuge now, one of the few remaining places we can go. In the shadows and trees, we stay as far away from the living as we can get.

The wood is not a large area, never has been. Even centuries ago, it only covered a few square miles. Half a dozen miles outside Dalry, it stands between the end of a pleasant area of houses on one side and farmland nearby. In the middle, Thistlemoor Wood and a narrow trail that grows to a real pathway the closer it draws to the houses. And it was to that pathway I ran after leaving the Meadows.

I did what I could to keep to the shadows cast by the houses, but once in the fields, I was totally exposed. Thankfully, Drude's howls were far behind. Even so, slowing down wasn't an option. I ran from the trail, dashed over the field and reached Thistlemoor Wood with the sun directly above.

I fell into the shade and quiet of the trees and lay on the earth, far too weak to move. A worm slid through rotten leaves not a foot away. The leaves shifted and crackled; the little sound ate into my head. The worm dropped into the earth and vanished. I tried to follow it, to vanish as it had, and something new drifted from the big trees all around.

"Benjamin?"

The word was a whisper, too soft to carry far through the woods.

The shadows shook. One of them formed a face, then the suggestion of a body.

"Dennis?" I struggled upright.

The body grew more distinct and Dennis stood before me. His smoky form grew an arm, then a hand. He held it out to me and pulled me upright.

"Benjamin," he said. "Welcome back to Thistlemoor. It's good to have you here."

"It's been a long time," I muttered. Years had passed since I'd been to Thistlemoor. Right then, I couldn't think of the last time.

"You look terrible," Dennis said.

"Thank you."

We embraced briefly and some of my energy returned. Not enough to consider anything other than sheltering in Thistlemoor Wood but at least it was a start.

"I'm sorry I left, Benjamin."

"No need to apologise. You were right to go."

"There was something in the yellow light, wasn't there?"

I smiled and nothing at all felt funny. "Teeth," I replied and Dennis shivered.

"What happened? It was in the house, wasn't it? The family with the baby."

Without speaking, I took his arm and walked us to the nearest trees. Being high up off the ground made it easier to feel comfortable. Despite the differences between Thistlemoor and the park where Dennis and I had spent many years, imagining we were back there before the Wilson family, before Cooke and Drude wasn't difficult

I told him the story. It didn't take long. He showed no sign of surprise when I finished. In the silence, I studied our surroundings. Nothing moved below. Even the woodland animals; the squirrels, the birds, the mice and foxes were hiding.

"I don't see anyone else," I said eventually.

"Too bright for them."

I nodded, realising this should have been obvious. Those in Thistlemoor Wood don't like the day and they especially don't like sunlight.

"Any news from here?" I said, not expecting much.

"Little. Walkers, kids, couples thinking they're alone." Dennis smiled. "They provide some entertainment when it's quiet."

"No, Dennis. *News.* What have you heard?"

He didn't look at me. Instead, he studied the ground below for long moments of silence.

"We heard the demon return," Dennis said eventually. "All of us."

"That's why nobody's here, isn't it? Not because of the sun or the day. They've all gone." He said nothing and I continued. "This was our place once, our city, and now it's just the two of us in a tree."

"They're not gone. Not all of them." Dennis faced me finally. "We heard the demon come and we knew what it meant. Some of them ran. The others are hiding. I suggest you do the same."

"What?" I shouted.

"Hide. Drude will come for you. All you can do is hide."

"No, all I can do is fight."

He stared at me. Clearly, that was the last thing he'd expected. Surprising him was a pleasure. I felt more in control.

"Fight? How?"

I didn't answer at first. What was against me was very clear: Cooke, behind him, Drude, behind him. .

.well, best not to think of it. Best to focus on the immediate problem.

"Benjamin?" Dennis said and I appraised him.

"Cooke thinks he is able to beat me? Well, I think otherwise. I say we give him a real fight."

Dennis tried to look away but my hand lunged and held his face. Squeezing his cheek, I leaned to him.

"I say we give Drude and Cooke a war."

Chapter Twenty-One

It must be said Dennis wasn't overly keen on my plan.

"What war?" he shouted and the leaves all around us shook. Whether that was down to his voice or the anger of the trees, I couldn't say.

"He's got the demon on his side. *Your* demon, I'd remind you." Dennis paused as if expecting me to shut him up. I'd let go of his face and made no move to touch him. I knew what he was going to say but decided to let him speak.

"If Drude is doing as this man Cooke asks, then what chance do you have? You've got nothing. It's over, Benjamin. All you can do is join us here."

"Join you? Join the exiles?"

"Is that what we are?"

"Yes."

He'd expected me to take it back, but there was no chance of that.

"You're hiding, Dennis. You've been hiding from Hell for years, just like me. That's all you know now and that's fair enough. Given the choice between Hell and this place, I'd be here, too. But I *do* have a choice."

I dropped to the ground. My strength had returned during our conversation and I kicked out at the untidy piles of dead leaves. Watching them scatter was extremely satisfying.

"They'll destroy you, Benjamin," Dennis called down to me.

"Maybe. But I'll give them a good fight."

I should have known better, but my conversation with Dennis took much of my attention. And, truth be told, the events of that day had disturbed me more than I wanted to admit. That's why I didn't hear him coming until it was almost too late.

Branches shook as they were pushed aside, and there, embraced by the sunshine behind him was Cooke.

"Get out of here, Cooke. You can't do anything to me here and I doubt anyone would welcome you."

Cooke said nothing. I glanced at Dennis. His eyes were wide with wonder and a fair amount of fear.

"Nothing to say?" I yelled to Cooke.

In reply, he said my name. "Harwood." It wasn't his voice.

"Drude."

"The one and only."

Cooke grinned. It split his mouth in a way that made him inhuman. There was nothing of the man in the smile. There was only the demon.

"He wasn't too happy with my suggestion," Drude said. "But he went for it in the end."

"Is that right? Or did you steal his form and leave him screaming somewhere?"

"He's here." Drude touched Cooke's chest. "Inside. He wants you, Harwood. You're to blame, after all. He wants you punished."

"How nice."

There was no way out of it. Up meant the trees, but Drude could follow me easily inside Cooke's form. Ahead meant going straight towards the demon.

There's one way out.

To my right. To the centre of Thistlemoor. The final sanctuary.

"So you've come for a fight?" I asked.

"A fight?" Cooke's face twisted again and there was a moment of pity that took me by surprise. He was part of things he'd never considered. The man was way out of his depth, but on the other hand, the silly sod had nobody to blame but himself.

"Is that a challenge?" Drude asked.

His arm lashed out to strike a tree. The trunk shook. Wood shattered and the trees moaned.

"Go away," I shouted and Drude bellowed his laughter. Although his form was Cooke's, picturing light glinting on his teeth when he did was easy, and seeing those teeth opening a baby's throat was equally as easy.

1663. The first of November. How cold that day was. How wicked. How sharp.

I ignored the memory. My business was here and now, not the dead years of my past.

"You have no power here," I yelled. "This is Thistlemoor Wood, home of the dead, shelter of the forgotten—"

Drude ran at a tremendous sprint, aiming straight at me.

I flew upwards to the tree where Dennis and I had sat. Dennis was gone, probably since the second Drude spoke through Cooke's mouth.

The demon gazed up. He could follow any time he wanted but seemed content to study me.

"What do you offer me, Harwood?" he asked.

"Offer?" I replied, knowing what he meant but hoping to buy some time.

"More lives. More babies. Make me an offer as you did in the old days." He cackled and spoke in my voice. It wasn't an impression. It was *me*.

"Take the woman. Take her and let me bring you others." He hissed his demon's laugh and shouted the last words. *"Take her or don't, damn you. I've killed men, women and children. What is one more to me? Take her and spare me Hell."*

He fell silent and in my memory the woman's face was flesh again, her mouth opening and closing without a sound as she pleaded with me not to do it, to kill her but not to hand her to the demon.

A woman had begged for her soul when that soul was in my hands. She'd wanted to be a nursemaid. I gave her to Drude and counted it as good work.

"If you really wanted more lives, you'd have come to me a long time ago," I shouted and Drude laughed.

"Maybe I decided to let you stay here. Maybe I watched you do your work." He lowered his voice; it carried all the same, full of sincerity. "What's time to me, Harwood? What are the days and years? Nothing at all. So I watched you hurt people just as you did in life. Every evil thing you did, I watched. And now here we are together again."

"Like old times," I said. Drude placed his fingers around the base of my tree. Wood snapped but the tree remained standing.

"Make it easy, Harwood. Come with me."

I didn't speak, wanting him to believe I was considering his invitation. Strength gathered in my legs and the tree moaned. The sound was a rustling of the leaves with no breeze to cause it. The demon couldn't hear what I heard—the natural world was alien to him—

but he saw the drifting leaves. I lifted my leg and Drude understood.

Slamming my foot down, I jumped. The branch that supported me fell in a mighty crash, wood breaking through other branches and the green mess falling to the ground vacated by the demon a second before. The noise was tremendous but I didn't stop to listen to the echo. The instant after breaking the branch, I'd launched higher into the tree, raced through its arms and leaves and flown down to the ground. My movement was soundless but Drude knew where I'd gone. Still inside Cooke, he raced forward me in a furious sprint, screaming, churning through the earth. Trees broke apart in his wake, shrubs and thick twigs flew from the ground to rain down in a patter.

I raced deeper into the woods and aimed for its heart, desperate to reach the place where Drude couldn't touch me. My route took me through trees and each one bellowed my name as I passed. I didn't stop, I didn't care about the trees. They were meant to be shelter for the dead, even the filthy dead such as I. If they wouldn't help me, I couldn't care for their outrage.

A massive explosion shook through the woods and I risked a look back. Drude had blown three ancient oaks apart to create a clearing. Shattered bark and leaves spread over a wide area and the howls of hurt ascended from the earth. Drude jabbed one of Cooke's fingers at me. I dashed to the side as Drude's fire burst from the finger and scorched a tree close to where I'd been a moment before. The tree flamed, and then fell into ash on the ground.

I wanted to call back to Drude, to taunt him for his aim, but I didn't. All my energies were focused on running from the demon.

Drude screamed. There was no need to take another look back to know he was coming for me again.

You must shelter me, I called to the trees. Their reply was simple negation. I called to the trees again and received only a soundless bellow to leave before I hit Thistlemoor's middle.

Damn you! I roared at the trees and their reply was my name repeated over and over between the leaves.

I ran on, using the last of my energy to up my speed, speeding over the earthy floor, through trees and outcrops of rock and coming to the core of Thistlemoor Wood.

The section was clear and no more remarkable than any other part. There was a distinct circle in the land, framed by the trees. Wood chippings and twigs lay in piles, as untouched now as they'd been for God knows how long. Even woodland creatures stayed away from the centre; it was for the dead, and for the dead, this little patch of damp earth and old trees was a refuge from everything.

I crashed to the ground, rolled over and tried to summon the last of my strength. It wasn't enough. A shadow hit my face.

"Damn you," I whispered

The shadow grew larger as it closed in.

Chapter Twenty-Two

"Get up, Benjamin."

I opened my eyes. There was a figure directly above. I struggled to stand but couldn't do it. The speaker took a few steps forward and emerged into full view. Andrew McMillan: a killer dead for best part of ninety years, and, I hoped, the last defence between Drude and me.

I managed to sit upright as Dennis appeared beside Black Andrew. He winked at me and the two men stood together. Their human forms faded, to be replaced by a buzzing fog in the shape of two men. Quite horrible to look at, or it would have been if my own true form wasn't the same.

The two fogs floated as closely together as they could and Andrew spoke to Drude.

You can't stay here. This is our place. You're not allowed here. Leave us.

I couldn't see Drude through the fog, and didn't need to. He knew perfectly well what Thistlemoor Wood was and what he was risking by being there. The trouble was, his defence was perfect; nobody outside Andrew,

Dennis and I knew Drude was in Thistlemoor Wood. As far as the worlds at the top and bottom were concerned, Drude was far below where he belonged. Far below in the Pit.

I made it to my feet and changed to fog, dropping a level from my usual state. The sensation was not a pleasant one, never had been, but it did the job. My energy returned much more quickly than it would have in human form. I drifted close to Andrew and Dennis, keeping behind them.

"You can't stay here forever," Drude said. His voice wasn't quite his own. It had become a mixture of his rumbling tones and Cooke's measured calm.

We don't need to stay here forever. You can't stay here at all. This isn't your place, Dennis said.

He and Andrew drifted closer to the demon and Drude saw me. He waved.

"Come to join us, Benjamin? Me and Cooke?"

Never, I said.

He eyed me. "That's a shame," he murmured.

The ground shook. None of the trees moved; the leaves remained perfectly still and I understood. The world I'd inhabited for so many years was the same as ever. This was another domain shaking, another realm ready to welcome me.

"Time for us to go," the demon said and there was nothing but finality in his words.

The fogs that were Andrew and Dennis fell apart. The two men stood, Dennis turning to me. Without a second thought, I reclaimed my human form and did the only thing I could: crashed into Dennis and Andrew and sent them flying towards Drude.

The shrieks from my friends met Drude's howls of delight. With the ground still shaking, I turned and ran.

And the only desire in my head was one word.

War.

Chapter Twenty-Three

Thistlemoor Wood fell behind quickly. I crossed fields and farmland, roads and rivers, always travelling north and never looking back. There was no need to in any case. Drude had lost my trail, although I knew that was at least partly deliberate. He wanted me to run. He was curious about what I would do next. Sacrificing my friends to ensure my escape had pleased him. There was no doubt of that.

I spent the first few days and nights making sure my route kept me away from towns. Staying hidden in woodlands and beside rivers meant there was less chance of being noticed, even in the smallest ways, by the living. I stayed in the empty places before eventually changing course, heading west and arriving at my first destination—a town not far from Manchester—six days after the events in Thistlemoor Wood. As bad luck would have it, I arrived there late morning on a Saturday. The streets were busy with shoppers and families which would have ordinarily been fine with me. However, I didn't want the living to sense me at all. My business was no longer concerned with the living anymore, it was concerned with my survival.

I crossed train tracks to reach the hub of the town and drifted in the middle of the road, high above the ground to avoid the traffic. The road reached a pedestrianized area rammed full of people, and shops offering everything from clothes to food to toys for the little ones. Two small fountains jutted from the middle of the square between larger flowerbeds – I floated to the flowing water and let the beads drop through me.

Jonathan Richmond, I called and turned in a circle. Life was all around, life was everywhere. The sights and smells of a Saturday morning hammered at me. Skin was on display, children laughed, and beautiful girls with their healthy teeth and budding breasts filled the streets. Such life. Such strength.

Jonathan. Come to me.

There was an old building opposite me, once a bank, now a Café Nero. I faced it and the pulse beat from the roof.

A patch of murky fog spread up there. Despite the distance, the fog's buzzing reached my ears as easily as it would have had we been next to one another. The sound was the dance of flies feasting on a corpse and celebrating their dinner.

Jonathan.

The fog grew into a human shape of a tall man dressed impeccably in a long since out of date suit. He brushed his full hair from his brow and gazed at me from the roof.

Jonathan.

He threw back his head and screamed. Only I knew it for what it was. A young mother with a baby in her arms stopped nearby, the child crying. Jonathan ceased his noise and the child did the same. It settled into a snuffling weeping, head against its mother's breast.

Jonathan continued to stare at me from so far away and I heard the undercurrent far below his raging noise, far below the reasons for it.

He's still strong. And he's not afraid to use his strength. He doesn't care about Drude coming for you.

My thought was a true one. I let none of it show on my face or rise any higher than the bottom of my secret mind.

Silence passed between us, the shoppers walked by, and the water fell through my form to run down into the tiny holes in the concrete. Eventually, Jonathan swooped from the roof, streaked towards me and landed on the paving. People walked through him and paused a step later as if someone had called their name. Jonathan paid them no attention.

"Jonathan. It's been a long time," I said.

"Betrayer." His word was utterly flat.

"I am. Amongst many other things."

"A recent betrayer," he said and I understood. I didn't reply, though. Best to let him finish. "Word travelled faster than you, Benjamin. I know what you did to Dennis and Andrew. I know you gave them to Drude to escape."

He fell silent as if expecting me to bellow my defence to him and the living around us. I didn't say a word.

"Nothing to say?" he asked.

I took several quick steps to him. A few inches separated our faces.

"Do you know the difference between us and all these people?" I said and it was Jonathan's turn to not speak. "They believe in goodness and decency. We believe in ourselves."

"Is that some kind of justification?" he said, and I was abruptly tired of the subject.

"You would have done exactly the same," I said.

His movement was almost too quick to register. He grabbed me by the shoulders and threw me to the ground. At once, I tried to stand, but Jonathan was too fast. His fists bashed on my face repeatedly and the impact was so much like Cooke's beating, surprise swallowed any reaction I could have made.

Jonathan's added his feet to his fists in pummelling me and I did nothing to defend myself even though I like to think I could have beaten him in a fair fight. He kicked me in the face, aiming for my nose. Pain flooded my body; I let it, resigned to the beating until he lost energy or interest. People unconsciously walked around us as if avoiding a hole in the ground. The beating went on for another few minutes before he gave up.

"Finished?" I said and stood with as much grace as I could manage.

"I would never have betrayed my own. They were your friends, Dennis especially. How long did the two of you share that park? Thirty years? Forty? And you gave him up to save yourself. I bet you didn't give him a second thought. And I bet you'd do it again if you had to."

I flapped a hand at him. "I'm not here for debate, Jonathan. And I'm definitely not here to defend myself to you. I did what I had to. That doesn't make it right, but since when were you and I concerned with what's right?"

He swore at me and turned. I let him walk away before calling his name. He stopped but wouldn't turn to face me.

"I'm sorry for what happened with Andrew and Dennis but it had to be done. This is bigger than them."

He still didn't turn. That was all right. He was at least listening and I knew he'd turn at my next words. I didn't have to choose them carefully. They'd been with me for days.

"This is about war."

Chapter Twenty-Four

We sat on the fountains at a spot close to two bins. The living congregated further away, put off by the aroma of the refuse. Water fell through us and ran away in thick streams. The sound was like rain and it made me think of the old days, my pub beside the river, rain hammering on the water. And, of course, I thought of all my killing.

"I'll give you a few minutes. But that's all," Jonathan said.

So I told him about Cooke and Drude, about my conversation with Dennis and the sprint from the demon through Thistlemoor Wood, running from him before he could tear me apart, as he should have done centuries before.

"What has this got to do with me? Why come running to me, Benjamin?" Jonathan asked.

"I'm not running. I'm getting ready for a fight."

"Of course you are. So why me?"

"Because I want your help. I want you to be on my side."

His laughter mocked me.

"Why would you expect me to do that, especially after what you did to Dennis?" he asked.

"Because what's to stop Drude coming for you once he's done with me? Why wouldn't he want you?"

"I'm none of his business," he replied.

"You *haven't* been his business but you're mine and I'm his. He'd see you as a bonus. After all, there's nothing to stop him coming for you when he's done with me." He opened his mouth but I went on. "Ignoring that side of things, what about Cooke? Are you telling me you can stand for that? He's pushed me out. After all this time, after all *my* time, how dare he? I can't stand it and I know you can't, either."

A shadow ran over the brickwork of the bank. There was nothing close enough to the building to cause the shadow. I looked away but kept the movement in view from the corner of my eye.

"Cooke is none of my concern," Jonathan said.

"Maybe not yet, but he will be."

"Why?"

I ignored his question.

"We have a visitor."

Jonathan turned from watching the girls walking past to stare at me.

"The bank," I said and turned to it, making no effort to hide my gaze.

The shadow grew into a roughly human shape. It stood over six feet high with two arms and two legs and appeared approximately human. I didn't need to see that there were no six-foot men close to the building to know it wasn't human.

"We should run," Jonathan said.

"We should stay," I replied and we said nothing more as the demon detached itself from the shadow. Like the darkness on the wall, it had a human shape and I wondered at that. Drude was the only demon I'd seen, Drude with his teeth, now using Cooke's body like clothing. This one was new. And its human shape made no real difference. It had still come from far below.

It stood motionless for a moment, watching us, giving us chance to study it. It wore a black coat as if the day was cool rather than warm and its hair was cropped to the point of showing the gleam of its skull. All in all, it looked no more like a demon than I did and that worried me.

"I'm going," Jonathan said.

"Move and it'll destroy you," I replied. That may have been true; I didn't think so, though. The demon hadn't come to hurt us, which didn't mean we were safe. It only meant we weren't in immediate danger.

My words silenced Jonathan. By then it was too late, in any case. The demon was crossing the road to us, paying no attention to the crowds. People walked around it and appeared to not notice doing so. The demon didn't change its path or speed; people stepped out of its way as if they saw him.

It reached us and the beads of water from the fountains shone as they fell through the demon. At first glance, it could have been reflecting sunlight. That wasn't the case. The demon lit the water as it fell and the effect was quite beautiful.

"Good morning," it said, and its friendly, human voice changed things for me. It became *he* and that also worried me.

"Hello," I said.

"Jonathan Richmond and Benjamin Harwood."

"That's right," I said.

"My name is Xaphan."

"How do you do?" I said.

The whole situation was all very polite, very civilised. I decided I liked this demon.

"I do well," he said and smiled, exposing sharp teeth. For a moment, I caught the feel of heat that had nothing to do with the morning sunshine. Something else; the demon's voice sounded slightly familiar. It made me wonder if I'd met him years before.

"Tell me, Ben," Xaphan said. "What's stopping me from taking you Below right now?"

"I've been marked," I replied.

"True."

"You can't touch me without word from Drude."

"Also true."

He didn't appear particularly bothered and I couldn't even take a guess as what to make of that. He wasn't threatening me. That much was obvious, even if little else was.

He smiled again. "Drude is a pain in the arse. He always has been. The trouble is, he knows what he's doing." He leaned closer to us. "Drude's mark on you is your protection, Benny, and that pisses me off."

"Why?" Jonathan said and Xaphan glanced at him as if surprised to see him.

"Because I outrank the little shit. He's causing me trouble and I should be able to stop him whenever I want." He sighed. "But rules are rules. You know that, don't you?"

We said nothing. I knew what Xaphan meant. A glance at Jonathan told me he wasn't sure. Xaphan stared at him.

"We can't kill; we can't hurt the innocent. And the thing is, most of us don't want to. We're happy doing our work, punishing the wicked and all that fun stuff, but then some of us are just bad. I mean, really bad."

"I'd noticed," I said, thinking of that long dead day when Drude appeared before me; an insane demon with the burning need to kill, to swallow souls, and a terrible frustration that he couldn't do any of that. With that single meeting, I'd become his hands and his will.

Xaphan flashed his teeth in another smile.

"Drude has his mark on you, Benjamin. I can't touch you and I can't stop him." He eyed Jonathan again. "You, on the other hand," he said and Jonathan tried to blurt out his defence, his reasons why he should be left alone. Xaphan waved the words away.

"Jonathan Richmond. Killer of the homeless. Murderer of twelve young men between 1923 and 1932. Killed by a fifteen-year-old boy. Thomas Parker, I believe."

Jonathan dropped his gaze. I listened with great interest. I knew Jonathan's story but to hear it put so baldly, put without Jonathan's bias, was something new. Xaphan continued.

"Parker managed to stick you with your own knife on a cold winter's night in the middle of Manchester." Xaphan grinned. The grin was distinctly different from his smile. "The last thing you saw was your own breath puffing out of your mouth, the last things you felt were the pavement below your back and blood pouring from your throat. Then what, Richmond? Who came to you?"

I answered for Jonathan, "I did."

"You did indeed," Xaphan agreed. "Come to save him from Below. How lovely."

"What do you want?" I said. "Us? Drude? What?"

If Xaphan took offence at my abrupt question, he didn't show it. "Drude, of course. You two don't interest me. Neither do any of your friends. Although. . ." He trailed into silence. It was quite on purpose and I refused to play his game. We eyed one another, his understanding of my thoughts dancing in his eyes.

"Okay. I'll ask," he said. "Why?"

"Why what?" Jonathan replied. I stayed quiet. I knew what.

Again, the demon and I locked eyes. It seemed only right that I reply, given he'd broken our last silence.

"Because it meant part of me would live forever. My actions, my influence, my impact on the world. That's what I wanted." I pitched my voice low and steady. There was no obvious judgement from the demon, but even so, I had no desire to defend my long-ago actions or pretend the world would not see them as horrendous. I didn't lie to myself.

"I thought as much." Xaphan watched the living for a moment. "Human lives are so brief, it's no surprise some want to have a lasting impact. . .as you put it. Fifty years. Sixty. Seventy or even eighty or ninety, they're not enough to really hit the world, are they? You want life to know you were here, that you happened to it rather than it happening to you, right? You want the fact you existed to be worth something when you're bones in the ground. Some people create." He finally turned his attention back my way. "You destroy."

"Same result in the end," I replied.

"If that's what you want."

He had a good poker face and despite any chilliness between us, I still liked him.

Clearly utilising the British skill of pretending an awkward situation didn't exist, Jonathan spoke, "So, what do we do?"

Xaphan answered him while his focus remained on me, "Fight the little shit. He wants you in the Pit, but he also wants a fight. He wants you to struggle, to go against him. That's the only reason you're still here."

Directing this to me made little difference, Jonathan knew the realities of our situation. "I can't leave, can I? I'm part of this." He was resigned to it.

"Afraid so," Xaphan told him. "Thank your friend here. Thank yourself for being what you are, Richmond."

"What about Cooke?" I asked.

"What about him?" Xaphan seemed unsurprised by my question. Nor did he appear particularly interested.

"What about him? He started this by getting Drude involved," I shouted.

"Cooke's your weapon, Harwood."

Whatever I'd expected Xaphan to say, that wasn't it.

"I'll let you work that one out for yourself. Can't make this too easy for you, can I?" he said.

"What—" I began and Xaphan stopped my words.

"Fight Drude. Stop him or he'll take you Below." Xaphan grinned again and everything turned cold. For a moment, all the demon's attention was on Jonathan. "He'll take you far below the Bottom. Below what you think of as Hell, that's where he'll take you." He was whispering by then. "Benny knows. He knows about the Pit, he's seen it."

He looked at me for the last time. "Your plan of a war is a good one. Stick to it."

Then he vanished. He didn't fade. He just wasn't there anymore and the shining drops of water were water again.

I stood and held a hand to Jonathan.

"What now?" he said. He took my hand and stood beside me.

"Now we find the others," I said.

In my mind, I saw them and saw us, walking through Dalry, walking to a particular street while all around us, buildings burned.

The vision was exceedingly pleasant.

Chapter Twenty-Five

Our first stop was only fifty or so miles distant. Even so, I said we could take our time. Jonathan didn't ask why but I told him anyway – I wanted to give Drude (and Cooke to a lesser extent) time to grow complacent. Drude would have expected me to make a move much sooner than this, not be running around the country several hundred miles from him and my city.

We went north-east, following the road towards Leeds, leaving the road when I said to and striking out over the hills and farms. Jonathan barely spoke, which was annoying. We were away from people; there was little chance of Drude knowing our location or my plan, and I wanted to discuss that plan and what this new demon Xaphan might mean for us. Jonathan wasn't forthcoming so I had to be content with developing it in silence.

We crossed the odd river, walked in the hills and spent our nights in tiny caves in the hills. Our journey was almost pleasant. Only *almost* because I wanted to be back in Dalry, to be facing Drude and Cooke, demanding Cooke tell me why he thought his actions were justified, and doing whatever it took to wipe the smile from Drude's face.

On the second day after our conversation with Xaphan, we re-joined the road to Leeds and passed through pretty villages, houses, homes, people. Jonathan didn't like the traffic so to keep him happy (as happy as I could), I took us further into the fields and hills that lined the road. Passing through hedges and woods slowed our speec, which wasn't a problem; I knew where we were going.

We arrived at the perfect time and on the perfect day. At half past nine on a bright weekday morning, we couldn't have picked a better time to find the old ladies walking their little dogs.

"Fulbridge Park," I said to Jonathan.

"Wonderful," he replied and managed to take any joy from the word. I ignored him and gazed at the park.

It didn't take up much space and to be honest, it really wasn't much of a park. A single pathway wound through much of it and curved to meet an entrance from a nearby road. High trees lined the park's border, a few benches were dotted around and there was a depressing play area of two broken swings, a climbing frame covered in flaking paint and a rusting slide. Two young mothers were attempting to entice their toddlers on to the slide and having no success. Overlooking it, three tall blocks of flats with cracked walls and dirty windows. I'd seen more dispiriting places on my travels, but not often; everything in sight was a product of no forward thinking, no consideration of the people who would call the area home over the decades. That, and clearly next to no investment in recent years meant that despite the brightness and warmth of the morning, the park was a gloomy place. I didn't care about that. It could have been on fire and I wouldn't have cared. It had what I needed.

"Old ladies walking their dogs," I said to Jonathan.

"Why are we here?"

Those few words were the most he'd spoken in days.

"Joining the conversation, are you?" I said.

He shrugged.

"We're here because the old ladies are here. And because the old ladies are here, *he's* here."

I pointed to one of the benches. Three ladies sat together, two with dogs at their feet. Behind them, a man they couldn't see leaned close to them as if eavesdropping.

"James Cairns," I said.

He was too far away to hear me. He saw us, though, and waved.

"Jimmy Cairns?" Jonathan said. "That child?"

"Dead at twenty-nine, Jonathan. Not exactly a child."

"You've brought us here for him? We've run all this way for *him?*"

I interrupted him. "We're not running. We're getting ready for our fight."

He snorted and let it carry his disdain. Keeping calm in light of that obvious disdain wasn't easy.

"You've had plenty of time to ask me what's happening and to give an opinion on it. You haven't bothered, so for now, shut up."

He glared at me and kept quiet.

I set out over the grass towards Jim with Jonathan following. Jim watched us come and only left the ladies when we reached the bench.

"Benny," he said and grabbed my hand. "How are you?"

"Things have been better. You?"

"Well enough."

He studied Jonathan and a slow smile spread over his face. "Johnny. You look terrible. Running out of the homeless to victimise?"

"Why don't you leave the old ladies alone? This is all very unbecoming," Jonathan said.

I waited for Jim's reply, readying myself to keep the peace if needed. Jonathan's words were light enough but there was also been a sneering layer below them. Jim wasn't the same sort of monster as Jonathan and I were, although that's not to say he wasn't his own sort. Back when he was alive, he'd spent years working on the elderly—women, most of the time. He'd befriend them, work his way into their lives and steal as much as he could from them. In 1951, his final lady caught him in her bedroom and chased him downstairs. Seconds from the door (and a relatively clean escape), Jim had pushed the old woman backwards. She'd hit her head on the stairs and whether she was already dying or not made no difference to Jim. He'd strangled her and run.

Straight into the path of a car.

At the time, he'd had no idea who the old woman was. Even when I introduced him and Jonathan, there'd been no connection. Somewhere along the way, probably a decade after their first meeting, the truth came out and their relationship rapidly went downhill.

Jim's final victim had been Jonathan's aunt, his last surviving relative. I considered it bad luck and nothing else. In the years since, I've wondered if death has a sense of humour or if there was some other reason the two men had to meet.

Although he'd been dead for more than sixty years, Jim hadn't changed a great deal. He spent his time whispering into the ears of old ladies, annoying their yapping dogs and occasionally stealing their precious belongings.

"They keep me busy," Jim said eventually. He smiled, a young man with a pleasant demeanour. His face was the sort young women would call cute, I believe, and was what the old ladies would call a rogue. Many had done just that before discovering *rogue* was too weak a term for his true nature.

"I can imagine," Jonathan said and turned away as if he'd seen something interesting at the other end of the park. Not for the first time, I wondered if bringing the two of them together would turn out to be a mistake.

"Walk with me, Jim," I said.

"Be happy to."

We left Jonathan with the women and moved several paces away. At the play area, a man let his dog urinate on the swings. I smiled at the sight.

"What's happening, Benny?" Jim asked me. Ordinarily, I won't be called *Benny*, but that was Jim's way and I accepted it.

I told him about Drude and Cooke as well as Xaphan. He listened without interruption and gave me his answer as soon as I stopped.

"I'd love to come. In fact, I *insist* I accompany you."

He smiled again. His teeth were perfect.

"I knew you'd say that," I replied and pointed to Jonathan. "Will the two of you be able to work together?" I gave him my sunniest smile. "Can you work with me after what I did to Dennis?"

"I don't see why not."

"That isn't a yes, Jim."

He clapped my shoulder. "It's a yes, Benny. You worry too much. Dennis knew the risks we take." His smile fell from his face. "Although I will say one thing."

"What's that?"

"You do know we'll probably lose against Drude, don't you? Fighting a demon, well, I've heard that might be difficult."

That wasn't what I'd expected him to say and he knew it. The little bastard was happy to surprise me. The little bastard had always liked getting involved in trouble. That was probably why he agreed to join us so readily.

"Maybe. But I'm keen to have a go," I said, eventually.

We walked back to Jonathan, at which point Jim delighted in telling him our party was now three strong. Jonathan nodded and didn't speak.

And with that, we left Leeds.

Chapter Twenty-Six

A day later, I first noticed who was following us.

We were heading in a roughly south-west direction, avoiding towns at my insistence, and not talking much. We crossed the county border around midnight and soon after, a shifting pulsed on all sides. It wasn't much more than a formless tremor, the sort of thing generated by thunder over another town or city. Jim halted and gazed at the inky sky brightened a fraction by stars and a small moon.

"What was that?" he asked.

"Hard to say." I deliberately kept my gaze straight ahead. We were on a track a mile or so from farm buildings. The only life anywhere near us was several rabbits lurking in the bushes and shrubs. Further into the fields and greenery, night animals were on the prowl for food.

"Have a guess," Jonathan said and there was an ugly suspicion on his face.

"Drude?" Jim ventured.

"No. He's miles away. He's waiting for us," I said. "It was nothing."

Jonathan drifted ahead without comment. The moonlight played through his form to brighten the trail.

"He'll be all right," Jim said, loud enough for Jonathan to hear. "We just need to find a few homeless people for him to stab and he'll be happy."

Jonathan didn't stop or even pause. Jim's face betrayed his disappointment at having failed to needle Jonathan.

"I'll have to do better than that," Jim said to me and flew ahead of us to swoop over the fleeing rabbits. The trail behind was devoid of human life, as was the rest of the farmland. Below the high sky, it seemed there were only three dead men and a few wild creatures remaining in the world.

I didn't believe that for a second.

Go away. You're not part of this.

Something replied. Jim and Jonathan gave no sign of having heard it, the reply was meant for me alone.

One word.

Coming.

It had been a long time since fear filled me as it did then. That fear was due to an advancing unknown. While I knew who'd spoken, what they wanted and what they meant was another matter.

What they mean for you is danger. That's all that matters.

I couldn't move. Dread rooted me to the ground and it would only be another few seconds before Jim and Jonathan turned back. I didn't want them to see me that way any more than I wanted those following to reach us, but there was nothing I could do. Fear held me hard.

Another voice spoke to me. The demon Xaphan.

Move or you lose everything, Harwood. Deal with what comes when it comes. That's always been your way, hasn't it?

The voice worked. I sprinted forward and forced myself to slow to normal speed a moment before Jim glanced back.

"Everything all right?" he called.

"Fine."

He nodded and faced ahead again. Not taking my gaze from the path, I sent a command to those far behind.

Go away. This isn't for you. Go away. Go back to the shadows.

That time, there was no reply.

We moved on, Jim behind Jonathan, muttering insults to him in a voice too low to quite hear. Hearing his words, now that *was* a comfort, oddly. It was something known, something I could focus upon and doing so helped to stop focusing on other issues. It wouldn't be long before Jonathan reacted in the way Jim wanted and I was well aware it would be up to me to sort them out, to keep the peace as much as I could.

As it turned out, the animosity between Jim and Jonathan should have been the least of my worries.

Chapter Twenty-Seven

The rest of our journey to Gloucestershire was uneventful. Jim and Jonathan continued their sniping at each other, I kept silent and pretended I didn't know we were being followed. The other two didn't pick up on it, and there were no more tremors like that first one. That changed little. Those following were still several miles behind and I grew more certain the further we went that their numbers had increased.

We stayed away from people, stuck to the fields and rivers, and we reached Bristol a week after leaving Leeds. The morning dawned dull. The late summer warmth had died overnight as it sometimes does in August. That didn't bother me, although I did sense something strange around us, something more than unseasonable coolness. I said nothing to the others and nor did I ignore it. I kept us moving through the early morning, keeping the three of us close together, despite Jonathan's distaste at being so close to Jim, and kept the conversation to a minimum by answering their questions with one or two words. They soon realised my attention was on something else and quietened without knowing more or asking for explanation.

Our route took us through the city and out to the suburbs. We reached the field behind a school while the city slept in the early morning; my interior clock told me six had not yet passed. At the same time, the sensation of something not quite right grew stronger. Despite wanting to, I couldn't ignore it.

"Stop," I said.

Jim and Jonathan did so and both gazed at me, patiently waiting.

"Either of you feel odd?" I said.

Jim shrugged.

"In what way?" Jonathan replied.

I arose and turned in a circle to study the area. The main building of the school was beyond the tennis courts. Not a soul walked there.

"What now?" Jim said and I dropped back to the ground.

"We wait."

An hour passed. Nobody spoke. The sun moved as if it had all the time in the world to slide across the sky; the temperature failed to improve. I listened to the steady breeze and listened to my thoughts. They helped to hide the tiny whisper of those behind us.

Occasionally, cars passed on the road beside the field. None of them caught my attention, until I heard one come along at the same time as a scent all three of us recognised.

A ghost.

A *female* ghost.

Immediately, I passed over the hedge at the edge of the field and saw the car as it followed the curving road. Hanging on to the roof, with long hair streaming out behind her, was a ghost. Instinct told me what to do.

"Come on," I shouted.

The three of us flew high and chased after the woman on the car. She turned as we closed in and her face, probably attractive in life, was made ugly by fear and surprise.

The car took a curve, she let go of the roof and flew towards the smart houses. I grabbed her before she reached the first building and threw my form on top of her. We tumbled over the garden and landed in the flowerbed, Jim laughing hard behind us.

"Fucking get off me," the woman cried.

I relaxed my hold a fraction, ready to grab her should she try to run. She stared at me, a woman forever in her early twenties.

I stood and pulled her to her feet.

"What's your name?" I asked.

At first, it seemed she wouldn't answer. Then she spoke quietly, "Tanya."

"Tanya. Pleased to meet you. Or I will be if you answer my next question."

Jim and Jonathan were close behind me. Jim had stopped laughing. The three of us stared at the woman while the morning ticked by on the pleasant, suburban road.

"Just let me go, yeah?" Tanya said.

I smiled. "What are you doing here, Tanya? This area is already taken."

She shook. "What?"

"Christopher Hopkins. This is his area. So, where is he?" I said.

"Who? Look, I've been here for a few weeks, yeah? I'm enjoying myself and I ain't seen anyone else, any other dead people. I don't care about them, anyway. I'm just here, having a bit of fun."

"Christopher Hopkins," I said. "Highwayman. Dead since 1781. Hanged by the neck until he was dead, and local ghost for this part of city ever since. Where is he?"

"I told you. I don't know who the fuck that is, or where, or what you're talking about." Her words dried up. Behind me, Jim and Jonathan waited for my decision. I made it without any interior debate.

"Jim. Jonathan. Go and find Christopher. Search his favourite places. Be back here inside an hour."

They went without a word, not even a joke from Jim. I waited until they were away from the garden and heading to a small cut between the houses. It led to a thick line of trees, occasionally populated with teenagers and their illicit entertainment of drugs and alcohol. There, I hoped Jim and Jonathan would find Christopher.

"So, Tanya," I said. "How did you die?"

She didn't answer. All she did was stare at me. No longer smiling, I stared back.

Chapter Twenty-Eight

I took her into the rear garden of the closest house and sat her on the grass beside a shed. The bulk of the shed and its shadow on the grass shielded the home from our view.

Standing over her meant she reached no higher than my knees. I crouched. She spoke first and did a fair job of coming across as brave and in control. "What do you want?"

"Probably not a lot. We're on the hunt for a friend. You can help us find him."

"I told you. I ain't seen anyone. I've only been here a few weeks, but I ain't seen anyone."

"Well, let's not talk about that yet. Let's wait."

"For what?" she asked, clearly doubtful. She wanted to hope but wouldn't allow it.

I leaned close to her. "For my friends to return. And depending on what they tell me, I might not need anything more from you."

She met my eyes for the first time in minutes and attempted to give me a flirtatious smile. It didn't work.

"I got nothing to give you," she said, and the tremble of her mouth took any of the strength from it.

"You can tell me your story. I'm always interested in a good story." Her face was blank, and I continued. "Your life, your death. Although I'm happy for you to spare the boring bits."

My smile showed her I was friendly deep down.

"Why?" she asked.

"I like to know who I'm dealing with."

My words came out as jolly and it worked. She told me her story quickly but without fear.

She was twenty-three and had died a month before, or at least she *thought* it had been a month. Being sure of it was hard; time was strange and she'd spent a good few days trying to get used to being dead. When it had sunk in as far as it could for now, she'd spent another week wandering around the city before ending up here. This part of town wasn't her usual area and she didn't care about that. She spent the weekends wandering through the neighbourhood, talking to the occasional cat that never drew too close to her, and the weekdays in the grounds of the school. She'd wanted, in a vague way, to become the school ghost, to become a story of a haunted building but hadn't known how to develop her abilities.

"What did you die of?" I asked. She'd not mentioned that and I had a strong feeling the omission had been deliberate.

"My appendix. It burst."

"Why didn't you go to a hospital?" I reached for the answer in her mind as I spoke and wasn't surprised to feel her putting up a wall.

"I didn't know what was wrong. And when I did. . .well, it was too late, wasn't it?"

I did my best to pick through her wall which was a new and extremely unpleasant sensation for her. She fought against me, eyes not leaving mine; I pushed harder and she let out a pained moan.

"Stop it," she whispered. "I'll tell you."

I waited and wasn't surprised when she said: "I was homeless. Spent a few years living rough, drinking, taking whatever I could get my hands on. When it happened, when my appendix. . .I didn't give a shit."

I understood why she hadn't wanted to tell me. Even though she hadn't been dead for long, she knew enough to see what Jonathan was and who he'd killed.

"Don't worry. I won't tell him," I said.

Timid hope filled her face. She was a pretty thing. Death had taken away the tiredness and muck that doubtless clouded her face in life.

"Really?" she said.

"Really. Jonathan was a bad man. I suppose we're all bad men, really, but he won't ask you any questions as long as you don't give him any reason to."

She relaxed. "I was scared as soon as I saw him. He's dangerous, right? Not dangerous to everyone, but dangerous to me."

"He would be," I agreed. "But I won't let him hurt you."

She relaxed a little more.

"So, talk to me, Tanya. Where is Christopher Hopkins?"

"I told you. I don't know who that is."

I nodded. "Yes, you do."

"No, I don't.

I sighed, weary and losing what little patience I had. "Tanya, please. All I need to know is where he is and we're away from here. We'll leave you in peace."

She wanted to say that was what she wanted, that she wanted us to leave her alone but then her attention shifted to focus behind me and the soft whisper of my approaching friends.

"Benjamin," Jim called to me.

I turned, already knowing what I would see.

Christopher Hopkins hung between Jim and Jonathan, their arms supporting him. His face hung down and right then, being dead already wasn't important. Christopher was as close to leaving the world as it was possible to be.

"Oh, Tanya," I said. "What have you done?"

She gave a feeble squeak that was supposed to be denial.

"Jonathan," I called. "Got some news for you."

Chapter Twenty-Nine

I sat Christopher in the pleasant shade of an elm tree with dozens of pretty flowers and sculpted hedges nearby. There'd been no sign of the living from the house of the grounds we'd invaded but they were there, all the same. Should they venture outside, they'd feel us but only as an unpleasant smell on the breeze, or a strange chill.

Christopher managed to lift his head, and registered who was with him. No surprise showed on his face. He simply gave me a weak smile and said my name in the croak of a man recovering from a long illness.

"Yes, it's me." I kept my voice low. "Come with a mission for you, Christopher. For all of us."

"I doubt I'm up for it," he whispered.

"You've looked better," I said, and he wheezed laughter.

He had no visible wounds, no broken skin. Whatever attacked him had done its damage internally.

"The girl?" he asked.

"Nobody. Jonathan's entertainment."

"Leave her alone."

"What?" It was possibly the last thing I'd expected him to say.

"Leave her alone," he said again, with more force the second time. His eyes met mine and the understanding from the long years of our acquaintance was like a klaxon in my head. A *warning*. There was no time to argue with him or the metal alarm. I whirled around as Jonathan gripped the girl's throat and her pleas dried up into nothing more than ash.

"Jonathan," I yelled.

He gave no reaction; he hadn't heard my voice. His focus on the girl was much too strong.

A blast of white light hammered at the air, invisible flames burned. Vision returned. Jonathan's hands were around Tanya's throat. He was smiling the smile of a man content with his lot and his work.

I left Christopher's side and streaked towards Jonathan as Jim reached to pull him from the girl.

We were too late.

Tanya managed to look at me for a second and even now I don't know if she smiled in triumph or the image was simple imagination. Then she blew apart in a dazzling crash of light as if the sun had burst from her body. That light enveloped each of us; we flew in all directions, unable to see or to stop ourselves until we hit ground.

I lunged upright and stared at the garden. My friends had been blown to three separate areas; the spot of grass below Tanya was now a gaping hole. Wind howled out of it and although it didn't have a shape, there was something inside the mad air, something alive. It arose, level with bedroom windows, and then dived back to the grass.

Land exploded, scattering mud and grass everywhere. The shockwave flew to the houses, smashing windows, splintering doors. Bricks and plaster coughed out of the buildings, leaving rents and scars in the frames, debris spilling in piles and crushing grass and flowers. Car alarms brayed into life, each shrieking like an old lady. I caught a glimpse of Jim, mouth wide open. Then the land at his sides fell into nothing. He managed to shoot upwards at the last moment before vanishing in a cloud of raining earth, then reappearing to drop and grab Jonathan. They streaked towards me and behind them the garden of the house we'd borrowed was abruptly aflame. The fire roared from nowhere to swallow the building in a moment, the towering wave of blinding yellow, red and orange consuming stone and roof with ease. Flames muffled the screams from inside. Another mighty crash boomed into the day, reverberating throughout the city – the house next to the burning one collapsing as if a giant had stamped on it. It didn't so much fall as detonate. Huge chunks of rubble hit the road, struck cars and overturned them, then landed to snap paving and tarmac. A second later, everything in sight was a rapidly spreading wall of dirty cloud and flying rubble with the shrieks of the living somewhere beyond the gloom. Jim and Jonathan were above; I flew to them, words impossible against the storm, and we dropped to Christopher's prone form.

As soon as the four of us were together, our hands linked, the living wind returned. It went off like a bomb in the grass straight in front of us and whatever beast capered inside the howling air roared in an unthinking animal's cry.

It blasted down on us, the land gave way and below us was Hell.

Chapter Thirty

There was no sound. All I had was sight.

Colours were on all sides in a dance of light, a spiral, a circle. It was all those things and more. There was no up, no down. The others were close by, even if I couldn't see anything other than those wild streaks of colour flowing faster and faster. My eyes wouldn't shut. A dozen different hues pounded my eyes as the light shook the world. I tried to scream Drude's name, to curse him while my voice was still mine. The colours blew apart into darkness lit with one tiny light. Direction returned. The light was above. That meant escape was above.

Shrieks rang out below and I looked down, unable to not do so.

There were no lakes of fire below, no rents and scars in an earth broken like a battlefield. Either might have been better.

Below me was a hole in the floor of the world. Something inside that hole looked at *me*. It knew me. Worse, it called my name; a shout, a howl come from so far away that it arrived to me as a simple whisper exactly as it had that first day on Azalea Drive.

please oh please get me

Light flashed from the hole, light the colour of bruises and regret, and it was still there, still with eyes bigger than mountains staring straight at me. Its arms extended from the hole in the world, punching through all that black and the hands opened for me, to take me as far from the tiny dot of light above as it was possible to get. That light was so far above, it may as well have been at the other end of the universe.

Movement streaked down, aiming for my head, and I could only watch it come and float before me in a constant, shifting shape. A dot one moment, a line the next, a blurred fog a moment after that.

Benjamin.

Nothing emerged from my mouth. Everything was frozen.

Benjamin. Look.

I did so. Straight down.

The hole in the floor of the world had gone. Hell was below, stretching far beyond sight, the massive city of Hell with its infinite streets and buildings of every design imaginable, each structure an echo of human history; a sample of one century right next to one hundreds of years before so skyscrapers of office blocks stood tall beside the black and white of Tudor homes, and those pitched next to a sea of spreading tents taken from deserts. There were more towers of brick and glass and alleys and twisting pathways than I could count in a hundred lifetimes. Hell with its innumerable souls and its demons, all busy and productive; the dead atoning for their life's sins by studying billions of human lives that needed help, the demons working with them to ensure they made up for a life spent doing wrong, demons as far away from Drude as it was possible to be.

But, far under the streets, the buildings and towers growing tall and far below the atonement of the dead, something desperately attempted to peer through the buildings, up to the dark where I couldn't move.

It knew my name.

It knew everything.

Atone.

The shifting thing in front spoke that one word and somehow my eyes moved again, looking straight up.

The light was still there, still no more than a dot in the ceiling.

The choice was clear: stay in Hell and atone as the shape said, or go to the world below Hell. The world of all the worst things I would ever know.

Go to the thing that knew my name.

Damn you. Damn Drude, and damn me. I will not.

A bare moment spun out and it lasted forever. The ever changing shape flickered and dropped faster than light.

It crashed into Hell, a shockwave roared out, blowing straight into my form. And I understood that the pinprick of light wasn't only simple light.

It was the sun. It was all the judgement I would ever know.

Then it swallowed me and everything was fire.

Chapter Thirty-One

My mouth was a cavern in my face and the screams didn't emerge. What did come was shock.

Whatever halfway point between two worlds we'd been in was gone. So was any sight of Hell far below. The garden and road were in full view, both unmarked by flame. Christopher was beside me, Jim and Jonathan and the girl, and nobody gave any indication that things had changed.

"Don't let him do it," Christopher whispered.

I left his side and smashed into Jonathan the second before he connected with the girl's neck. He bellowed his outrage, pushed away from me and stood, brushing his chest and arms down.

"What the hell are you doing!?" he shouted.

Off to the side, Jim watched this little scene, not smiling. It would have been better if he had. At least it would have made sense.

"Get up," I said to the girl.

She struggled upright, weeping again. "Please. . .please. . .I. . .I. . ."

I held up a hand and she was silent. "Go, now," I told her. "I don't care where. Just don't haunt this city again. There's a whole world you can haunt. Stay away from here."

She fled, a white shape skittering over the green, towards the road and from there to wherever she could.

Jim was the first to speak, which was probably for the best. "Anyone else having as much fun as me?"

Jonathan crossed the grass. We stood within kissing distance. "Benjamin, would you like to tell me what that was about?"

I glanced back at Christopher. He remained in the shade of the tree. "Trust me. It's for the best you don't know," I said.

Jonathan shook. His clenched his fists an inch from my chest and he spat the words at me, "Who are you to decide what's best we know?"

The morning sun shone on us and I pictured that tiny moment it claimed me, my form sent streaking into it by a shockwave from the streets of Hell. It hadn't been a vision; it had been as real as Jonathan at my side.

"I am Benjamin Harwood. Never forget that, Jonathan."

He opened his mouth and I overrode him before he could speak. "Do we have any problems?"

Jonathan gazed at me for a long moment. "No, but perhaps you'd like to explain what's going on, at the very least."

I couldn't. I had to hope Christopher could.

Chapter Thirty-Two

We squatted beside Christopher, he was almost unconscious but came around fully when he sensed us close.

"Is she gone?" he muttered.

"Who did this to you, Christopher?" Jim said.

He lifted his head again and the answer was in his face.

Drude, I whispered inwardly. *You bastard.*

Christopher dropped his head again.

"Talk to me, Chris. What happened?"

He coughed a few times.

"Drude did this, didn't he?" Jonathan said.

Christopher managed a weak smile. "Came at me a few days ago," he said. I held his hand. "At night. I didn't see him before he was on top of me. I tried to fight him, but he's strong, Ben. Very strong."

"We're stronger," Jim said. "All of us together."

"The girl," Christopher began. He stopped and eventually managed to speak. "The girl. She was here when Drude found me. He did something to her. . .I don't know what."

It took Christopher a few minutes to tell us. Drude had hurt him in ways only the dead can be hurt, left him weak and then worked on the girl. Somehow, he'd turned her into a door. Christopher knew that much even if he had to guess as to where the door opened. He fell silent and I briefly considered telling the others what happened when Jonathan attacked the girl. A moment's interior debate decided me against it.

"I don't get it," Jim said. "If he knew we were coming here, why not wait? Why not hang around until we arrived?"

"He's playing with us, isn't he?" Jonathan murmured. "He's having his fun. Even if his plan with the girl hadn't worked, he doesn't mind too much. He's enjoying all this."

Jim let out a sorry laugh that said he was close to giving up. "Devious little shit," he said.

"It's not as simple as that. He's planning something," I said quietly.

All through this, Christopher didn't speak. His eyes asked his questions.

Still holding his hand, I told Christopher what was happening, of Drude's hunt for us, of Xaphan's words that our plan of war was a good one and my personal battle with Cooke.

"Are you with us?" I said and he gave me a weak smile.

"As much good as I am to you, Benjamin, I'm with you."

"Good man. Now on your feet."

I helped him up and tried not to notice what an effort it took for him to remain upright. Jim and Jonathan gazed at me and their naked emotions were all over their faces. In his current state, Christopher would be more of a hindrance than a help to our cause. Even so, I didn't change my mind. We were four. And I was determined to make Drude pay.

"Who's this Xaphan?" Christopher asked me.

"In all honesty, I have no idea, but he seems to be on our side."

Jim giggled for a long time at that. I waited while he regained his composure. When he spoke, all his laughter had gone.

"Side, Benny? We have no *side*. There's just us. Whatever Xaphan wants, you can be sure it's for himself. He'll be using us to get what he wants."

"What he wants is Drude away from this world, so I think for the time being, we can work together. Agreed?"

Jim shrugged as if the subject wasn't anywhere near as important as it truly was.

"There are others," Christopher whispered suddenly. For a second, I pretended only I caught his words. No such luck.

"What?" Jim said.

"Others," Christopher said and coughed hard.

I heard them again, those following us. Jim and Jonathan didn't. Not yet. But they would.

"Let's go," I said.

"What others?" Jonathan said.

"Nobody. He's just confused."

"Benjamin—"

"Let's go," I bellowed. Beside me, Christopher groaned. The mindless twittering of the birds stopped. Even the breeze playing around us paused.

"Of course," Jonathan said. "Work to do."

"Where to next?" Jim said. His almost constant smile had vanished and all at once, I was a tired, old man.

Exeter was the word ready to come from my lips. Instead, I held a finger over my lips, lowered it and mouthed *north*.

They understood. The chances were high that Drude wasn't close to us, which meant very little. The trees were listening, as was the wind. Word could spread fast.

We left the garden and the houses, Christopher held between us as we went north.

Chapter Thirty-Three

Four days passed before we reached Shropshire. As before, we kept to the secret places, away from people and we didn't talk much as we travelled. Christopher gradually healed; by the third day, he could move unattended. A lot of the energy I'd known in him for two hundred years was gone. In its place was a dispirited man, a man forever thirty-five who carried himself as if he was fifty years older. Despite knowing his energy and zest would return, it depressed me a little, which I didn't show. I couldn't afford to, not with so much at stake.

The others hadn't asked where we were going or who was next on my list. They understood the reasons for my silence—or believed they did. The truth was, another reason existed for not telling them and it had nothing to do with Drude. They wouldn't be happy with my next choice and I wasn't eager to get into it with them until doing so was absolutely necessary.

That time came when we stopped in a small town another day's travel from Shrewsbury. We'd journeyed through the town and paid no attention to the people or the cars, not talking, not looking anywhere except straight ahead. We halted behind the buildings of a retail park half a mile from the nearest busy road. The end of the working day was close by then. Workers and shoppers headed for their cars. Behind us, fields marched away to hills. Early evening shadows were already creeping in off the sloping green and the woodlands.

"Where to?" Christopher asked.

Jonathan gazed at me with an expression that said he knew what was next and he wasn't happy about it. I prepared for their arguments.

"Philip Matthews," I said.

"What?" Jim spat. "That filthy bastard?"

"Yes, I want him."

"But. . ."

"I know what you're going to say, and I know what he is. Even so, I want him with us."

Barely fifteen seconds had passed since I'd said his name and already, they had bunched together. All of a sudden, our situation was them against me and there was no way around that.

"Benjamin, I have to protest," Jonathan said.

"Why?" I knew why, of course, but my temper was close to boiling and I wanted him to say the words. After our days on the road, and even after the undercurrent of animosity between Jim and Jonathan, I'd believed we were a small army ready to fight Drude, Cooke and anyone else who judged us. Now, with the simple act of me stating a name, we were falling apart.

"Why?" Jonathan shouted. "Isn't it obvious?"

"Yes, it's obvious. It's also ridiculous. By any man's definition of morality, you are all bad people – as am I. We all know the truth of what we are and of what each is capable, and yet, here we all are. As always. We stay together because of the things we have done. We are outside the rest of humanity and always have been. Life or death, it's never made a damn bit of difference to us. We none of us have ever cared about morality and don't pretend for a moment it's otherwise."

Their faces were those of sullen children. Questions of right and wrong or good and evil had rarely troubled us during the long decades and centuries of our deaths. We simply *were* and decency belonged to the rest of the world. Lowering my voice, I went on. "I stand here with a robber, a man who terrified and threatened hundreds of people, who shot and killed dozens. He stands beside a man who killed the poor and the wretched because he believed it was the righteous thing to do. And lastly, we have a man who abused the trust of the old and the innocent, a man who murdered a woman who was a mother and a grandmother. These three men are filth. They are murderers and thieves and stuck in a world that rejects them every day. And they judge another man for his appetites, his disgusting need for children." I barked laughter. "Three killers judge a man for what God made him, just as the world judges them for what God made them."

"We may be killers. We may be filth," Jonathan said. "But we are not Matthews."

Christopher spoke for the first time and to hear his lack of support for my plan hurt deeply.

"I agree with Jonathan. Matthews is not the sort of man we need for this."

I gazed at each of them in turn and chose my words as carefully as possible. "Where do you draw the line? When does murder become acceptable but abuse of children is not? Matthews is a monster. I don't argue with that. But is he any worse than us? Killers, thieves, monsters." The last of the cars were leaving the giant car park, the noise of the vehicles fading. "I brought you here. I brought you together. This is my battle; you're here to help me. If you won't, then leave."

None of them moved.

"I'm going to find Matthews. You'll wait here. If I return and you are gone, then our business is done. *All* of our business. I will have nothing to do with you, no matter who comes for us."

Still none of them moved. I turned and left them in the shadows.

Chapter Thirty-Four

I walked into the town, strolled with drinkers getting ready for the coming weekend and resisted the urge to cause trouble, to start fights in the groups smoking outside the pubs. While it would have released some tension, the chances were it would have brought unwanted attention my way.

I called to Philip as I walked and received no reply. It wasn't that he was ignoring me exactly; I sensed nothing at all and as time went on, I couldn't help but wonder if he was still there, doubtful of it despite instinct's voice telling me he hadn't left the city or the area.

Proper night descended, the pubs and takeaways grew busy and taxis filled the roads. I left the busier streets and kept to the quiet places of the suburbs, always on a constant move. The sense of those following us had faded in the last two days and as much as I didn't want to admit it, that awareness returned during those hours. They were still miles behind and were staying as far back as they dared. Now they were moving again, hiding in farm buildings and trees, walking beside silent rivers and streams miles from people, massing into one solid wall coming for us, coming for me.

The image made me cold and I doubled the strength of my focus on feeling for Philip. Nothing came. And there was nothing from the others, either. There was no sense of them going away, but nor was there any feeling of support. If they were where I'd left them at the retail park, they were keeping silent.

Midnight passed by. The pubs disgorged the drunks and the rowdy. One in the morning passed. Then two. I walked. Three. Half past. Silence in the streets. Rain fell. I'd left the busiest areas of the town far behind and come to long roads of Victorian houses backing on to allotments. I entered the allotments and walked. Silence surrounded me. The others—if they hadn't gone—were miles behind. All that remained was the night and quiet.

I rested beside a rusting shed and didn't have a clue what to do next.

###

"The Pit," Xaphan whispered to me.

I was in a dream. I knew that immediately. And that didn't make a bit of difference. Fear swallowed my entire soul, my being. Fear? No. This was terror. *In that terror, Xaphan's few words echoed around my head, echoing as if he was at my shoulder.*

The Pit.

The Hell below Hell.

There was no fire in the Pit, no cackling demons with their pitchforks. Worse than any torture, there was no comfort from knowing what the real Hell was, from seeing a fraction of it in the last seconds of my life.

A universe devoid of all life, all form and shape and home to a spirit's most personal torment – whatever form that might wish to take.

It was opening a door, blinding light a snake at the crack between door and frame; illumination ever-present and solid so it would stop my eyes from shutting against what waited for me so very close by.

There would be no atonement for me, no penance, and no work to make up for a life's sins as was the case for most of the dead who went Below. And nor would there be anything as cliché as eternal fire. No. What was reserved for me was the real *Hell, the section of Below given to the few true monsters like me.*

The light.

The staring eyes peering into that light. The hole below the world.

My own screaming voice calling out my name over and over into my own private universe, forever unheard because there was nothing there to hear. Nothing but what waited for me.

The Pit.

Chapter Thirty-Five

A shadow on my face woke me. In the moment before my eyes opened, I saw Drude from the first day we'd met, grinning with his dozens of shining teeth.

"Sorry to wake you," Philip said.

I stood and brushed myself down. The act helped to brush the dream away, as well. Forcing a focus on the present and not my nightmare, I glanced around. Dawn hadn't long arrived to lighten the pavements and the high walls of the terraces. The last of the night was fading, giving everything a tinge somewhere between blue and purple. The living hadn't yet emerged but it would only be a matter of time before we'd have the old gents walking their dogs or those who'd woken in the beds of strangers staggering home.

"No apologies needed. Glad you're here."

"Can't say I feel the same way, Ben."

I nodded as if his reply wasn't a surprise.

"I spent all last night looking for you. This is a wretched town." I stretched, doing my best not to be on edge. Philip was with me; that was one side of my business taken care of. The other of Jonathan, Jim and Christopher long gone wasn't so definite.

"You think so?" he said and smiled. Or at least, his mouth moved. "And I thought it was just me."

"Walk with me." I took his arm.

We followed a side street to the allotments, crossed the mud and grass, sliding through vegetable gardens and flowers without a second look. Neither of us spoke until we were off the allotments and on to another street. A woman entered her car not far from us; she pulled away to leave the area quiet again.

"You're here with a mission, aren't you? A quest?" Philip said.

"Nothing as grand as that. Some business is all."

"And this business, you want my help with it?"

"I do."

He sighed, a weary man faced with a mountain of hard work. I studied him. He'd always been large, as long as I'd known him (which was over a hundred years), he'd stood an inch taller than me and was much wider. Appraising him that early morning, I wondered if he was shrinking as the living do or if it was just the way he stood with head bowed and shoulders slumped. He wore the same Victorian clothes he'd died in and he looked like what he was; a relic from long ago.

"Let me show you something," he said and marched ahead. I followed. He led me through the streets, along roads gradually becoming busier, across a footbridge and to a wide path snaking between houses on a miserable estate. He pointed ahead of us.

"See there?" he said.

I did. "A school?"

He walked ahead again and aimed for the squat building on the other side of a wide patch of grassland. Low hedges bordered it and the path we were on narrowed to a single line entering the school grounds. We stopped at the back of the building. In front of us, an electricity substation blocked from the grass—and children—by a high wall. Barbed wire unfurled on the wall all the way around it.

"My home," Philip said. "My prison most of the time."

He didn't need to elaborate. The substation was the perfect prison for him. If he held himself in there, then he'd have no choice but to take the sounds of the children playing so close to him. He wouldn't be able to see them or whisper to them or do anything but let their voices float over the grass, through the barbed wire and crash down on him. The children, all so close he could reach out and touch them if he wanted to. Out of all the lonely, forgotten places in the town, he'd chosen the one that would cause him the most suffering.

"Your punishment," I said and his lips split in a hurt smile.

"Exactly."

In a decidedly odd way, Phillip had proved himself to be something of a surprise. I would never have put myself up for punishment (after all, there were plenty who would say my fight with Drude was nothing but the avoidance of a long-deserved punishment) and my companions whom I'd left several miles away had avoided retribution for many years. I'd been right when I described them as not caring for morality. While each knew exactly what it was, the issue had next to no bearing on their decisions or actions. Matthews, on the other hand, had embraced his self-inflicted sentence: a monster trialled, judged and found guilty by himself. No torture inflicted by Drude or his kind could be worse for the man.

"Do you want to know why I'm here?" I asked, shaking my thoughts loose.

"Not particularly."

He took a few steps closer to the substation and I checked my interior time. Still an hour or two before the children were due to arrive and he was already desperate to lock himself away.

Not caring about his lack of interest, I gave him the details quickly and only left out the others' reaction when they'd discovered who we were in Shropshire for. It didn't change a thing for him.

"Not for me," he said without turning.

"This affects all of us, Philip. It's not only me Drude wants. He'll take all of us if he can."

"So be it."

"Good God, man. Are you seriously standing here and telling me you're willing to let that bastard destroy us?"

"It's what I deserve."

The complete lack of strength in his voice infuriated me. I wanted to grab him and bash his skull against the wall of his precious prison.

"For what you did?" I said and he finally looked at me. For the first time since I'd woken to see him standing over me, there was light in his eyes but the light was cold.

"For what I did. And for what I know I would do again if I had the chance. For all the lives and the children I hurt." He ran at me, grabbed my neck and pulled me as close as he could. "All those children I hurt in ways they didn't have a chance of recovering from. I did what I did because of what I *am*, not what I was, Ben. I'm still the same, even though I'm dead. Being dead makes no difference. The last hundred and thirty years makes no difference. I'm the same monster I was in life and I deserve nothing more than whatever Drude wants to do to me."

He let go of me and again faced the wall of the substation.

"The others think I'm running from Drude, but I'm not," I said.

Philip made no move to turn towards me.

"I'm getting ready for him, Philip. I need your help to do that. You can't stay here."

His reply possessed all the fatigue there could be in one man. "I stay here because I love the children. I stay here because I don't want to hurt them."

That was the last he would say on the issue. He drifted towards the substation, paying me no more attention. I left him with his prison and the time ticking away until the first of the children arrived and his long sentence began again.

Although many years had gone by since I'd been to the town and Philip had taken me to an unfamiliar area, it didn't take me long to get my bearings once I was on the move. The retail park from the day before was five or six miles from Philip's prison. I took my time on the return journey and that was only partly down to the fear that the others would be gone by the time I returned. I refused to let my fear tell me what to do or push me any faster than I wanted to go and I didn't consider what my contingency plan would be should the others have deserted me. All that mattered was the knowledge of Drude coming, always coming and the only weapon I owned was my little plan.

The town was coming to life by that point. Cars and people and buses passed by; I ignored all of them exactly as I ignored the few dogs barking as if to frighten me away.

I reached the retail park at ten o'clock. The car parks were full. People went from building to building; lorries took their loads and departed. There was no sign of my little group of thieves, murderers and bastards.

Still not hurrying, I slipped between cars and drifted towards the final ugly building in the long row, abruptly convinced Jim, Christopher and Jonathan would be gone.

I reached the building, turned and looked towards the little patch where building met grass.

"Thought you'd never come back," Jim said.

Chapter Thirty-Six

Things were better for us during that reunion. We shared a few moments of stilted apologies; they were sorry for how it had been the night before and I was sorry for leading them such a long way for no result. We talked about my meeting with Philip while the living made their noise not far enough away and the sun's light beamed through patchy clouds. The sense of urgency had gone and I was at least temporarily glad of it. It was nice not to have the voice of instinct hammering at me to keep moving, to stick to the quiet roads and empty fields. Gone, too, was the sense of those behind us. They were still following, I was sure of it, but they'd lost the feel of me if only for a short time. Even so, knowing their whispers and entreaties were far away was enough to keep me happy.

"So," Jonathan said when a silence fell. "What next?"

"One more," I whispered. "One more should do it."

They gathered close, interested, and I mouthed a name. *Sally Winchester.*

Jonathan blinked, surprised into silence. Jim giggled a nervous laugh and Christopher smiled. There was a lot of happiness in that smile. He and Sally had something of a history, or as much of a history as the dead can share.

"Benjamin, no offence, and none to you, Chris, but she's a tad unpredictable," Jonathan said.

"I wouldn't have her any other way," I replied and Christopher snorted.

"Same for me," he said.

"Are you sure?" Jonathan said and I reminded myself he was a cautious fellow, much as Dennis had been. Never mind his murdering and the blood he'd spilled, Jonathan never took a risk unless there was no other way.

"Sure as I've ever been. We need her. She'll do a lot of good for us."

"I still think—" Jonathan said and froze.

We all did.

The sounds of the living and their vehicles persisted, all as garish and jangling as ever. The constant steady passage of the clouds hadn't stopped and the temperature remained stuck somewhere between mild and cool.

Even so, something was different.

I titled my head like a dog as my instinctive voice came alive.

"Run," I whispered.

"What?" Jim said, panic blooming on his face.

"Run," I said again and raced forward, desperately hoping the others would follow instead of going the other way.

They were close behind. The five of us flew into the car park in a silent streak. We stopped beside a dirty van and I stared back the way we'd come. Some of the greenery behind the buildings was visible, but not much. Not enough.

"Who is it?" Jim asked, probably aware his question was a stupid one.

"We should get into the fields. Into the hills," Christopher said.

"No," I said. Jim moved as Christopher spoke, desperate to be away. I put a hand on his shoulder.

"We stay here. We stay around people."

They understood my plan. I thanked whatever luck I could that my friends didn't need everything spelling out for them. Even so, Jim wasn't totally convinced. Maybe his own instinct was telling him the hills with their scrubland, their little woods and streams would be a safer course of action than this—in full view of the approaching demon.

"We can hide out there," he said and jabbed a finger towards the green.

"We're safe here. Drude won't attack when there are people so close."

I let go of his shoulder and stayed ready to grab him should he move.

"There," Christopher said and extended a trembling finger.

West of us, the familiar waft of heat shook above the ground.

"If we move, go for people," I told them.

The heat sped towards us in utter silence. The living went on with their business, all oblivious to the approaching demon. For a second, I envied them.

The streak stopped at the exact spot where grass met concrete. Drude appeared. He'd left behind the suggestion of his form living in the flickering to assume a human shape. A shape is all it was. He was no more flesh and blood than I. He floated a few feet above the ground as if unwilling to touch it.

"Hello, boys," Drude shouted.

At the junction where the entrance to the park met the proper road, two cars collided with a hollow thump. Breaking glass tinkled, followed by shocked screams. Drude gave us a sunny smile. I remembered Cooke as I'd last seen him, a human-shape with Drude inside him. Drude was now a demon inside a man-shape.

"Go away, Drude," I said.

"That's not very friendly."

He rubbed his hands together. The whisper of his skin made me want to vomit.

"Cooke not with you?" I asked, stalling for time.

"No. He's. . .busy."

"Is that right?" Without taking my eyes off the demon, I tried to think of an escape plan. In all honesty, there was only one. I didn't relish what I'd need to do if were to survive the next few minutes.

"He has his own work to do so it's just me, I'm afraid." Drude appraised us. "So, boys. How are things?" He sounded bitterly jolly.

"Grand. They'd be better if you went back where you came from."

"Can't. I've got stuff to do here."

Jim took the bait and I mentally cursed him. "What stuff?" he asked.

Drude's mouth widened in a hungry smile. "Tearing your souls into a million pieces," he replied.

I willed the others not to speak. It turned out either my will wasn't strong enough or Jim didn't get the message.

"Come on, then," he yelled. "You ugly bastard. Come and get us."

Drude howled once, a mad shriek that broke through to the living. People stopped outside the closest building and scanned the area around them, the sky above and each other. Then Drude flew at us.

"Move," I bellowed and crashed down beside the entrance to a huge DIY shop, Christopher beside me. Jim sped towards a pet shop and Jonathan flew through the windows of a garden furniture shop.

Christopher yanked my arm; we flew into the building, streaked over the tills and landed in an aisle lined with paint, rollers and brushes. We'd been too fast for Drude. He called to us. It sounded as if he was still beside the entrance.

"Don't do anything," I whispered to Christopher. He nodded.

A middle-aged man passed by close, pushing his trolley and examining the cans of paint within. I considered using him as our defence, but knew we could do better.

I gestured to Christopher and we floated to the next aisle. Drude's angry mutters were still audible from the same place. I pictured him there, scanning as much of the shop as he could, cursing us, desperate to have our weight his hands as he tore us apart. I grinned without feeling at all amused. I was reasonably sure there were only seconds left before my end, but annoying Drude could only be seen as a plus.

We slid alongside the paint thinner, the trays and step ladders and our perfect defence appeared behind a group of young men. The young woman, twenty-five at the most, steered a pushchair with one hand and held her empty basket with another.

"Her," I whispered.

We raced to the woman's side and bracketed her. She kept walking and the only obvious sign she felt our presence was her suspicious glance at the other customers. We reached the end of the aisle; the woman steered her pushchair towards a display of garden benches and I called as loud as I could.

"Drude."

He howled again and sped towards us from his spot by the doors. As soon as the demon registered the woman with the pushchair, he froze.

Silent joy filled me. Christopher would never have guessed my plan had been based on a hopeful guess Drude would adhere to the rules. We were protected by sticking with the woman because Drude wasn't allowed near her. She was an innocent and whether she knew it or not, she was protecting us simply by existing. Briefly, I offered silent gratitude to whomever or whatever would take it that demons had to abide by the rules of the living and the dead.

"Leave us, Drude," I shouted.

"You don't tell me what to do," he ranted.

"I do, so go away." That was a bluff and I knew it. Despite it being easier to face Drude when he dressed in such a nondescript fashion as a human man, the demon still terrified me. If he had been thinking rationally, he probably would have remembered that.

Spitting, he tried to float closer to us. He made it more than a few inches before he was forced to stop. The woman we were beside was still close to the benches. I kept half my attention on her, ready to move the second she did.

"You can't stay with her forever," he yelled.

"I don't need to. You're on a time limit, aren't you?" I made a show of checking my wrist as if I was wearing a watch. "How long until someone misses you? How long before the other demons want to know where you are? How long before one reports your absence to one of the high-ups? You know what happens then, Drude. You know what happens to you if they find out you're here."

Drude came down. He crashed into a high shelving unit and flew out of sight as the unit tilted and tipped, spilling tins, brushes and rollers in an almighty crash. Howls drowned out the din and one old man didn't get out of the way fast enough. He fell below a massive pile of cans, head crushed into an interesting shape while the blood spraying from his skull turned the floor bright red.

The woman we were bracketing was seemingly frozen. People sprinted away from the falling cans and more howls of terror rang high. A running man smacked into the woman's pushchair and the baby added its own screams to the chorus. Drude reappeared over the melee and glared at us. Christopher gave him a jaunty wave and Drude struck another unit. It tilted, hit a third and both crashed down on three women. The noise was tremendous. All around, people ran screaming and jumping over the fallen, all desperately attempting to make it to the other end of the shop.

The woman we were beside finally made a move; she yanked on her pushchair, trying to turn it and move backwards at the same time. Moving as little as I could, I whispered to her and she froze. She wept and didn't move. Drude saw what I'd done and spat laughter. He pointed to the shelving units.

"What are you going to do if I decide to knock those on to her and her baby? Keep her there? Keep her as your protection? *Coward.*" He spat the last word as if genuinely offended by our actions.

The last of the terrified shoppers ran towards the far end. To them, the only life remaining in the middle of all the mess was one woman with her baby. A few people called to her, pleading with her to run; she made no move to do so.

I spoke before Drude could. "You've blown your cover now. None of that was allowed."

"I don't care about what's allowed. I want your soul, Harwood."

The anger was gone. All that remained was certainty he'd won.

"I don't think so," I said and stared without blinking at the demon.

His face could have been chiselled from rock for all the reaction he made.

"Last chance," I told him.

"For you."

I shook my head as if saddened by his words. "No. For you."

As fast as I could, I whipped my head around, swooped close to the woman and bellowed into her ear. The shout had no words. She understood, though. So did Drude.

As the woman obeyed my command and yanked her baby free from the pushchair, Drude gave a final bellow. From the corner of my eye, I saw him coming and reaching for me, no longer caring about the rules that said he couldn't directly harm the living.

The rest of the woman's movement was strangely graceful even though it was almost too fast for the human eye to see.

She turned on her heel, arms flying out from her body, all her strength behind the throw. Her baby soared high, straight towards Drude's grasp. He pulled back at the last second, shrieking his fury as he came within half an inch of touching the child. That was half an inch too much for him. He flew backwards, crashed through the window and vanished in sunlight and breaking glass.

The baby dropped, hit a huge pile of paint cans and was instantly silent.

Mind you, its mother's screams more than made up for it.

Chapter Thirty-Seven

"**W**as that absolutely necessary?" Christopher asked.

I didn't move from sitting on the pavement, head resting on my knees as I silently tried to get my strength back. Screaming at the woman and influencing her to such a degree stole a great deal of energy.

"What would you have done?" I muttered.

"I don't know."

"There's your answer."

I studied them; the men I'd brought with me to face off the demon who wanted their souls, men who'd killed and killed but who were now looking at me as if I was something worse than them.

I suppose they had a point with that idea.

"He did what was needed," Jim said and kept his focus on a group of crying women beside one of the many ambulances. The police were also there, and several of them were with the now childless mother in one of the ambulances.

"Thank you, James," I said and he turned to me.

"Answer me one thing, Ben."

"Of course."

"Did you know your plan would work?"

That was what I'd expected and my lie was ready. "Yes. There was no way Drude would risk alerting the higher demons to what he's up to. Destroying the shop was bad enough; killing those people who couldn't run fast enough was another. Letting the baby touch him would have been far too much. He knows the rules of what he can and can't do. He knew all of that and he knew we'd beaten him, so all he could do was run."

"You think Hell knows where he is and what he's doing?" Jonathan said.

"Possibly. At the moment, though, we should assume not. Nobody else in Hell would stop him from getting to us. He marked us, after all, but he's not allowed to do all that."

I jerked a thumb to the mess inside the DIY shop.

"The chances are he'll stay away from us for some time. If anything, he'll be less sure of himself now. He wasn't expecting me to do that. It took him by surprise and that can only be a good thing for us."

I stood as straight as possible. My strength wasn't back yet but standing was wonderful.

Jim faced the hills in the distance. "So, Sally Winchester," he said.

"Sally." I nodded.

"Do you still think we can beat Drude and Cooke?" Jonathan muttered.

"Yes. If I didn't, I wouldn't be here."

He seemed satisfied with that. I wished I could be.

"To Sally," Jim cried. "A fine woman in need of a good man." He glanced at Christopher who gave him a small smile. They embraced in a rough manner before setting out together.

"A shame she won't find a good man in any of us," Jonathan said.

He drifted after the others. I followed and we left the grieving and the bodies behind.

Chapter Thirty-Eight

Our route took us south. We travelled for a day and a night without stopping before Jonathan said he needed a rest and we sheltered in a farm building on the county border. Leaving my motley crew at the rear of the building, surrounded by rusting machinery, I stood beside the doors. They were rotten and hanging off the frames, but they'd keep the night out for us.

The sun was going down; there was an uninterrupted view across wheat fields to the red on the horizon. The colour shone through the sky in a pleasant fashion, the sky met the earth and all that was between me and the line at the end of the world were miles of farmland, empty, quiet, free of the dead and demons.

Such melancholy wasn't like me. I shook it off and took a moment to appreciate the last light of the day burning into the red of the sunset. That was when I heard them again, much louder than before.

They were at the horizon, running and jumping through the land between here and there, skimming over rivers and lakes, shifting into the gaps between trees, flying through valleys and hills. They were coming for us, coming for me.

"Go away," I whispered and sensed movement.

It was Jim. He'd approached as I'd been staring outside. As I'd been so engrossed in the view and those approaching us, I hadn't heard him until he was almost on top of me.

"Evening," he said.

"Everything well?"

"Everything's well with us."

I turned to him, glad to have my eyes on something other than the burning sky.

"Meaning?" I said.

"Meaning what the hell is going on, Ben? And don't tell me nothing is, because I know that's a lie."

"Would I lie to you?" I attempted a smile and almost managed it. Jim didn't return it.

"Yes," he said.

"True."

Jim smiled that time, showing the face of the handsome, easy man the old ladies had all trusted. I pictured him beside Jonathan a few days before, back in the garden with the girl, Tanya who had been a door into Hell. Even though the others hadn't known it, she'd been an opening to Below. More than that, she'd been a warning. Carry on fighting Drude and I was practically guaranteed my own destruction. If I'd followed the opening all the way down, we'd now be in the Pit. Not much of a choice.

"So, what is it?" Jim said, bringing me out of my head.

I heaved a heavy sigh which wasn't much of a pretence. I was tired. Fighting Drude and taking revenge on Cooke for starting all this was still what I wanted to do, but if truth be told, I was playing a young man's game. Here I was, almost four hundred years dead and still fighting the good fight. But then, what other option was there?

"Give me a few days, Jim. That's all I need. As soon as it's the right time, I'll fill you in." I lowered my voice as if the rotting doors and grass outside were listening. "Besides, word spreads, doesn't it?"

He got my meaning and nodded once.

"Have Jonathan and Christopher said anything to you?" I asked.

"No, but I think they're wondering the same as I am. Chris, especially. Jonathan is too tired."

"Say nothing to them. It's not the right time."

He offered me one nod again, turned and headed back to Jonathan and Christopher, their dim forms almost lost in the murky light of the old building.

I gave the horizon a final look (by then, it had become an explosion in the sky and would remain so for another few minutes before night fell), listened to the whispers of the coming hordes and again told them to go away.

It didn't work.

"We will be ready for you, Drude. Understand? We will be ready for you. You best be ready for us." My whispered words floated in the gathering gloom as I thought of Drude somewhere across the country, cursing me.

I slinked away into the shadows and joined the others.

Chapter Thirty-Nine

Jonathan spent the next three days telling us he was too old for such a journey and we needed to rest every few hours. I had none of it. Time was growing short and I pushed us onwards, travelling south across farmland, hills and empty spaces between towns. We rested for a couple of hours before dawn on the morning of the third day but that was it. There was work to be done, I told them, and we wouldn't succeed by sitting in the trees or in the long grass beside rivers. Jim and Christopher had very little to say over those few days. They spent most of their time in silence or occasionally appraising me when they thought I wasn't looking. Those following us were still coming, still whispering on the wind. The others knew it, even Jonathan by that point. None of them mentioned it, though. Whether that was because they all knew I was aware of it and was keeping quiet for my own reasons or because they didn't want to alert Drude, I don't know. Anyway, we kept going, kept quiet and reached Exeter six days after leaving Shropshire.

And Exeter was where I planned on recruiting the last of our little group.

Of course, plans rarely work as one imagines.

###

We left the towns and cities of Devon behind during the day and ended up in the countryside as the afternoon wound down to evening. The weather improved during our journey from Shropshire; the sun had been brighter than recent days and the temperature increased to more respectable late August levels. Even so, there was a coolness around us that was perhaps simply down to the exposed land.

Our route took us by the side of a busy road, which gradually narrowed the further we went. Traffic decreased; we moved closer to the road by unspoken consent and eventually walked on it rather than on the embankment. Each of us walked with our private thoughts and if any of us pictured Drude, we didn't speak his name.

As proper dusk fell, I gestured to the others that we should leave the road. They followed me to the fields and fell behind in a line. We snaked over the grass and shrubs, still moving with the line of the road but also heading further into the darkening green.

After we'd gone a short distance, I stopped. The others did the same and floated close to me.

"Sally Winchester."

The two words of my shout hung above us and while they didn't echo, I did have the feeling of them bouncing off each other like pebbles. I waited for them to spread across the moorland and drew breath to call her name again.

"Wait," Jim said and pointed.

There was a lone car on the road. Its lights speared the gloom, taking away any sense of peace and isolation.

Although the driver would have had no idea we were a quarter of a mile from the road, his presence gave us problems. Sally wasn't a fan of people, not since she'd been burnt alive. This one idiot and his car, the first we'd seen in two hours, would doubtless drive her away.

We stood in silence, waiting for the vehicle to be out of sight or at least far away enough for Sally to not see it as a threat.

It slowed at a point almost level with us, stopped and a man got out.

"I don't believe this," I muttered. For a discomforting moment, I'd wondered if Drude had tracked us down again through the lonely countryside. That worry was needless. The man stood where the road met a sharp dip to grass and nettles and urinated in a high spray.

Jim let out a healthy volley of laughter. Jonathan, always more refined than any of us, hissed his disgust and turned away.

Music from the man's car stereo drifted to us and I lost what little patience I had. There was no way Sally would come to us with this idiot pissing into the wind and his stereo playing some vacuous dribble of a song.

"Want me to get rid of him?" Jim said. He was eager to do so. Even Christopher's expression suggested he wanted to be part of any fun Jim had in mind.

I shook my head. "Keep an eye out for Sally," I said and flew over the grass. The man was still urinating, aiming his spray in a fine line. I swooped at him from behind and stopped as he finished urinating. Jim, Christopher and Jonathan were watching me which was slightly irritating. If Sally came to them as quietly as she could, they wouldn't see her.

Ringing sang from behind as the man's phone in his car brayed into life. He returned to his vehicle, answered the call and stood on the side of the road, completely oblivious to the problems he was causing us. I floated beside his ear and breathed. His words faltered for a second. I let him talk for another moment, then did it again. That time, he stopped and stared at the fields he'd parked beside. The growing night stared back; my friends stared with it. They were grouped together, all facing the man. It took a lot from them, but they still managed to show themselves for a fraction of a second. The man let out a noise somewhere between a moan and a hiss of fear. The person on the other end of the phone was asking if he was all right; the man was sweating now and I heard the strong beat of his heart.

I whispered to him again, telling him of the night coming, the massive open spaces where anything might walk in the night, anything in the lonely places between houses and roads. Creatures of childish stories made flesh and creeping ever closer from the lonely and forgotten corners of the land. Shadows moving despite the lack of life; slithering horrors dripping ice-cold water as they emerged from ponds and streams, where the only witnesses were the dangling arms of the trees, and the sky, so impossibly huge like an unblinking eye watching for *him.*

He saw it all, saw the things he didn't believe in when he was at home with his lights and television, and the animal inside his rational brain took control of everything.

"I'll call you back," he said to the caller and pocketed the phone. His eyes were two wide holes in his face. I followed him as he trotted back to the driver's side of the car and tossed his phone to the other seat. He slid inside and I whispered to him for the last time in a wordless growl.

His lips tightened into one line, almost a slash in his face. He slammed the door closed and sped away, veering all over the road. I waited a minute to see if he would steer properly or crash. After he'd gone a few hundred yards, he straightened his course and accelerated. I offered him a jaunty wave and sensed him look to the rear-view mirror as I did so. The car almost hit the narrow embankment before he straightened again and disappeared towards the horizon.

I turned back to the others. My three were now four.

Sally was with them.

Chapter Forty

Probably without needing to be told, the men had grouped away from her. Sally didn't like anyone getting too close and the others knew that, even Christopher. His face told me he wanted to go to her, to put his arms around her but didn't dare. Wise man. I'd seen what happened to those who got too close to Sally Winchester when she wasn't expecting it. Such transgressions rarely went unpunished.

"Good evening, Sally." I bowed my head to a respectful degree.

"Good evening, Benjamin," she replied.

"Are you well?" I asked.

"I am."

"It'll soon be night. Would you care to come with us? There is a woodland nearby."

"I know."

"Your home?"

"As much as it can be."

We were talking as if night wasn't almost on top of us, as if Drude wasn't somewhere probably close by. Jim, Christopher and Jonathan, knowing what I wanted, stood beside me. We faced Sally. Her face was almost invisible in the dusk. For a moment, she showed us the burns she'd carried for almost four centuries. Then she turned from me to gaze at the countryside she'd haunted for so many years.

"You need me, do you not?"

"I do, madam."

"Then I'll come. But I will leave if you lie to me."

"Thank you."

She drifted past us; I mentally told the others to wait for a count of ten before we followed in a loose line of the dead floating across the Devonshire moorland.

The woodland was an ugly area of skinny trees and tatty scrubland of barely half a square mile. We floated through the pitch-black, none of us caring about the thick cloud blocking the moonlight, and halted in a tiny clearing. Again, we men stood together and faced Sally. Ghosts give off a certain illumination to other ghosts; we saw each other quite clearly. Sally's burns were gone for the moment and I wondered why she was hiding them. I doubted shame had anything to do with it. Sally didn't believe in that. She took my appraisal without comment for a moment. Then, "I dress when I'm at home."

"Understood."

"Tell me what you want," she said and lifted a hand as I tried to reply. "Not you. Him." She pointed one long finger at Christopher. He glanced at me, asking for approval with a look. I didn't nod. He had my approval but I couldn't be seen to give it. This was Sally's moment.

"Speak, Christopher. Speak if you love me as you said you did once."

Christopher blushed. You wouldn't think the dead could or would, but we know embarrassment. Christopher shook his off and spoke. He didn't start with Drude as might be expected. He started with Cooke.

"A man came to Ben, a man who prided himself on being good, on his good deeds. A self-righteous man."

A light shone from Sally's face. I smelled flames as heat radiated from her. Christopher continued.

"This man Cooke fought Ben to stop him, to do the right thing. He took it upon himself to do work that wasn't his to do and to be a judge when he has no right to be one." Christopher's own ire had grown. It wasn't forced for Sally's benefit. He was truly indignant at Cooke's presumption.

"He brought the demon into this, didn't he?" Sally said and I took over from Christopher.

"He did. Drude. Cooke wanted him to take me to the Pit; Drude's mark is on all of us and I intend to fight him with your help, Sally."

The light burning on her face, light from those consuming flames all those years ago, faded. It returned when I stopped talking.

"A self-righteous man. A judge."

Her few words were laced with something extremely dangerous. There was no madness or rage. Her words held no light at all.

"I know about the self-righteous. I know about those who judge."

She touched her face and all at once, the light below her skin was above it. A wall of fire held her; flames burst from her features, consumed the night to scorch and swallow. None of us moved. I doubt any of us could do so.

The fire raced upwards to climb into the sky; orange and yellow tongues licked at the tops of the trees, coated bark and leaf and birds' nests as if they were nothing. Sally voiced a giant scream, tearing it out of her throat and we saw—*a decaying cottage, a garden growing wild, a narrow line of a path snaking to the front door, a woman running to that door and hammering on it, howling a name, screaming for her husband. And behind her, coming fast, a group of men, soldiers, the woman at the door screaming for her husband while behind the door, a woman and a man frantically dress in a tiny room that still smells of their spilled fluids, of their sinful love and the soldiers are advancing and the woman outside the door screams for her husband, curses Sally's name with hate and judgement and wails one word in accusation, in total condemnation.*

Witch.

The soldiers reach the path, come to the door and hammer on it, prepared to bash it down, and the man with Sally is yanked outside to fall at his wife's feet, to feel the sharp night prick at his naked flesh while the soldiers grab Sally, pull her from her little home to the villagers and their hate and judgement.

Witch.

Witch.

Witch.

A fire lights the day, the villagers are around the fire and some cheer the flames and some yell for Sally to burn in Hell.

The fire.

Burning.

Screams.

Sally.

Fire and witch and burning and judgement and death.

Sally's fire died. It faded back into her as if she controlled it through simple breath. Not a one of the trees was marked. There was no sign of the conflagration, no noise of burning wood. The entire time had been silent.

Sally gazed at us.

"Wise woman, they called me. They came to me with their aches and illnesses and private problems. They came when they were sick or confused and I cured them all. I loved my friends, my villagers." Her eyes were far away. "I loved one too much. But I never judged a soul."

Out of all of us, Christopher was the only one who could have gone to her then. He drifted to her side and bowed.

"We can't know your pain. Nor would we try to. It's a woman's pain. Men, as foolish as we can be, we know of other pain. We know of those who look down on us. Others who judge a man's life. We know about that, Sally." He swallowed. "Will you come with us? Will you use a woman's strength to fight a demon's?"

Had I been alive, that wait between Christopher's question and Sally's reply would have frozen the breath in my lungs.

"I'll come," she said. "And I'll come gladly if it means judging those who would judge us."

She kissed his cheek.

That's us complete, I thought.

Sally pulled back from Christopher. "Who are they, Ben?"

"Who are who, Sally?" I said and knew what she meant. There was no way I could pretend I didn't know just as there was no way out of it.

"Those behind you. Those who've been following you."

Chapter Forty-One

The wind passed through the trees in a powerful rustling that would have, I imagine, terrified the living. For us, it was only the sound of the unthinking night.

But that wasn't right at all. The sound was the murmurs of those Sally said were behind me, those following.

Those coming closer, now Sally named them, coming much faster, all speeding through woods similar to the one we stood within, watched over by the massive sky and all its black glory.

"The Lost," I said and Sally echoed my words.

"The Lost. The shades."

She stopped and I willed her not to finish her thought. She did, though. "The ones who want a leader."

"What's all this about, Ben? Who's behind us?" Jim asked.

"The ones outside Heaven and Hell," Jonathan answered the man.

"That's right. The Lost. They're the ones who've rejected Heaven and Hell for too long, they're now the eternal ghosts. They want you as a leader, Benjamin. They're coming to make you that leader." Sally said all this without any emotion.

"I don't want them. I never have!" I shouted.

"How long have you known they were coming?" Jim said. He was always slow to anger; it was there then, though. It had probably been days in the making.

"He's known the whole time," Christopher said wearily. "Don't be foolish, Jim."

Jim eyed me silently. In his silence, the crushing weight of his feeling was terrible.

"We're not enough for you?" he said. "Us, all thieves and murderers? We're not enough?"

"Wait a moment. I never planned on using anyone else."

"But you're going to, aren't you?"

"He will if he wants me to come," Sally said.

I faced her, glad to no longer see Jim's appraisal. The leaves rustled again, much louder than they had any right to do, given the almost still night. Our group was silent and my mind sped through my options.

Run. Leave them in Sally's woods and run deep into the countryside and keep running so Drude would never find me.

Stay. Argue with Sally. Tell her I didn't want a mass of ghosts looking to me to be their leader. I wanted the few I'd chosen, the few strong enough to stand against Drude, not those too weak and indecisive to move on to the next worlds.

Or stay and agree to Sally's condition.

There were no options, not really. An eternity of running or becoming what I'd never wanted to be.

Sally smiled.

I turned away, held out my arms and called to the rustling in the leaves and in the shadowy pools beside tree stumps.

"Come on then. Come and follow me if you want me."

The rustling stopped. In the following silence, countless spirits waited. Sally spoke, amused.

"If you're here because you want a fight, then you must do better than that, leader."

I cursed her and I cursed myself. Nothing changed. It never does.

My next words were a shout. "Come to me. I'll lead you against the demon. I will take you to a war. I will lead."

The shadows opened and they came.

Chapter Forty-Two

Dawn grew grudgingly. Dirty light slipped over the moorland, flittered through the trees around our little camp and glided into the roof of the wood. The light did nothing to improve the sight or my mood. If anything, I would have preferred not to see those watching me from the little gaps between trees, the ones who tried to skitter out of sight when I glanced their way.

Jonathan approached first. I'd known he would and it cheered me a fraction to be proved right. Behind, Jim and Christopher spoke in low voices that still managed to carry to us. They weren't talking of anything important, nothing about Cooke in any case. Sally was nowhere to be seen and I couldn't find much inside to care about that.

"Good morning, Benjamin," Jonathan said and I nodded my greeting. He let a silence play between us for a moment, long enough for me to take a guess at his next words. As it turned out, I was wrong.

"Fancy a stroll?"

I laughed for the first time in weeks, maybe months.

"Something funny?" he asked.

"Not really." I laughed again. "I expected you to ask me about them." I flapped a tired hand at the nearest shade in the trees. It vanished.

His mouth opened wide. "Probably not the best place for such a chat, is it?" he said.

We walked together, leaving Jim and Christopher to doubtless debate my next secret move. To be honest, I was wondering the same myself.

Jonathan and I stopped a quarter of a mile from the woodland. The land raced away, big land below a big sky. We faced one another.

"Talk to me, Benjamin," Jonathan said.

"About?"

My reply was the wrong thing to say. His face flushed and he forced his feelings back inside. He swallowed them, leaving me curious on how far I could push him before he pushed back.

"Apologies," I said. "I shouldn't be making stupid comments."

"Accepted."

"You want to know what I don't like about this. You want to know why I don't want what is effectively an army of ghosts against one ghost."

"Yes."

"Because this is for us. This is our business, our strength against Cooke's strength. For all this time, we've been outside Hell, outside what we know in a fair and balanced universe is the punishment we've managed to avoid for centuries. We've been better than Heaven or Hell, better than life or death. We've managed to beat the system by being strong and clever and quick. Now the system wants to beat us. Well, let it try, I say, but we fight back on our terms and those terms don't include me as a pretend leader to a load of directionless souls."

"Why not, Benjamin? Why not have more of us against Cooke?"

"Because they're not us."

"No, they're not," he agreed. "They're their own. But that doesn't mean you can't use them."

"He's right," Sally said behind me.

I didn't jump or cry out (other than rogue demons attempting to condemn you to an eternity of damnation, it takes a great deal to scare the dead). I simply turned and studied her. The land around us was featureless. She'd come from the land, come up out of the grass like smoke.

"Good morning," I said.

"He's right," she said again. "You can use them. You *will* use them."

"Or you won't come."

"That shouldn't be your biggest concern. You should concern yourself with Cooke and what he means to you, not whether your ego can deal with working with such as yonder rabble."

That stung simply because it was true. The quest that I'd imagined the last few weeks to have become was me and my friends against an outsider. There was no room for more outsiders even if they did want to support me.

"There are a hundred ghosts in there," Sally said. Her voice changed to a kinder tone. "A hundred souls ready to do your bidding. There's a long way between here and Dalry, a long way between you and Cooke. If we leave now, if we march on your home, we'll pick up more as we go. And then what will this Mr Cooke do? What *can* he do when faced with such a large number of the dead ready to fight him and punish him for his presumption?"

She stopped. I didn't reply and she answered for me.

"He'll have to run, just as you did, Benjamin. He won't have any choice."

"It might not be as easy as you expect," I told her. "He's clever and he's angry. That makes him dangerous."

"As dangerous as the five of us? As dangerous as murderers and monsters like us?" She smiled with a precise lack of warmth. Despite it, the beauty she had been in life was still there, way beneath her face. "And that doesn't include those in the trees. They've been outside light and the living for so long, they won't remember what it was like. They won't care to. All they know about is loneliness and the dark. You can give them more than that at least for a short time. And so what if Cooke manages to fight back and destroys some of them? They won't care about that any more than they care about what it's like to be alive. They've forgotten how to care."

Jonathan stood forgotten beside us. All that was left was Sally in front of me and the silent land flowing away to the living miles away.

"Are you a monster, Sally?" I said.

The touch of the fire that ended her life returned briefly. It crackled against my face and a touch of her rage hissed in the crackles—rage at her killers, those who judged her love as immoral to the point of death; the same people who had come to her to cure their ills had been afraid of her and she paid for their fear with her life.

The flames faded. Her grin went with them. "They called me a monster, so perhaps that makes me one."

"No, woman. They were wrong." I held her. "But that doesn't mean you can't still stand against those who judge now." I welcomed my righteous indignation. "Those who judge us."

Sally's eyes gleamed.

"Come on," I said.

The three of us walked back to the woods and Christopher and Jim. Behind them, the shades grouped in the branches or tried to hide in squat bushes. I didn't speak until we reached Christopher and Jim; all of us faced the aimless dead and a few of them peered down from the tops of trees or from the tattered edges of bushes. They were all formless shapes, all no more than smoke with eyes, and I had to wonder for how long they'd been dead; for how long they had continued to walk in a world that forgot them all, centuries before.

Wondering made no difference. I had no idea.

I spoke and knew full well that my words were more than just speech. They were an address.

"We're going back to Dalry. All of you are welcome to join us. We will meet more on the way and they are welcome to join us, too. If you go ahead of us and tell them, we will be that much stronger. We will return to Dalry and we will tear it apart if we have to. We will teach Mr Cooke a lesson. He will learn it is not his place to judge. He'll learn it even if it's a hard lesson for him."

Two of the shades slid away from a thick tree trunk. They held hands and drifted towards us. Their sex was impossible to tell, as was their age. All that was visible was wafting smoke. They were older than me, much older. The slits in the smoke that were their eyes gazed at me and me alone. I saw the centuries they'd spent as part of the secret land, the spaces between cities. It was a glimpse of what it meant to reject Heaven and Hell for all that time. That glimpse gave me months and years and centuries; it gave the boundless green spaces of a country older than the living could comprehend. For a few dizzying seconds, I went back in time to the centuries before my life, before my death. The

Reformation came and went in a spinning blur; kings lived and died, and the country burned in the Black Death. Further back to the Dark Ages; further back to the waves of invaders from Europe, from Scandinavia and on and on through the snow and sun and fog of years unremembered by any of the hundreds of ghosts I'd met throughout my death. The wide-open spaces of Britain grew larger—green upon green, woods upon woods, and fewer and fewer of the living to fill those spaces. Time became meaningless. We were back before records, before the Romans, and everything around us was fresh, clean and full of the possibilities of all the long days and years ahead. The long time the shades would know, because this was *their time.* This, thousands of years before my parents and grandparents, was their life. Under a huge sky, the ground cooking below a blazing sun and the small settlements sleeping beneath a younger moon, they lived and had no idea of the loneliness waiting for them millennia after their bones and bodies had been reduced to less than memory or dust. Or the horror of forgetting what being alive meant.

The horror of forgetting they had ever been anything other than wisps of forgotten mist, too inconsequential to be called spirits.

That was what those few seconds gave me. That was all these shades had.

The aimless dead. The ones lost from the world. The words clanged around my head.

"Will you come with me?" I said to them.

One breathed a word from its smoke. *Yes.*

"Thank you," I said and meant it. My panic and bad feeling of recent days had decreased. It hadn't gone by any means, but I could deal with it. Even if it meant they'd made me a leader.

"We'll go now," I thundered. "And we don't stop until I have Cooke's head in my hands."

There was nothing else to say as we began our final trek east.

Chapter Forty-Three

I almost ordered us to stick to my word of not stopping until we reached Dalry. After six days travel without a single break, I knew we'd need our energy and focus to face him, so I called a halt to our journey. We spent the night eighty miles from Dalry in a condemned factory, which was home only to spiders and mice. The next morning, we travelled with the dawn at a slower pace than recent days and reached our final stop hours after sunset. Theoretically, we could have continued non-stop (after all, it's not as if any of us had any muscles to strain or blisters on aching feet) but we were emotionally and mentally tired and that was enough. We set up a rough camp on a golf course about ten miles from the edges of the city, lights from the motorway gleamed and the fairly constant traffic sent its noise into the cooling air.

Most of the shades stayed together. They rested in little groups, keeping as low to the grass as they could. The few braver ones wanted to join us and I probably would have welcomed them. Jonathan wouldn't let them, though. He told them to give us space and they did, perhaps thinking their leader being treated as such was only fitting.

Jim, Christopher, Jonathan, Sally and I sat in a loose circle, the grass below our backsides and legs. Tiny voices rose from the blades of green all around; it wanted us away, didn't want our filthy touch. We ignored it.

"Cooke will know we're close," Jim said.

"True. He's not stupid," I said. "Which doesn't concern me. We were never going to have much element of surprise working for us."

"You think he's prepared?" Christopher asked.

"Probably. Which shouldn't change anything for us. We'll fight him until the end. That was always the plan."

Sally asked the only remaining question. "What about Drude?"

I'd been expecting that. We hadn't spoken much of the demon in the last few days. Sally's question was a fair one.

"I don't think we need to worry a great deal. Drude knows the rules. He knows if he breaks them, he's as much an exile as we are. He won't risk that. Everything he's done and everything he *can* do is purely for show – even all that business back in Shropshire. Remember that and we'll be fine."

"What's that?" Jim said.

He was looking over my shoulder towards the motorway. The lights on the road did little to dispel the shadows and illuminate the area. Even so, the movement of something over the grass was visible.

"Stay here," I said and stood.

"Maybe we should send some of them." Christopher gestured to the closest shades.

"No. Stay here," I said again.

Everybody watched me go. Nobody followed, though. They hadn't heard my command to stay and yet, they had. Word travels fast when you're dead.

I passed beyond the last row of our quiet army and crossed the golf course. The land dipped and spread in small mounds and the moving thing didn't fade or come any closer to me. The night grew out of it in streams. I stopped and it formed a face, a body. In seconds, it appeared human.

"Hello, demon," I said.

Xaphan bowed. "Benjamin Harwood. Nice to see you again."

"Is it?" I said. My one meeting with Xaphan seemed to have happened to someone else. We'd travelled so far since that day and now that our journey was close to its end, I wondered again if this demon had ulterior motives for his support of my plan.

The demon smiled. "It's *always* nice to see you. Again."

Chapter Forty-Four

He wanted me to walk with him, to walk and talk. I said no and he didn't appear surprised.

"Want to stay in sight of your friends?" The demon gestured to the ghosts across the golf course.

"Yes," I said. There didn't seem to be much point in lying.

"Fair enough. Can't say I blame you."

He sighed and more of his features became visible. As it had been during our first meeting, his face was fine-looking, although still lined and tired. His pale features and almost bald skull shone in the dim moonlight.

"You're an interesting man, Harwood."

"Thank you."

He grinned again and showed his perfectly even teeth. "That doesn't make you likeable, of course, but you *are* interesting. A killer, a butcher, a murderer, a monster. They've called you all those things, haven't they?"

"And more, I don't doubt."

I was relaxed, which was partly down to a sneaking resignation. If Xaphan wanted to break the rules and take me, there would be almost nothing I could do about it. Ignoring for a moment what he told me about not being on Drude's side, I didn't think he was there as Drude would have been. If anything, he possessed none of Drude's madness. What he did have that Drude didn't, was a sense of self-control.

"I told a friend of mine I was coming to speak to you and he said you were one of the worst excuses for a human being he'd ever heard of," Xaphan said. "But then, he always was melodramatic."

"He could be right. I may be just that."

"Probably."

He lit a cigarette. No pack emerged from his long coat and there was no reaching for a lighter. Instead, cigarette and lighter were in his hands as if they were no more unusual than his long fingers.

"A bad habit," he said and inhaled. "But we have to have some fun, don't we?"

His eyes shone red for a tiny moment and fear touched me. Below the light voice and joking comments, Xaphan was as much a demon as Drude.

"Anyway, enough of this. I've come with a warning, Benjamin."

"Which is?"

I wanted to be away from him, to be back with the others.

"Don't underestimate Cooke. He knows you're coming and he'll be ready for you. He'll be prepared."

I frowned. A warning that would do me some good, even though I could have guessed as much, wasn't what I'd expected the demon to give me.

"Why do you say that? Why would *you* warn me?"

"You still think I'm here to do Drude's work? No chance. Even if I wanted to, I couldn't. You're his. I can't touch you. You know the rules, Benny."

"Yes, I do."

I didn't lose my fear or drop my guard. Xaphan was telling me the truth. Even so, I was careful. I hadn't stayed out of Hell for four centuries by being careless.

"Don't lie to me. You must have another motive for all this. You must have something else going on." I paused deliberately. "So I ask you again, why tell me?"

"Because I don't like Drude and it would make me happy to see him lose his hold on you. Because Cooke is a boring bastard. Because *I'm* bored and this is as close to entertainment as I can get. Because I want to see what shit you can cause. Because, because, because."

He leaned close to me and I held my ground.

"Because I can. How's that?"

"Not good enough."

A bright smile made his mouth open. "Okay, you win. I'll spare you the details. Let's leave it at Drude pissed me off a long time ago. Doing all this will go towards getting him back. Good enough?"

"Good enough."

He backed away. The light from the tip of his cigarette glowed red and I pictured his eyes. They were no longer visible. Nor was his human like shape. All I saw was a fog merging with the night.

"Be careful, Benny. You've come such a long way. It'd be a shame to come this far and lose."

He was gone.

Chapter Forty-Five

The others wanted to know every detail of my conversation with the demon, especially Sally, Jim and Christopher, who hadn't been with me the first time. Out of all of them, Jonathan was the most obviously worried by the demon's involvement, despite having met him all those days before. He stared across the golf course as if Xaphan was still watching us. For all we knew, he was.

"This changes everything," he said and I spoke over his next words.

"It doesn't change a thing. We still have more than enough ghosts here to take back to Dalry and destroy Cooke."

That was the wrong thing to say and I knew it. Xaphan's words had unsettled me more than I wanted to admit.

"He said this wasn't about Cooke," Jonathan said.

"I know, but I'm going to make sure Cooke is part of this. He started it and there's no way he's getting out of it now."

"What about Drude?" Sally asked. The light of amusement was in her eyes and I didn't care for it.

"Drude knows the rules. He won't break them."

"Well, if you're sure," she said and turned her back before I could reply. She crossed to a few of the shades she'd befriended and each of them faded away. I faced Jim, Christopher and Jonathan.

"Are you with me?" I said.

"You really have to ask?" Jim said.

"I wish I didn't."

"We're with you," Jonathan said. "But I don't like this. I really don't."

Neither did I. And I think he knew it.

Chapter Forty-Six

The whispered word went around for a few days leading up to our stop at the golf course; it didn't reach me until the night before we returned. Our army wanted to travel at night, to come to Dalry in the quiet and stillness of three in the morning. Whether that was because they thought it would work to our advantage or, as I privately believed, because it would mean fewer people for them to be around, I didn't care. We arrived on the outskirts of the city half an hour after dawn and that was exactly how I wanted it. To bring our fight to Cooke in the light of a new day would be too much for him.

A motorway was a few hundred yards in front, already busy with cars despite the early hour. On both sides of it, green fields spread in great swathes while a completely clear sky extended from one end of the earth to the other. It really was a beautiful day.

With the others beside me, I faced the milling shades on the grass.

"We're almost there. We're almost at the man who would judge us, who would keep us outside because he thinks this is where we belong. I say, we teach him a lesson."

Briefly, I wondered what really made Cooke tick. A need to beat me? The righteous judgement held by so many when it comes to a bad man like me? Or he was simply insane? Sent over the edge by refusing to accept the things I'd done. More than that, sent there by *my* refusal to apologise for them? There was no way of knowing. Cooke had started this – I would finish it.

A mutter ran through the shades at my last words, sunlight blanketed their thin forms and coated the grass. The army of ghosts were almost invisible even to me. They didn't want to be out in the sun, they wanted to hide in the quiet places untouched by human life, as they had been doing since the land around us was healthy grass and young trees.

"Stick with me," I called to them and turned back to the road.

We drifted alongside it for several miles, the flow of traffic grew even heavier and I didn't turn around despite the little worry that told me the shades wouldn't cope with such a close proximity to the living, that they would all scatter now my back was turned.

Sally read this worry on my face and slid close to me. "Don't worry. They won't leave."

"I don't worry."

She smiled. "And you don't lie, do you, Benjamin?"

She floated back to Christopher's side. Jim took her place beside me.

"May I say something?" he asked.

"Of course."

Jim let a few moments pass before he spoke again. We floated under a footbridge and the ghosts let out a soft murmur of gratitude for the respite from the sun.

"You haven't told us what happens when we get back to Dalry," he said.

"I know."

"Are you going to?" he said and it made me happy to hear a fragile layer of amusement in his voice.

"No," I replied.

"No?"

Any amusement had vanished. I'd annoyed him with my one word and if I didn't change my angle quickly, that annoyance would grow.

"Not yet, Jim. Soon, but not yet."

He stared at me. "This isn't just your fight, you know. You've got us involved in it. It's our fight, as well."

"I know."

"I doubt that."

I expected him to move away, leaving me alone at the front of our group. He stayed with me, though, and I gave him a few minutes to calm down.

"Watch me," I said, voice low. "You'll know what to do. Just watch me."

Jim said nothing. I had to take that as answer enough.

Chapter Forty-Seven

Dalry.

It felt as if I had fled from it hours before, not weeks. The roundabout on Thorpe Road was exactly as it had been for years; the parkway ran off it, the road beyond the roundabout headed into the centre of the city. We were three miles from our destination and I wondered how close Cooke would let us get before he made an appearance.

We drifted on, Jim still by my side. I led them along the road and ascended two dozen feet. It gave me a good view of the way ahead and the vehicles and large houses on either side. More than that, it was chance to watch for Cooke. Christopher said my name and I glanced down.

"He's close. He knows we're here," Christopher said.

"Good."

Sally's eyes were all over me. For once, she wasn't smiling.

"Sally?" I said.

"Don't underestimate Cooke."

"I don't underestimate anyone, madam," I said and knew the reply was simply a formality.

We passed the roundabout and soon reached the bridge. Below us, traffic passed in and out of the city centre. The noise was tremendous. There couldn't be long before the shades would lose their strength and retreat to the quieter areas. Their urge to punish Cooke for becoming involved in issues which were far beyond him could only stand up for so long when put against the modern world and all its noise.

"Dalry!" I shouted to them and pointed ahead. "Memorial Square. Long Gate. Bishop's Gate. Mid Gate. All the little streets and buildings and old places. They're yours."

I lowered my voice so only Sally, Jim, Christopher and Jonathan heard me. "Tear it apart."

A slow grin spread over Jim's face.

"Is that your sign?" he said.

"It is."

"About bloody time."

He shot ahead, flying over the speeding cars. Christopher and Sally followed him silently. Jonathan hung back and wouldn't look avert his gaze.

"Do you know what you're doing?" he asked.

I echoed Jim's grin. It felt good to smile. "I always do."

Jim turned to the shades and called to them. En masse, they streaked forward, a wall of grey in the morning sun. They swooped past me; Jonathan led them over the rest of the bridge, crested a large roundabout and hit Bishop's Gate.

Cooke. Come and get us.

I followed my ghosts into Dalry.

Chapter Forty-Eight

Sunlight. Warmth. And people ready for their working day, not a one fully awake, all coming and going into Memorial Square.

We raced down Bishop's Gate, passing estate agents and parked cars, we flew in a howling wind the living couldn't hear. Even so, a few people on the pavements stopped to study the sky, as if a thunderstorm had formed in the blue yonder.

We came like Hell.

Memorial Square was exposed and beautiful in its complete lack of defence. We hit the road and several dozen of the shades fell under the ground. Rumbling grew from below, a slow crack snaked from the road to the fountains and then towards the stone steps of Memorial Hall. The few people didn't notice; maybe it was too early in the morning for them. They didn't even notice when the crack reached a bench and one of its supports gave way, spilling the thing on its side. The rest of the supports broke and it collapsed to the paving.

The remaining ghosts stared at me; I tried to see their eyes in their smoke. I caught a glimpse of one or two, but most were no more than wafting fog in the sunlight, formless and faceless.

"Make me proud," I bellowed.

In silence, they filled the buildings, the banks, the record shop, the mobile phone shops, and the jewellers. There was a beat of nothing. Then windows exploded and music equipment, mobile phones and jewellery flew from the wrecked shop fronts.

People screamed; some ran for cover in Memorial Hall, others ran for Long Gate and others couldn't move even as the rubble and broken glass scattered in a deafening storm. They watched with their mouths open wide, watched as goods from the shops rained around them. Staff from the record shop dashed to the street, a few chased after their flying stock and managed to grab some from the road. Two smartly dressed women emerged from a jeweller's, their faces dazed, their steps silenced by the roar of the exploding glass.

The crack in the ground abruptly widened, the damaged bench split in two and the steps of the Hall snapped open. Chunks of rubble collapsed, dust flew and the remaining people ran.

Memorial Square had become, in under a minute, a warzone.

"Impressive," I murmured.

"What next?" Jim said.

"Enjoy yourself."

Whooping with delight, Jim swooped over a burger van. I imagine it took most of his energy but he managed it all the same.

The van tipped with an almighty crash, spilling meat, sauces and oil. The mess spread in a wide pool around the van and looked quite disgusting.

"Bravo," Christopher said and flew to the fountains. The water rose and fell in a constant gentle stream. As soon as Christopher fell on it, water exploded in all directions, showering shop fronts and the stock on the ground. Christopher claimed the second fountain and did the same. The water now resembled a wall; the fountains were buried below it. I caught a glimpse of the fountains cracking, of stone, earth and dead flowers pouring out.

The water rushed into the cracks in the ground, filled them and flooded back out. Two minutes after Christopher's first move, the large pedestrianized area of the Square was flooded and the living were left to watch from the shops and road. They'd stopped screaming,; a few shouted their fear and panic, but most simply stood without speaking – it was as if all the sudden violence and destruction had made them mute. People who hadn't been in the Square, who'd come running to witness our actions, were on their phones, speaking rapidly. Others were filming the chaos on the same devices. It wouldn't be long before the authorities arrived. The *living* authorities, that was. I didn't care about them. The *real* authorities were who interested me.

"Where are you, Cooke?" I whispered.

I'd forgotten Sally was close by. She'd remained there while the boys had their fun, floating behind me. She heard my question and asked her own.

"Are you scared of him, Ben?"

I eyed her, trying to work out if she was joking. There was laughter in her face.

"No. Should I be?"

"I don't know. I *do* know I have a feeling that says it's perhaps wise for you to be scared."

"If it keeps me going, I'll be scared. In the meantime, feel free to join in the fun."

She didn't move, but the ghosts who'd crept back up from the ground did. They fell into the streaming water from the wrecked fountains, put their collective energy into each single drop and sent it flying in massive spurts towards the living. The reaction was spectacular.

Each man and woman scattered as if the water was fire, most shrieking. Those shrieks hit a new pitch when the ghosts kept the momentum of the water going, aiming the liquid at the fleeing people. They ran, soaked and coated with pieces of road. In seconds, there was nobody within a hundred yards of the Square. The dead let the water drop and it struck road and pavement with a resounding *smack*.

Sirens sped closer. Jim and Christopher drifted down from the windows on the high floors of a bank, and Jonathan raced towards me from the Burger King.

"To me," I called to the ghosts.

They drifted like fog. A few people wept; all stared at the mess of the Square they'd known as utterly normal for years.

The sirens drew closer.

"A job well done," I said. "Now. Get ready for part two."

Chapter Forty-Nine

The police arrived. Ambulances followed barely a minute after. By then, the crowd had grown from the few who'd been there when we'd started to seventy or eighty. The police blocked off Bishop's Gate and Long Gate, leaving the Square as sealed as it could be. They took the crowd further down Long Gate to where it met Mid Gate. They'd placed bollards on the road and erected a low fence around the Square. I'd caught a few words from them; they thought the whole calamity was down to a gas leak, an underground explosion, and there was talk of evacuation.

We grouped in the Hall and took in a fine view of the Square as the living attempted to impose some order on the mad events. It couldn't be done, but they did their best, as they always do. Twenty minutes after the police arrived, I breathed two words to the assembled dead beside and behind me.

"Part two."

We drifted out of the Hall and floated towards the police.

They'd arrived with four vans and several cars. We closed in on the nearest van. Beside it, three officers spoke in low voices while another sat in the driver's seat. There was more talk of a natural explosion. It sounded as if the policeman wanted to convince himself as well as his colleague. That was fine with me. He was welcome to any comfort he could take.

"Jim," I said. "On the left, if you please. Jonathan, the middle."

"What do you want me to do?" Christopher asked.

"The driver."

Each of them floated close to the men I'd directed them to. Sally hung back. I spoke without turning.

"Sally, would you mind joining the men in that car?" I pointed to the nearest vehicle. Two men stood beside it, one speaking into his radio.

"Not a problem," Sally said. "Where to?"

I pointed to the second van.

Sally drifted towards the vehicle. In the centre of the Square, the crowd of silent ghosts waited. They knew their role and I had a feeling most of them were looking forward to it as much as they could.

"Do your best," I breathed and closed in on the remaining policeman. Jim, Christopher and Jonathan slid in beside the other men and Sally floated into the car.

At the same time, we spoke to the policemen. It took a great deal of energy from all of us to do so, but we were boosted by our work and by the coming result.

We whispered in the officers' ears. We told them secrets, dark things they didn't want to know, but couldn't help but hear. Their faces went slack, as if the strings holding their muscles had been cut, and their hands hung at their sides.

We whispered. Their wives, their families, their loved ones were against them, had betrayed them in the worst ways they could conceive. The Law failed them; the line they fought to keep the world crossing over was a sham. The public loathed them. They did no good in an uncaring world. That world was an unforgiving place and they were lost inside it. Worse, they'd lost the world they wanted to help through their own failings. They'd brought it down with their weaknesses, their mistakes, their faults, and all they had now was the blame for not only how they were seen but for the state of all wrong things.

The one I floated beside wept. He was silent as he sobbed, which was quite a sight. His hands still hung like dead fish at his sides, and he didn't see his colleagues also beginning to weep, didn't hear them, either. A voice crackled out of his radio and he gave no response. All he saw and heard was the pain my whispers gave him. And that pain brought rage.

It grew slowly at first but expanded quickly like a flame exposed to a steady flow of oxygen. His tears ceased. He gazed at the other men, seeing them for the first time since I'd come to him. They stayed back. Jim and Jonathan moved away from them and Christopher slid out of the car.

Each policeman held his breath. The radio spoke again, and again it went unanswered.

I gave my last whisper to the man beside me, flexed my energy and gave the same ugly words to the other officers.

Three of the men collided in a howling mess of arms, fists and teeth. The man in the car flung the door open, staggered out and barrelled into the fighting men. They dropped to the road, tearing at each other. The first of the blood flowed and I called to Sally.

She soared from the car as officers ran from the bollards. There was an abrupt screech as the car Sally had been inside lunged forward. It was aimed directly at the second van.

"Beautiful," Christopher said.

Car hit van with a strangely hollow crash. Screams echoed from all sides, although the men below us didn't stop their fight. More blood streamed from their growing wounds, and one of them was perhaps already unconscious.

The running officers reached their colleagues and could do nothing to separate them. Hands were fists and mouths were biting teeth. We left them to it and went closer to the wrecked car and van. Neither had exploded upon impact, which was definitely disappointing. The driver of the car was a mangled shape halfway through the windshield. Much of the van had been crushed. Glass and twisted metal lay in heaps around both vehicles and there were no signs of life.

"Well done," I said to Sally and she curtsied, which made me laugh.

More police raced towards the chaos from Long Gate and Bishop's Gate. They were too late for the officers beside the first car. None of them moved despite the efforts of those who'd come from the bollards. There was a terrifically strong smell – a mix of spilled blood, crushed metal and panic. I let it drift over me for a moment, proud of our work.

"Job's not done," Jim said close to my ear and I smiled.

"True," I said and gazed at the police fence. There were still more police there than I would have liked, but we'd achieved quite a bit. Their numbers had been more than halved by those who'd come to aid their fighting and dead colleagues. Behind the remaining police at the bollards on Bishop's Gate and Mid Gate, rapidly growing crowds of the public stretched back. All of them wanted to see what was occurring in Memorial Square, and doubtless all of them felt they had a *right* to see, to be part of what had happened.

"Friends," I called to the silent shades. "Your part of this is here. Do this and your work is done."

A few of them moved, but that could have been down to a nervous shuffling rather than any eagerness.

"I know this is difficult. I know this is the last place you want to be but I also know you wouldn't be here if some little part of you didn't want to make them pay for their arrogance and presumption. I know you want that, so I ask you to do your work, do your best and punish them all."

The first line of the wispy shades drifted in a long line. They were all almost in perfect synchronisation, a breath of smoke crossing the Square, heading on to the road and aiming for the bollards on Bishop's Gate.

"Is this going to work?" Jonathan whispered.

"I have no doubt," I answered and he knew I wasn't lying, because I believed it myself.

Another line of the ghosts followed the first, then a third. A fourth and fifth went towards the people on Long Gate. After that, the rest followed like a cloud.

"If you're going to make a move, Cooke, about now would be the best time," I whispered.

If he was listening, he didn't reply.

"Do it," I said.

As one, the shades dropped over the people.

Chapter Fifty

For a count of five, nothing happened. Then everything happened fast.

Screams were first, then shouts. There weren't any words in the noise, just a tidal wave of fear and rising temper. The perfect soundtrack to our work. In the crowd on Bishop's Gate, several people bolted, hit the shop fronts and fell to the ground, crying. A few policemen ran to them but couldn't do any good. There wasn't time.

Both crowds surged forward and ran over the police, over the bollards and through the fence. Complete chaos was coming to Memorial Square, coming in a fast jumble of running people. They'd seen their private nightmares. The ghosts gave them the same Hell the five of us had given the policemen, and the public reacted in the same way. They thundered into the Square from Bishop's Gate and Long Gate as we floated above the ground, not wanting to get in the way. The shades joined us from our vantage point. Even as the surviving police shouted for order and tried to physically stop the terrified stampede, both sets of crowd saw the others and everybody blamed everybody else.

They halted and nobody made a move. The police were still calling for everyone to calm down, to lie flat on the ground and remain still. Those not shouting at the public were on their radios, calling for backup, yelling for support. Let it come, I thought. The more, the merrier.

A queer silence enveloped the police as they saw the lack of reaction from the public. Each man and woman stared at those in the other crowd. The police shoved a few down to the ground and could only watch, dumbstruck, as those pushed stood to stare at the other crowd.

"Come on, Cooke," I whispered. "Come and save them."

The shades were waiting. I stayed utterly still.

"Come on. Do your best. It's what you do, isn't it?"

Still nothing. Around us, the sour, electric smells of panic and fear grew rapidly. The police were pushing more people to the ground and those people went down silently. As soon as the police were off them, they rose again and gazed at the opposite crowd. Seeing this, the police tried a new move. They formed a human barrier between the crowds; there wasn't much space but they managed to do it. Twenty of them formed a line crossing over a small fraction of the Square, ten facing one crowd, ten facing another.

"Everyone move back now," one officer ordered. He had a strong, carrying voice. Ordinarily, they would have followed this command probably without question. Nobody obeyed. The shades drew close to me, now eager to complete their work.

"Benjamin," Jonathan breathed and I smiled.

Cooke. Come and stop me. Come and stop a bad man.

An officer spoke into his radio. I didn't catch his words and didn't need to. His tone was clear: shock and panic.

Jim climbed higher and gazed towards Mid Gate. He let out a long, hard laugh.

"Ben, my friend. I think you'll like to see this."

I joined him and we stared over the heads of the police and the public.

Richard Cooke was coming to us and the mess and hurt we'd created. He saw me and despite the distance between us, the hardness of his expression was clear.

Unable to stop my grin, I shouted to the shades. "When I say so, please finish your work."

As one, they breathed their happiness.

"Ben?" Jim said in a soft voice completely unlike his usual tone.

I turned back towards Cooke and understood Jim's tone.

Cooke wasn't alone. There was a third crowd coming to join the two in the Square.

And all of them were floating high.

All of them were dead.

He's been busy. Remember what Drude said? Cooke had his own work to. The clever bastard.

"Ben?" Jim said again. Jonathan, Christopher and Sally joined us. Sally let out a tired, hurt sigh. Her breath was the only sound any of my group made.

"Now," I whispered.

"What, Benjamin?" Christopher said.

"Now." I whipped my head around to the shades. *"Do it now."*

In Mid Gate, Cooke howled, the cry of a good man. The shades loomed above the people on the Square. At the same time, Cooke was a blur speeding towards me. Behind him, the dead flew, all howling my name.

Chapter Fifty-One

There was no time to think then, to wonder who the other spirits were. All I could do was charge against Cooke as he raced towards me.

We hit one another high above the heads of the police and civilians. Behind, the first screams began as the people charged at one another and paid no mind to the bellows of the police. The racket grew louder but all I could really hear was Cooke raging at me.

"You're sick, Harwood. You're a monster."

His fingers linked around my throat, began to squeeze and I threw him to the side.

"We established that when we first met," I said to him and five of his people struck me.

I flew and hit the side of a bank. A dozen ghosts advanced on me. Cooke swooped down in front of them and blocked them.

"Friends of yours?" I said.

"They're decent people, Harwood. Do you know what that means? They're the ones who know what you are, who came to me when we heard you were coming back. They're the people ready to kick you out of the world because they won't stand by and let you cause all this pain."

He came at me again. Behind him, dead men and women were howling abuse, calling me a monster, an evil bastard who deserved to rot, a killer, a bully and a coward.

As one, Sally, Christopher, Jim and Jonathan dropped, shielding me from Cooke. I went a fraction higher and Cooke froze. His advancing souls did the same. I glanced at either side and mentally swore. Cooke's people had boxed us in by forming a semi-circle that shoved us against the buildings. None paid any attention to the battle raging in the Square. I was in their sights and I was everything wrong with the world.

"Decent people?" I shouted to Cooke. "They'd tear me apart in a second. So how does that make them any better than me?"

"They'd do it for justice. Not for fun, you sick bastard," Cooke bellowed.

He had me there. He and his group moved again, closing in on us. The only obvious way out was down to the people on the street who didn't have any idea the dead were battling not far above their heads.

I spoke as quickly as I could. *"Jim, Chris, left; John, Sally, right."*

They surged in the directions I'd said and took the ghosts by utter surprise. Jim and Christopher smashed into those on the left, broke them apart and several fell, howling. An instant later, Sally and Jonathan blew apart the dead on the right.

Cooke froze. He stared at me and I took great pleasure in knowing he'd expected us to duck and run.

I soared to him, gripped him more tightly than I had anyone in my death and we streaked upwards.

Immediately, he was a screaming voice against my ear. I ignored him and took us higher. We climbed above the rooftops and flying birds and flew into the blue. Dalry was a picture below, framed by its fields and trees and tiny lines of rivers. Then we saw the county; then the region; then just land in blurred colours. I let go of Cooke and shoved him away. We stared at one another as we floated several thousand feet up, our only company the clouds.

"Why do you hate me, Cooke?" I said.

"Because of what you are."

I lost my temper at that. To be honest, I think I'd done well to keep it as long as I had. "Don't be so self-righteous!" I shouted.

"I'm not. You're a killer."

"Oh, for God's sake, will you stop that? Stop being so blinkered. So what if I'm a killer? Who are you to judge me? Who gave you that right? I've done bad things and I admit them. I did them because I wanted to. I had the power to do them and they were all my decisions. I accept that. Why can't you?"

He shook. I went on. "Down there, the living are tearing each other apart and my ghosts are fighting the ones you brought to battle. And not one of them has the right to judge. We're dead, Cooke. We're ghosts. And the fact that we're still here is the work of something above us. *Something* left us here and if they judge, then fine. I'll take that, but I won't take your judgment."

"You kill. You ruin lives, you hurt children."

"Yes, I do, but your decent people. How do you know they haven't done the same? Did you vet each and every one of them before leading them to me? Did you check if any of them are child molesters or rapists or murderers? Of course you didn't. You accepted them as *decent people* because they were against me and that was all it took. That was all that mattered. They're decent people because they're different to me, right? Well, let me tell you, in all the years I've been dead, I've not met a single person I'd call purely decent. Nobody is that one-dimensional. Not even you. You want to stop me. Fine. That's understandable. But don't pretend you and your people down there are pure and noble and decent and nothing more than that. Nobody is." I drifted closer to him. Miles below, the ghosts of Dalry were wrecking the centre of the city. For the moment, though, I didn't care about that. "I enjoyed what I did in life, Cooke. That power. That. . ." I splayed my fingers. "That power in my hands. Power over people. Power over lives and time. Truth be told, I've missed it. And I should probably thank you."

"Me?" he whispered.

"You. If you hadn't come to me, I wouldn't be back to who I was. You made me remember that."

He was silent. Whether through choice or not, I didn't know. Around us, the massive blue of the sky was dazzling.

"I do bad things, Cooke. You do good. But I think it's fair to say there's good and bad in both of us. What do you think?"

"Good in *you?*" He jabbed a finger at my chest. "There's no good in you. There never has been. You were born without it. And you died without learning that."

"What would you have me do, then? Just fade away? What about my friends down there? Bastards, all. What should they do? Give themselves up? Turn to Drude and welcome his judgement with open arms. They will not. And it isn't because of fear or the desire to stay out of the Pit. It's the same reason I've kept going for so long, and why I was that man in life." At another time, I might have laughed, I might have enjoyed the moment and the naked curiosity on Cooke's open, honest face. As it was, all humour dribbled away, leaving me with a simple statement of fact.

"I don't care," I whispered. "And neither do my friends."

"There really is nothing good in you, is there? Nothing of any worth." Even after all our time and everything he'd seen, I'd disappointed him.

I nodded. To be honest, his reply was about all I'd expected. "I tell you what, Cooke."

"What?"

It seemed he'd lost the ability to blink. I smiled for the first time in days. "Let's go and ask your people how *good* they are."

He saw me coming and tried to back away, but there was nothing to back away to.

We dropped back to earth in a howling streak and the bellows of the living and dead greeted our return from the blue.

Cooke got away from me as we fell and I hit the ground alone. Briefly, I was aware of nothing but earth and stone and the silence of underground.

I lunged in a direction—it was impossible to say which one. Vibrations shook from what I guessed was above and I scrambled that way.

At once, light slammed into my skull as I slid up through the road. Cooke was nowhere to be seen. On all sides, the living were doing everything they could to kill each other; the police powerless to stop it. Above, the ghosts were doing the same as the living. And yes, it's possible to kill someone already dead; that was exactly what was happening. Ghosts on my side and Cooke's brought to nothing and an incomparable, savage happiness burst out of me.

"Kill them," I shrieked.

I streaked upwards, as Jim and Christopher fought a group of men and women outside Burger King. They were outnumbered by twenty or more, but they kept going, fists punching the ghosts' forms, finding another and punching again. I roared their names, unable to contain my joy. My voice was lost below the violence below, the violence all around.

"Benjamin." It was Sally coming from above.

She smacked into me an instant before three of Cooke's people hit the space I'd filled a second before. Sally pushed me back as hard as she could, whipped around and raged at the approaching dead. Flames leaped from her mouth to scorch the air. The spirits retreated fast.

"Come with me," Sally yelled.

"Where's Cooke?" I yelled back.

Sally ignored that. She took me up and we flew to the melee Jim and Christopher were involved in. They saw me approach, Jim cheered and several of the opposing ghosts fled. Below us, the living were still kicking, punching and doing everything they could to beat each other into oblivion. The shades I'd brought across country fought Cooke's people almost in perfect quiet. They may have been weak but they made up for that with enthusiasm. Ten of them buried two men in a dirty black fog. The men's sobs were lost in the racket of the battles.

We fought as hard and as low as we ever had, and my group did me proud. Sally burned a dozen of Cooke's people outside NatWest, Jonathan sent another five crashing into the living below. Jim and Christopher stayed with me as Cooke's people attempted to close in. We spread over the Square, let a dozen shades join us and flung them down to the ground when four police vans arrived.

The officers in those vans joined the chaos in less than a minute.

Everywhere was a battle zone. The broken windows and cracks in the road mixed with the still bodies and the splatters of blood, the screams merging with the stink of tears and sweat and the dying. Water from the wrecked fountains streamed to the shop fronts and when the shades took control of it, the water flooded an electrical shop. TVs, stereos and computers exploded with a dull thud and fire licked out with hungry tongues. It was grand.

"Harwood."

My name fell from above, bellowed to me from on high. I stared at the sky and saw nothing but blue. That blue was as far opposite to the mess on the ground as it could be. Pure, clean, unmarked. It rose to the top of the world and my name was screamed from there a second, then third time.

Cooke stood on the roof of the shopping centre, staring down at me, showing his hatred. It turned his pleasant face into a hole.

And behind him, the air, so cool and pure and blue, was turning a deep, bloody red.

Chapter Fifty-Two

There was no need to call them. Sally, Jonathan, Christopher and Jim were with me before the echo of Cooke's final cry had faded. The fights continued around and below us and we didn't care. All that mattered was Cooke on the roof, and the strange light breathing in and out behind him. He pointed at me with an inflexible finger. I felt as if I'd been stabbed with his digit.

Forcing a smile, I waved. He wouldn't give me the pleasure of a reaction.

"I don't think he likes you a great deal," Jim said and cackled.

"The light. There's something wrong with it," Jonathan said

He was right. The light above wasn't the horrible bruise-colour I'd expected, but it still wasn't right.

Instinct told me to look to Sally. She hadn't reacted. I didn't like that, just as I didn't like the fear on her face.

"Sally? What is it?" I said.

An odd noise hit us. I risked a look around, not happy to take my attention off Cooke. Christopher did the same and he whispered his amazement in a hurt breath. "What's happening?" he said.

The fighting ceased. The noise was a steady murmur coming from the living and dead, a constant low pulse, as if they were humming the same note as one.

The unsettling shade of red behind Cooke had grown into a circle chasing itself, eating at the blue and growing faster. The living drew apart. None of them stopped making that odd humming, even when they pulled the bodies from the Square to the road, clearing space. At first, only a few took the bodies, but others joined in. The shades drew back from Cooke's ghosts and both sides retreated. Jonathan shouted at the shades, but they kept going. It wasn't long before we were the only ones left on or above the Square.

"Be ready for anything," I whispered.

The red circle behind Cooke exploded into a rapidly turning spiral. It snaked down from the roof of the shopping centre, a spinning tail touching the ground.

A ball of light no larger than a bulb emerged from the ground, ascended through the spiral and burst out of the turning red to float beside Cooke. I stared at him and he smiled the smile of a madman. And all the while, the spiral grew.

The light coalesced into a form; head, massive chest, thick legs – and nothing about it was close to human.

Drude stood beside Cooke and gazed down at us.

Chapter Fifty-Three

"Your time's up, Harwood," Drude shouted and although there was no way the living could hear him, a few of them stopped their humming and wept.

"I don't think so," I said. There was no need for me to raise my voice; he'd hear me.

He laughed, his mirth rich and deep, and I gazed at his new shape. The *thing* that he really was behind the teeth of Dennis' nightmares and the wavering air was gone, and here was a striking figure full of friendly smiles.

"Who are you to argue with me? You're nothing without my help. You wouldn't be here if it wasn't for me."

"And you can't do a thing to me. You know the rules, Drude."

He nodded. "Of course I do. And I know when they can be broken."

That threw me, I must admit. Even so, I didn't move or blink. I shifted my attention to Cooke.

"Not really the work of a decent man, is it? Working with a demon? Not very *you*."

"You deserve this," he bellowed. "I'll do whatever I have to, if it means you're punished."

I shrugged, a lazy, insolent movement designed to infuriate him. "Fair enough. Just don't come crying to me when Drude decides you owe him your soul."

Momentary doubt slipped over his face; Drude whispered something to him and the doubt was gone.

"Come with me, Harwood," Drude said.

"I don't think so."

"Come with me and these people, these living and dead, they'll be safe."

Joy filled me. He was bluffing and had exposed it in the most obvious way. "Is that right?"

I flew higher, as if I was a king looking down on my city. To be honest, that's exactly how I felt. Dalry was *my* city and the living were under my control. For a moment, I relished the feel of the years rolling behind to the seventeenth century just as I'd often felt the potential of the years ahead for the people I killed—years they no longer had, because *I* had them.

Focusing again on Drude, I called to him. "Well, what do you say to me telling you that is a pathetic attempt to coerce me? What do you say if I say I know the rules and I know you have to live by those rules? You can't do a thing to anyone here."

Drude appeared to consider this. Around him and Cooke, the red spiral turned and turned and a fierce wind took over the day. Within a few seconds, it grew hot. Too hot.

Drude smiled widely. He was mad. Even with the distance between us, his insanity shone brightly in his grin. "I say, fuck the rules."

The twisting spiral abruptly increased the speed of its revolutions and became a red mouth. Still, the heat fell out of it to crash down on us.

"Time for you to go home, Harwood," Drude said and his face changed. The human mask fell off and he was exposed as the beast he was. Darkness in a rough circle stared down at me, darkness speared with a million eyes. Those eyes were wide open, and a boiling, shrieking wind blew out of them. It carried the moan of the emptiness beyond everything. That black swallowed the daylight. It even swallowed the red in the mouth of the spiral.

The hole that was Drude's mouth didn't open; it didn't need to. I still heard him say one word.

Open.

And the mouth of the spiral was the mouth of the Pit.

Chapter Fifty-Four

Jim was the only one of my group who managed to speak.

"Run," he screamed and turned to do so. It was the last conscious movement he was able to make.

The wind blowing from Drude's face became a vacuum, inhaling the Square and pavements around it. A surging crowd of the dead—mine and Cooke's—were yanked from the ground to fly, screaming, into the spiral. Cooke sped down from the roof of the shopping centre, yelling my name as if Drude's work was my fault. I didn't have time to reply. Jim streaked past me, wailing. I reached for him and could do nothing as the spiral claimed him, as my friend fell into the red.

The others had deserted me. There was a huge, clear space on all sides and still, Drude's vacuum sucked up dozens of ghosts. A faraway voice echoed my words from a few minutes before to Cooke.

You accepted them as decent people because they were against me and that was all it took. That was all that mattered.

It didn't seem to be important to Drude. He took righteous and unrighteous alike and let the red spiral eat them. What it meant for himself clearly wasn't important to him, either.

Cooke streaked towards me in a blur. I offered no defence as he struck me and we rolled in a tangle of arms and legs to crash against the record shop.

"Stop him. He's taking everyone," Cooke yelled.

Stop him. A joke if ever I heard one.

I couldn't say the words. The implications of the demon's actions robbed my voice.

There was a fresh cry of my name. Christopher was in the middle of a group of several shades, fighting through them, almost at the edge of the struggling ghosts. He was calling my name as if expecting me to help him. I could do nothing, and I think he knew that at the end. For a second, maybe two, he gazed at me, thirty yards away and as far out of my reach as he could be; he looked at me and there was nothing on his face. Then Christopher let go of the shades.

He was gone before I could blink.

Cooke tried to move, maybe to fly up to Drude. I yanked him back and we slid against the remaining glass in the window behind us. He struggled to get out of my grip. I tightened my hold and the only thought in my head was that if I was going, I was going with Cooke.

The number of the dead in the Square had been cut in half. Some were still being sucked into the spiral; the innocent and the guilty – it made no difference to Drude, and that made everything worse. He had no interest in the rules. Not by that point.

Something made me look to the roof of NatWest. Later, I wondered if it was because she'd called my name. Perhaps I simply expected to her to be there.

Sally was on the roof, not quite opposite to Drude. The Square and all the damage we had inflicted lay between them like an old battlefield. He was still focused on the rapidly decreasing number of ghosts below and Sally took her chance while she could.

She sailed upwards almost too fast for me to focus upon, a bright trail of flame radiating out from her the higher she rose. She hung in the perfectly blue sky, tiny drops of fire falling from her. Then she streaked towards Drude in a silent, burning ball.

In the hole that was Drude's face, I fancied something changed. Maybe it was simple surprise.

Sally struck Drude; fire exploded over the roof and consumed the centre. There was no need to wonder if the living saw the conflagration. They pointed to the building, or ran from it or simply screamed. They couldn't see the demon or the dead; they saw the fire and what they made of it, I don't know.

Drude and Sally were nowhere in sight. The spiral remained; it spun and the thick, bloody red was still horrible, but the remaining souls were no longer being dragged into it. Those who'd been halfway or closer to it found themselves free. They swooped down to the ground and joined the exodus of spirits fleeing to Bishop's Gate and Long Gate. As if knowing the area was theirs again, the people crept on to the Square and picked their way through the rubble. A few ran to the centre entrance to bring others to safety. Some were on their mobiles and others stood in little groups, embracing each other.

The spiral slowed, and then stopped. It fell into the ground as if it had never been. I wanted to call Sally's name, I wanted Jim and Christopher by my side, all of us ready to fight. Jonathan was nowhere in sight and the closest ghost to me was Cooke—the man who'd led me to this point.

Sally. Come back.

My answer was a shriek from the fire on the roof. Flames rained to the ground, sending people running to all points of the compass. A section of roof caved in, glass exploded from the few remaining whole windows and the roaring fire devoured all other noise for a moment.

Whatever was in the flames shrieked again. Staring into the flames, a human shape was visible. Sally.

She wasn't on fire. She *was* fire. It made her body, dancing orange and yellow forming her arms and legs and head. Even so, I saw her below the flames. She screamed my name over and over. Behind her, a huge cloud pooled from the remains of the roof, formed a humanoid shape and extended its head to her.

The cloud's mouth opened wide, revealing a cave full of teeth and a curling tongue, miles long. Its tongue slid through the air, seeking, searching.

Drude swallowed Sally and still, I heard her. From the hole that had been his face, Drude stared at me and eternity was in his hold, eternity below.

"It's over, Harwood," Cooke whispered. He was quite mad. I was sure of it.

"Probably," I said.

The rest of the shopping centre caved in. Smoke hung over the Square, the whine of sirens competed with the bellow of the fire. Despite the thickness of the smoke above, Drude still stared at me. Anything approaching hope vanished. Cooke was right. It was over. By bringing Hell to the living, by claiming those he didn't have any right to touch, Drude had exiled himself from Hell and didn't care about the cost. He'd got me and he would have me forever.

I stood as straight as I could and stared at him.

"Come on, then. Do it."

Drude threw back his head and roared. NatWest, the record shop, Greggs, Superdrug and the handful of estate agents all detonated.

With a tremendous noise that buried everything else, brick, rubble and glass flew to all points of the compass. The living were by then far back on Long Gate and Bishop's Gate and out of reach of the debris. Even so, they ran, trampling each other in order to get away. Rubble rained through us; seconds after Drude's scream, the ground of the Square was a massive crater.

"You're finished," Cooke whispered.

"Yes," I said and dropped my head. My friends were gone; Cooke had beaten me with his righteousness and his decency, and Drude would swallow my soul for all time.

"Ben."

A figure picked its way through the mess. The voice didn't belong to that figure. It belonged to the one behind her.

The one leading her to me.

Chapter Fifty-Five

The girl stopped several paces away. She couldn't get past the large rent in the ground that ran the width of the Square. I stared at her through the dust of the wrecked buildings. Hayley Wilson.

"Hayley?"

She didn't react, which made sense. She was alive and she'd see me only if I made an effort. Her face was dazed and pale. She swayed as if drunk, but there was no intoxication involved.

"Ben. I brought her."

"Philip? What are you doing here?"

Philip Matthews: paedophile, murderer, scourge of the children and the man who'd put himself in a prison beside a school. The man who hadn't wanted to be part of my little army had come at the last minute to join me. Here he was with a child.

Drude howled and I understood everything. At that moment, it was all there in front of me.

My hand fell on Cooke's arm; he tried to pull back but I held him as hard as I could.

"Come with me or go to Hell," I hissed.

The smoke parted as Drude flew at us, racing down like a bullet.

I pulled Cooke; we flew through the dust and smashed into Hayley together. There was a second of nothing, and then I saw through her eyes. The girl staggered and managed to stay upright. Cooke sobbed from somewhere below me. I let him. There was no time to do anything else.

Drude hit the ground where we'd been a moment before. More rubble scattered; he turned to us and saw a teenage girl staring back at him.

Go, Philip. Go now or he'll destroy you.

From behind us, Philip floated down to the ground and faced Drude. He drifted forward and I was helpless to stop him.

"I brought the girl here despite what I wanted to do. I brought her to give Benjamin a way out. You can't touch him; you can't harm the child. So end me now. End me and let it be done."

Drude hadn't reacted to Philip at all. He'd left his nightmare shape on the remains on the shopping centre. Now he was normal Drude again, human-shaped and smiling.

"Philip Matthews. Dear Philip. Uncle Phil, they called you, didn't they?"

I wanted to back away. I wanted to grab Philip and run. I wanted Cooke's endless sobbing to stop.

I did nothing.

Philip shook. The demon's words hit the right spot.

"Uncle Phil to all those children. You made them call you that, didn't you, Uncle Phil? Uncle Phil. Uncle Phil."

Drude's voice changed to a child's, high-pitched and trusting, calling him *Uncle Phil* again and again, now weeping, a child undone by the adult world and all its filth, a child hurt terribly in ways they'd never lose.

Uncle Phil.

Philip screamed a noise of loathing aimed squarely inward.

"You want peace, Matthews? Peace for you? I don't think so," Drude said.

He extended an arm and held Philip as if he weighed nothing at all.

"All that lovely flesh. All that gorgeous flesh. All that given back to you," Drude said.

Philip changed. He was still as much a ghost as I was or Cooke, but at Drude's word, his form grew heavier. He became a ghost formed of skin, blood, bone and flesh.

"All that flesh given to the parents."

Drude threw Philip. He sailed far above us, a flailing figure rising, now falling, coming down to land in Long Gate. The smoke moved, perhaps at Drude's command, and he was clearly visible.

Philip lay on the road, a slowly advancing group of the living coming to him.

"Kill him," I whispered and Drude ignored me.

The living reached Philip and their eyes were my eyes: a man on the road, a monster in a man costume. There was no way they could know what he was, no way other than what Drude wanted.

Someone screamed. I think it was a woman. They knew.

Through Philip's eyes, I watched them fall on him and I watched them tear him into pieces.

He screamed for a long time. Even as they tore his head from his body, he continued to scream.

Chapter Fifty-Six

"**N**ow. What next?"

Drude finally turned from the mess that had been Philip. He gazed at Hayley and saw me. His face was almost kind and not without humour. Philip's destruction had put him in a happier disposition, it appeared.

Cooke heard that good mood and reacted violently. *Let me out of here, let me out, get me out of here now, you have to let me go—*

Drude sighed and Cooke fell silent.

"Keep him quiet, will you?" he said to me. I didn't need to. Cooke couldn't speak. For whatever reason, he'd believed Drude was on his side. Now he knew different.

"What next?" Drude said again.

Leave me alone.

"I can't do that, Benjamin. Not after all this."

He gestured to the destroyed Square and buildings. Several fire engines had arrived; men were doing what they could to put out the burning buildings. From every angle, people wept or held one another. New police officers filled the area and were trying to get sense from their ruined colleagues.

You did this.

"So I did, but I did it for you."

You took Sally, Christopher and Jim.

"*You* are responsible for them by getting them involved in this, Ben. You can't deny that."

I couldn't. And that was the worst.

"So, why not call it a day? Leave the girl. Leave Cooke and come with me."

A flame of hope flared inside. Philip's work hadn't been in vain. He'd brought the girl to me and I was safe inside her.

At that thought, Hayley stirred, as if she was gradually waking from a deep sleep. That was close enough to the situation to be true. The invasion of two spirits into hers had knocked her emotionally and mentally unconscious.

Relax. We won't be with you for long, I told her.

Crying out inside, she reached for me and I hid my identity. There was no way I could afford the girl realising who had invaded her.

Where am I? What's happening? I can't move. Oh, God. I can't—

Trust me. We'll be gone soon.

"Last chance, Harwood," Drude said.

I steadied my nerves and took control of the girl's mouth and tongue. Doing so was almost impossible but I managed it and won a small victory. She was trying to scream and could not.

"We're going now, Drude. It doesn't matter if you follow us. You can't hurt the girl and you know it. Give this up, now."

He gazed at me and I felt his judgment like a weight. He'd never give up. He was as much an exile from the world of light and love as I was. Worse for him, he was now an exile from his home.

"We're going," I said and turned my back on Drude.

Cooke tried to speak and I silenced him. Hayley was more awake and subsequently more frightened. Her head was a run of panic and questions; who was I, what was happening to her, where were her parents?

I didn't reply to any of her questions. All my attention stayed focused on making the girl's body take step after step. Cross Street was no more than fifteen paces in front and although a collapsed wall partially blocked it, enough space remained to squeeze through and be out of Drude's line of sight.

Fourteen paces.

Thirteen.

Twelve.

"Ben," Drude called. He didn't shout it and that was somehow worse than if he had. "Ben."

Ten steps. Nine. I passed over a tall mound of rubble. Much of the dust and smoke had cleared and eyes were all over me. Not just Drude; the living watched me.

They're watching the girl, Cooke told me. He'd stopped weeping and there was a flat resignation to his voice. It brightened my mood briefly. I wouldn't have any trouble with Cooke, maybe ever again.

Someone called to the girl, warning her to be careful, to come away from the holes and the broken bricks. I made her walk on. Cross Street was five paces ahead. Dust free light winked out of the narrow entrance.

"Ben." Drude could have been right at my shoulder. "Benjamin?"

Not Drude. Jonathan.

I made the girl turn. Drude was where I'd left him. He held Jonathan as he'd held Philip. One massive hand held my friend, and it was obvious Drude was ready to tear Jonathan in half if I moved.

What are you going to do? Cooke asked. He sounded honestly interested, which was bizarre. Even Hayley had fallen quiet; there was no way she could have known what was going on, but she instinctively knew something in her situation had changed.

"Come out of the girl or I'll destroy him," Drude said. He increased his grip on Jonathan's neck.

I made Hayley's mouth move again. "What guarantee do I have you won't kill him whatever I do?"

"None at all."

"So, why should I?"

He shrugged. "At least if you do, you have a chance of saving him."

Taking control of Hayley's voice was far too much effort. As much as I didn't want to show Drude any weakness, I could only think.

That's not good enough. I want your promise you won't hurt him.

"Fine. You have my promise I won't hurt him if you leave the girl and come with me."

I considered my options while we faced one another on the Square. It didn't take long. With Drude's focus squarely on me, with the people being pushed back by the police and the few officers trying to cross through the rubble to Hayley, I looked Jonathan in the eye. *No.*

The mask Drude used as a face clouded over and that was it. "What was that?" he asked pleasantly.

I said no, Drude. If that's not clear, then try this. For just a few seconds, I could ignore my fear and my exhaustion. *Go to Hell.*

His hand tightened on Jonathan again. My friend closed his eyes, unable to keep them open after my betrayal.

"Last chance, Benjamin," the demon said.

The police were coming closer, calling to Hayley. I had enough control over her to ensure she didn't reply or face them, but there wasn't much time before the police reached us.

With a bravado I completely lacked, I said to Drude: *Do what you have to. I'm not leaving the girl.*

Deep inside, Cooke swore at me, calling me a filthy bastard, a betrayer, a monster. I closed my ears to him as Drude let loose a horrific cry. The police stopped and looked to the sky. I glanced that way and wasn't surprised to see it then as a thick shade of black.

Drude fell silent.

And threw Jonathan.

Chapter Fifty-Seven

Jonathan landed at my feet. The impact would have killed a living man. As it was, he was upright in seconds, holding Hayley's shoulders and weeping. She couldn't see him, but she could feel him. She started screaming again and I did my best to ignore her as I faced Drude on the Square for the last time.

"Take him. Take the friend you betrayed. See what good he'll do you, Harwood." He smiled. "Consider this a head start."

He dropped into the ground, a puddle formed like an ugly stain and then vanished. Jonathan continued to weep as Hayley screeched, and Cooke was far below me, still calling me names.

Across the Square, the police were closing in fast.

I grabbed Jonathan's arm, turned Hayley around and ran for Cross Street with the shouts of the police chasing after the child.

Chapter Fifty-Eight

Hayley's strength gave up a few miles from the Square. By then, we were near the end of the Meadows, sheltering in a thick line of trees while the sunlight eased through gaps in the leaves and made the day sparkle. The position gave us a decent view of a wide field of long grass that finished at a hotel car park. We stopped there and I thought through my panic.

There was no doubt Hayley's disappearance from her home would have been reported to the police. It wouldn't have taken them long to connect her to the running girl in the Square. There was little I could do about that except try to keep away from people.

I let the girl rest against the foot of a tree and spoke to her.

Listen. My name is Benjamin and I need your help.

That was as far as I got before Cooke shouted over me.

Don't listen to him. He's a murderer and—

Shut up. For once, just shut up.

Wonder of wonders, he did. Hayley wanted to hold her head and squeeze her skull. *The thought was unformed but I still caught the suggestion of it.*

She'd gone insane. That explained the voices, the blackouts, the whole thing. She was mental.

No. You are not, I told her with as much gentle care as I could manage. *This is real. You are safe with us.*

Jonathan sat on a tree stump, gazing at us. Hayley was close to physical collapse and it took my mental support to literally keep her upright.

I'm sorry we did this to you. I'm sorry we got you involved, but I need your help.

"Who are you?" she whispered.

Cooke hadn't thought to tell her she'd dealt with me before. It was only a matter of time before he realised, though.

A ghost. I'm not going to hurt you. The other one, the noisy one, he's a ghost, as well. And so is the one you're looking at but can't see.

She grew cold which did not surprise me. She was a child in the woods with dead people and she was terrified.

We're not here to hurt you. We're here because we had nowhere else to go.

She dug her fingers into the cool earth and found dry leaves. They crackled. The green smells of nature were strong and I tried to recall if I'd ever smelled them when I was a child like Hayley. The chances were I had not, sadly.

My name's Benjamin. The other one with you is Richard and the one over there is Jonathan. We're on the run from. . .

I stopped because I had no idea how to finish. Telling her we were dead was one thing. Telling her a demon had destroyed the heart of her city was another. In the end, I went with the truth. There wasn't a great deal of point in saying anything else.

We're running from a demon named Drude. He can't hurt you; he can only hurt us and destroy things like he did in the Square. We're with you to keep us safe.

Her mouth twitched and that was all. Dull surprise filled me. She was either working hard to keep calm or she was extremely self-contained. Based on the time I'd spent haunting her and her family, the latter was much more likely.

Jonathan stared at me. His eyes were on Hayley but it was at me he stared.

Give me a minute, I said to him.

"What?" Hayley said.

Not you. Listen. What happened to you? How did Philip find you?

"Philip?"

The man who brought you to the Square.

That was the wrong thing to say. She drew in a sharp, frightened breath.

He's not here. He's gone.

She knew I was telling the truth and relaxed as much as her strained nerves would let her. Around us, birds sang their pretty songs as evening approached. Even in the shade, warmth touched us.

"Are you going to let me go?" she said. Her legs tensed as if she was about to run. There wasn't any point and she knew it. As long as I was with her, she couldn't do anything I didn't want her to.

As soon as I can. Now I need you to tell me what happened. How did Philip find you?

Perhaps thinking it would lead to a quick escape from us, she told us our story.

She'd been standing at her bedroom window, facing east, looking to where all the noise was coming from.

Sirens and panic were inseparable; people on her little street walked out of their homes to check the sky and talk to their neighbours. The sirens were constant as if police and ambulances were coming from all directions to head east. She'd called down to a neighbour, asking what was happening, but the neighbour hadn't known.

After checking her phone for information and finding little, Hayley went downstairs as quietly as she could. Her mother was asleep (she didn't need to tell us her mother slept a lot; I knew it from the tremble in her voice) and she didn't want to wake her.

She went to the living room, turned on the TV and found nothing on the news. She'd thought about calling a few friends but movement at the window caught her eye and the phone was forgotten.

Her first reaction was to run, but her feet wouldn't move. Her second reaction immediately followed the first and filled her with complete fear. She was back in the middle of the summer and that horrible time with her dad, with the baby getting sick and the house full of . . . .*something*.

She'd tried to call for her mother, and all that she could manage was a tiny squeak. A cloud filled the window, blocking out all daylight. And a dead hand on her shoulder, a voice in her ear.

She had no recollection of what followed; she must have left the house because her next memory was of walking on Park Road, half a mile from her house and heading east. On the road, police cars raced past while dozens of other people ran towards the noise and the rising smoke. None of them paid her any attention and for certain none of them saw the dead man beside her.

She couldn't see him either, which made no difference. There was a dead man beside her with his hand on her shoulder. It wasn't like before, not when the house had been haunted. This was worse.

Hayley felt something coming from the man. It wasn't simply because he was dead. There was something below the dead, a bitter and secret shadow. It made her think of those horrible moments when her father's eyes were all over her. As horrendous as that had been, this was somehow even worse. She knew that time with her father hadn't been down to him; something had forced him to be that way and anything he was doing was tempered by his love for her and hers for him. This *thing* beside her was a monster and it was only his will to take her somewhere that was stopping him from. . .what?

She didn't know, didn't want to know. If this man was alive, he'd eat her with his eyes again and again and when he couldn't wait any longer, he'd take her to a terrible and secret place and he'd lay her down and he'd and he'd and he'd. . .

She'd tried to scream then and found she couldn't. All she could do was walk into the centre of city, past the police cars and the people lying in the road, closer to the Square or what remained of the Square, closer to the burning and the massive rents in the ground until the one holding her stopped and wave after wave of his stink and his *need* for her ran over her, ran up her nose and below her clothes to her core, to between her legs; his stink was in there and she was screaming inside.

"That's when you came," Hayley said.

Her voice was completely flat. I'd expected fear or at least panic when she finished her story. Instead, I was left with a teenage girl too numb to find any emotion.

We're not like him. We won't do anything to you, I said.

She gave no sign if she believed me or not.

Jonathan. Show yourself.

He stared at me.

Jonathan, please. I'm sorry for what happened, but believe me, it was a gamble I had to take. I knew what Drude would do and I had to make him think I was willing to risk you.

He didn't speak, but slowly, his form grew visible. The only sign of Hayley's fear was a massive increase in her heartbeat.

Jonathan faded.

I can't show you myself, but trust me when I say we're not here to hurt you.

Cooke spoke for the first time in what felt like hours. *Tell her who you are.*

I flexed my will over Cooke's, which was difficult. He'd anticipated that and fought back. I was stronger than him, or maybe I had simply had more practice. Either way, we engaged in a silent fight while Hayley asked question after question, wanting to know what he meant, when she could go home, who I was. That, more than the other questions. Who was I? She *suspected*, which I had to admit wasn't a surprise. After all, there couldn't be that many ghosts ready to interfere in her life.

I gave up on Cooke and he fell quiet. Perhaps he knew what I was about to say.

Opposite us, Jonathan shifted. He didn't look away from me, nor did he speak.

Inside Hayley, I saw the slow seconds of the last four centuries. It was beyond black there.

And it went on forever.

Hayley was still talking, still full of panicked questions.

I said, *Listen to me, child. If you want to live, stop your questions and listen.*

My name is Benjamin Harwood. I was born in 1611 here in Dalry, and died when I was fifty-five. That's best part of four hundred years I've spent haunting this city, four hundred years of thinking about what I did.

I killed people. A lot of them. I don't remember how many. And really, after all this time, who cares? In any case, I had my reasons for doing what I did.

I know you're scared. You should be, although not of me. Be scared of Drude. He's still looking for us. He'll always be looking for us.

So you listen to me, girl.

You need to listen to me if you're going to survive this.

Chapter Fifty-Nine

It took me some time to tell her my story. She listened without any interruptions, the only response I got was a silent disgust as I spoke. By the time I finished, the afternoon was dying and evening was closing in. Morning felt as if it had happened years before. It had been hours since I'd lost Jim, Christopher and Sally, and that also felt as if it happened years before.

When I finished my story, I waited for Hayley to speak. It seemed only fair after my words.

"You were the one in my house."

She said this without any inflection at all. It reminded me briefly of Sally and I tried not to think of her and where she was by then.

Yes.

Hayley was upright so quickly, I didn't have time to react even though I'd been expecting her to move. She lunged forward and I fought for control. She trembled and managed to keep moving. Amazed, I tried to keep her still again. Youth was on her side. More than that, she was a burning mix of emotions. Outrage and horror pushed her on despite my efforts and she staggered forward another few steps before Jonathan swooped down in front of her. She ran into him, stopped and gagged.

Hayley vomited a thin line of spit and fell against a tree. Jonathan drew close to her and became visible. It would have taken a vast amount of energy for him to do so; I didn't need to ask if he was still on my side and sent him silent thanks.

"Get away from me," Hayley whispered. It wanted to be loud and furious. However I'd managed to regain my control over her and it was no louder than her breath. Before I spoke, I closed her mouth.

Listen to me, Hayley. I don't apologise for my actions. I know the only thing you want to do with me is to see me punished and I don't doubt you'd be happy to see Drude claim me right now. But I'm not going anywhere. Understand? I'm with you; Cooke is with you, and so is Jonathan. We're not leaving you.

Fuck you, she thought at me and I honestly couldn't remember a time in my death when someone had spoken to me with such unadulterated loathing. For a child, she knew far too much about the adult world of resentment.

Fuck off and leave me alone. You're nothing, you bastard. You're dead and you can't do anything to me so just go to hell or wherever you should go—

I can find another one like Philip, I told her and she was immediately silent. I wasn't proud of having to use such threats, especially when Philip had saved me from Drude and paid for it in such a brutal way, but there didn't seem to be much choice.

Philip's gone, but there are many others like him. They'd all like to meet you and have you alone. So you listen to me, child. Hate me as much as you like, but don't fight me. Don't ever fight me.

You made my dad. . .

I did nothing to stop her thought; she stopped it on her own. She couldn't bring herself to complete it.

And Cooke stopped me. Admitting that was a sore point. I did my best to ignore it and considered before speaking again. Shadows were gradually filling the woods and the voices coming across the big field became less frequent. Night would be on us in two hours.

Cooke stopped me and you should be grateful for that, but don't believe he can help you now. If he could, I'd be long gone and you'd be free.

She sobbed. Hot, unwilling tears fell down her cheeks and I remembered Hayley as she'd been the first day I'd seen her, new home at her back.

See what you've done. See what you cause, Cooke whispered. He was miles below and his voice reached for me across all that nothing between us.

You've done enough, Harwood. End it now.

I ignored him. Hayley spoke. *The demon. The demon in the Square.*

What about him? I replied.

What did he do? What happened with all the damage and all the mess?

She impressed me and again I recalled the first time I'd seen her with her family, ready to view their new home. I'd thought then that she was a strong one.

He brought Hell here, I told her. *He did what he's not allowed to do. If he'd carried on, well, you can guess.*

He wants you that much?

He wants me that much. I stopped and couldn't help but to verbalise my unwilling thoughts—unwilling because it meant all the rules were beyond broken now. It meant the game was on and I had no idea how to play.

He broke all his rules by opening Hell to get me. By doing that, he's exiled himself from Hell, which means he'll never stop coming after me. He's got nothing else to do.

Hayley considered this. *So that means he'll always be after* me?

You're safe, child. Even if he wanted you, he can't touch you. You're alive. What's more, you're an innocent. That's not to do with the rules; it's just what he can and cannot do. He can't hurt you.

End it, Cooke moaned. *End it now, Harwood.*

Again, I ignored him.

Jonathan. Will you do something for me? I said and Cooke's mutters faded. Jonathan stared at me. Any light had vanished from his face since the events on the Square. He appraised me and nothing moved around us.

Will you go to the girl's mother? Will you stay with her?

At this, Hayley lost any interest in Drude; she begged me to leave her mother alone. I tried to tell her I didn't have any interest in harming her mother. Of course, she had no reason to believe me and continued to beg for her mother's safety.

Jonathan, please, I said over Hayley's voice. *To the mother. Prepare her.*

He stared at me for a long time. Shadows grew around us as the last of the day slipped away from the sky. I stared back at Jonathan, waiting. My betrayal festered between us in the shadows, and despite my best efforts to not think of it, my head was full of the scenes of our battle on the Square, of Hell opening before us, of Drude willing to take exile, of my friends swallowed by the red spiral.

Eventually, Jonathan spoke. "One chance, Benjamin. That's all you get."

He was gone like a ripple of murky water.

Chapter Sixty

Despite wanting to be on the move as soon as Jonathan left, I made us wait another two hours. Hayley spent the first half an hour telling me she'd do anything I wanted if I left her mother alone and I did my best to tell her I had no interest in harming her mother. Eventually, her entreaties faded and she dozed against the tree. Night descended fast over the woods and the field. The night was moonless and the only visible light belonged to the hotel beyond the half empty car park.

Animals rustled through the undergrowth. None came near us. They knew I was there and they stayed away from me, not Hayley. Cooke tried to convince me to leave and I didn't bother replying. To be honest, I was slightly regretful I'd brought him into Hayley as I'd fled from Drude. I took comfort from knowing where he was and knowing he couldn't do anything without my knowledge. On the other hand, it would have been easier to concentrate and plan without his muttering voice.

He gave up after the first hour; I pictured him far below, my shape high above him like a massive cloud.

Thinking of him that way was as easy as believing recent events had driven him mad. I'd thought the same during the battle on the Square, and I wondered how true that was during those two hours. His single-minded quest to see me punished was unnerving, as was his complete refusal to see me as anything other than a monster. That was only fair, I realised. After all, all he'd seen me to do was ruin lives and work to keep myself safe from Drude. Plus I'd involved an innocent girl in my plans – I was using her as a shield from a demon and that was doubtless as low as I could go in Cooke's view.

I shifted inside Hayley, uncomfortable although there was no physical reason for it. It didn't take much time for me to admit the situation was not ideal. Hayley's pain was of no matter to me and nor were Cooke's whispers. I hadn't survived four centuries out of Drude's grip by listening to my conscience. On the other hand, nor had I been so involved with any of the lives I'd affected before Hayley and, to a lesser extent, Cooke. People were for my amusement. I knew their names when I haunted them, but to be with them as I was with Hayley was new. I didn't like it.

Jonathan's had long enough. Time to move. At that, I woke Hayley. Her sleep had been thin and she came to full consciousness quickly.

"What is it?" she said.

Time to go home. We're going the long way so we're not seen. You won't do anything I won't like, will you?

"No," she whispered and could have been so much younger than she was.

Good.

Hayley turned towards the field and gazed at the hotel. I turned her around to face the shadows in the woods.

This way.

She whimpered. The waiting darkness inside the woods appeared impenetrable.

We're with you. Nothing will hurt you in there.

She wanted to believe that and could not.

Come on.

She crouched, brushed aside thin branches and we entered the shadows in the trees.

Chapter Sixty-One

The journey back to Hayley's house from the woods—a distance of three miles—took us four hours. We crept through the woods and walked alongside the river, level with a dual carriageway. Hayley wanted to risk running over the road and swore it wasn't to attract attention. I took her another half a mile and we crawled along a creek that ran under the roads. The shadows were thick down there and I fought to keep Hayley going. She sent her mind away until she was no longer aware of the night and the stones and the trickling water around her. She stayed away for another hour by which point, we'd left the carriageway behind and run at a crouch over the fields behind Cromwell Hall. The old building was as distinct in the night as in day; lit windows glared down at us and the dash over the grass left me feeling horribly exposed.

We stopped beside a few young trees at the perimeter of the Hall's grounds so Hayley could catch her breath. She had no idea how ill and tired she appeared, and that was a good thing. If she caught sight of her reflection, it would take the last of her strength. I let her rest for a few minutes while waiting for a break in the traffic. As soon as it came, I sent her scrambling up the low embankment to the road and over it at a mad sprint.

She bent, holding her knees, and gasped for breath. Perspiration, dirt and several scratches marked her pretty face. Her clothing was torn in several places; the night air found those rents with ease. I'd forgotten how fragile flesh could be, how easy it was for discomfort to rob the mind of clear thought and the body of strength.

"Please," she whispered.

Almost home.

"Please," she said again.

please oh please get me

In my head, I was back on the garden with Tanya, Jonathan closing in to strangle her, Christopher a wounded animal on the grass and the normal world of sunshine falling into the holes below the land. The shifting shape that didn't know what it wanted to be was a speeding blur, the opening below Hell, the huge *thing* inside that hole staring at me from across all the time there was, and the tiny light miles above, the light of the living world out of my reach until the shockwave sent me crashing up into it.

"Please, I can't do it," Hayley said and I returned to my surroundings and Jonathan staring at me.

What was that? he asked.

I don't know.

That wasn't exactly a lie. While it had been a vision of Hell, I didn't know what it meant for us.

Hayley barely registered any of this. A stitch stabbed her side. Gasping for breath, she rubbed it and did her best to tell me she needed to stop. The night held hard to us and any choice there might have been in that vision of Hell was far away.

Come on, I told Hayley.

She groaned but had no choice but to move. We ran on and stuck to side streets for the rest of the way. By then, midnight had passed and the roads were empty. At first, I'd planned on coming through the park, but I felt a strange aversion to doing so when we came in sight of it. The park and all its trees and grasses were no longer the home they'd been for all those years. Instead, I turned my back on it and took Hayley around it. Occasionally, taxis drove by. None stopped, despite the oddity of a young girl out alone so late. We made it to the end of Azalea Drive at ten to one in the morning and I gazed at the house where my adventure had begun.

"Home," Hayley said and wept.

Home, I agreed.

I took her to the door, not liking the whisper that was purely my own telling me Jonathan wouldn't be waiting for me inside.

And that Drude would.

Hayley staggered up the drive and knocked on the front door.

Chapter Sixty-Two

Hayley's father was gone, of course.

Nobody said so, nobody mentioned his name. During my weeks haunting the Wilsons, the feel of a complete family was with them all the time. Now there was the missing husband and father, flesh and blood hurt by my actions.

I felt inside Hayley and got a glimpse of a memory from the days after my departure. Her father had gone to live with his brother in another city. She hadn't seen him since, although they'd spoken on the phone, each conversation as uncomfortable as their previous words.

The baby was gone, as well, now staying with Hayley's grandmother. I hadn't asked Jonathan to arrange this and he hadn't spoken of it; I didn't press the issue, knowing it was for the best.

Tracy had aged badly in those few weeks. Thick strands of grey streaked her hair and heavy bags hung under her eyes, and those eyes couldn't focus on any one thing for more than a moment. They constantly darted around the room as if she wanted to be sure everything was where she remembered it.

Or to make sure there was nothing new in the room.

She sat opposite Hayley who lay on the sofa, legs curled beneath her. Tracy clutched a mug of coffee with both hands despite its heat. A cup of tea stood on the floor beside the sofa, untouched by Hayley. All the downstairs lights were on and I suspected most of the ones upstairs were also blazing. The television broadcast a twenty-four hours news channel with the volume low enough to be almost inaudible. All in all, we were in the home of a woman who could no longer stand the night or the silence inside the night.

"I wanted to call the police," Tracy said abruptly. Her voice held a peculiar note as if the words were frightened to come out.

Hayley shifted and I flexed my control over a fraction to keep her still.

"He told me not to," Tracy said and sipped her coffee. Beside her, Jonathan met my eyes for the first time since Hayley, Cooke and I had entered the house. Disgust was all over his motionless face, and not all of it was aimed in my direction. Plenty was turned inwards. He'd wanted to leave, I knew. He'd wanted to abandon me as I'd been ready to abandon him. For whatever reason, he hadn't. I could only wonder at that reason and hope he'd tell me soon enough.

"I told her that her daughter would only be safe if she kept quiet," Jonathan said. "All very cloak and dagger."

I laughed. It was mannered and almost false but better than nothing.

Does she know the rest of it? I said and Jonathan nodded. *Good. That means she'll ask fewer questions.*

"When are you going to leave us?" Hayley said and Tracy's hand shook around her mug.

As soon as we can. Just be glad you're home and you're both safe.

Jonathan's still face asked a question. I nodded. Jonathan dropped his hand from Tracy's shoulder and she stared at the space he occupied.

"Go to her," Jonathan said and Tracy heard his words in the creak of settling floorboards. I made Hayley rise despite her protesting muscles. Mother and daughter faced one another.

"I thought you'd been killed," Tracy whispered and her next words were a hot, furious rush.

"I thought when the ghost came that you were dead, that he'd come to tell me you were dead and I couldn't handle that, I couldn't, Hayley, I really couldn't."

I took Hayley from the sofa. She fell against her mother and they hugged and wept while we ghosts didn't say a word.

Chapter Sixty-Three

I let them talk and hold one another for a few hours. Tracy made sandwiches which Hayley only picked at; they talked more and Tracy's eyes continued to flick around the room to where she thought Jonathan might be. She didn't address me directly, more than likely because she was unable to consider the idea of me lurking inside her daughter.

By five, the sky had lightened quite a bit. As time passed, the birdsong grew louder. I went to the living room window and studied the street through Hayley's eyes. There were no people outside yet which wasn't really a great help to us. The day was beginning and that meant our time was short.

Tell her, I said to Jonathan.

He drifted to Tracy. She was dozing on the sofa and woke fully when Jonathan took the seat beside her. He whispered in her ear. Tracy's face remained still. Jonathan stopped talking and waited for me to speak.

She knows we have to be quick and that we can't be seen? I asked.

"Yes."

Good. Then let's go.

I made Hayley stand and spoke in a calm, quiet voice to her. *We're all going now. We have to do it without being seen, you understand? If we're seen, then Drude will know where we are. He'll come after us and he won't care about keeping your mother safe. He can't hurt her directly but that doesn't mean he can't be indirect. Do you understand?*

Yes.

Speak here, child. This is your home.

"Yes," she whispered.

"Hayley?" Tracy said.

"It's okay, Mum."

I tried to make her move and registered her unwillingness immediately. It was like trying to bend a sapling.

A problem? I asked.

I need. . .

Yes?

She was silent. Tracey watched her daughter, clearly wanting be part of the conversation, perhaps too afraid to ask what was happening.

Still, the girl was quiet, and something – possibly the memory of what it meant to have a physical body – filled in the blanks.

The lavatory? I asked.

Her reply was emotional rather than verbal. Shame, embarrassment, anger: all the particularly powerful feelings.

I understand. Let's go.

Not while you're – She tried to stop the word but was slow to catch herself. *In. In me.*

She blushed, dull anger stronger than shame.

Believe me, child. I have no wish for this. But it is what it is. Soonest we leave, soonest I leave you. Now. The lavatory.

"What is it?" Tracey whispered.

I pulled back, letting the girl answer her mother. "I need the loo," she said it in an utterly flat tone; I exercised my will slightly but had no real need to. She strode to a door in the hallway, pulled it shut with force and stared at her reflection on the wall beside the lavatory.

Can you shut your eyes or something? she asked.

No. It was an honest answer. I had little desire to lie to her. *But I can look away if you do.*

I really hate you.

I know and I understand.

She believed me. It seemed lying to each other might prove impossible and I wondered if that was such a bad thing.

Tilting her head back so she peered up to the ceiling and the small lightbulbs, she lowered her jeans and sat.

Silence.

This is like someone watching me. I can't do it.

Close your eyes, girl. I see what you see, remember.

At once, she did so, turning my perception solely into sound. A few moments passed before the noise of the obvious reached her ears and mine. Mentally, she groaned and I considered offering some words to reassure her, then thought better of it. We were not friends; she was an embarrassed child, and as soon as she was clear of the lavatory, that embarrassment would revert to fury at me.

The suggestion of my thoughts reached her and she shouted at me to shut up.

We have few secrets from each other, I told her as she finished and reached blindly for the lavatory paper.

Just shut up, she said with almost no energy.

Out in the hallway, she finally opened her eyes, bringing light back to our eyes.

Tracy stood against the wall, twisting her fingers together. The pallor of her cheeks and the bags hanging under her eyes made it appear she had recently recovered from months of illness. In a way, that was close to the truth.

"Come on," Hayley muttered.

We're going to the car and we're going to drive, I told her. *Once we're a few miles away, we'll tell your mother where to go.*

Jonathan floated close to the front door. At my silent command, he went through it and returned a moment later.

"A man walking his dog," he said and I cursed. "He's at the end of the street, coming this way. We'll have to wait for him to pass."

"How will he know?" Hayley said. "How will the demon know you're here if we're seen?"

I wasn't going to answer her at first, but changed my mind almost immediately. She was involved, the question was a fair one and she had a right to ask if not know.

People won't see Jonathan and me, not as they see you, but they might sense us. And if they do, Drude will know. He'll have his own eyes all over the city.

"What about the other one? The one with you," Hayley said.

I didn't know what to say. Cooke had been silent for a long time. There was a strong possibility the events of the last few hours had been too much for him. It was certainly possible he'd faded away inside the girl. In which case, the remnants of his spirit would leave hers without her noticing. She would simply slough it off like dead skin.

He was there, still miles below, still in the void. He stared upwards, trying to make out anything above the thunderously dark sky.

I don't know if they'd see him. He's not altogether there, I said and it was an honest answer.

We waited another few minutes, then ran to the car on the empty street. None of us said a word until we were out of the business side of Dalry and driving with the early morning traffic towards Thorpe Road. The day was pleasant; it held the last of the summer in its gentle warmth and unbroken blue sky.

"Where are we going?" Tracy asked.

Tell her to relax and just keep on this road, I told Hayley. She did so. Then as soon as she finished speaking to her mother, she said to me:

Turn the radio on.

I gazed at it and couldn't think of a reason to do so.

Why?

For the news. Maybe there's something about what happened yesterday. Maybe you can use something from it about your demon.

Surprise came in a flood; I tried to give none of it away and failed, of course. Keeping secrets was almost impossible for our linked spirits.

Why would you suggest that? Why would you want to help me?

I don't, she said with complete honesty. It was laced with a strong dose of anger, too. *But if you* can *use anything from yesterday, then that means you'll be away from me sooner.*

I thought about this for a few moments, wondering if it could hurt me. Eventually, rationality stepped in. The girl couldn't lie to me. She hadn't suggested it to help me, but her reply was still a help.

I didn't speak to her; she turned on the radio, scanned through it until she found the local station and explained to her mother what she was doing. Tracy took this news without comment. All her attention was on the road and the traffic. We drove, passing houses and allotments, until the music stopped and the news came on.

It was full of the previous day's events, of course. Details were thin and the police apparently weren't saying very much. Previous theories of terrorism had been rejected and the current idea was several explosions caused by gas leaks were responsible for the damage, and a mass hysteria resulted in people attacking each other in the ensuing panic. More than a hundred people had been taken to hospital and were being treated for injuries, some serious, and shock. Memorial Square, Long Gate, Bishops Gate and Mid Gate were sealed off while the authorities searched the damaged buildings and rubble in the streets.

I turned off the radio and Jonathan said: "It could have been much worse for them."

True.

"Drude causing all that, Ben. . .you believed he was bluffing, didn't you? All the way through?"

True.

"And he wasn't even close to bluffing. He's locked himself out of Hell for you."

True.

Jonathan's frustration exploded. He lunged for me and froze half an inch from Hayley's neck. She stared towards him, heart hammering, even if she wasn't quite sure why.

"Don't treat me like this, Benjamin. Never do that."

His words were soft. Dislike drifted below them. It was not quite hate. Not yet.

I won't, Jonathan. But you need to understand we have to be in this position. If we'd done anything even slightly differently, we'd all be gone by now. We'd all be in the Pit.

Tracy indicated right, changed lanes and gripped the wheel as tightly as she could. We were minutes from Thorpe Road.

"I'm supposed to believe you knew he was bluffing when it came to me?" Jonathan asked.

I took a moment before replying, fully aware I needed to choose my words with exceeding care.

It was a gamble. I admit that, but Jonathan, you need to know I'm not in the business of losing. Nor do I betray my friends.

"What about Dennis?"

Dennis was not a betrayal. Given any other option from keeping Drude in his place, from keeping him from the things he's done, I would have taken that option in a moment. Dennis would have done the same.

We gazed at one another.

"As I said." Jonathan leaned towards Hayley and held up a single finger to her face, to me. "One chance, Benjamin."

I understand.

"Good. What's his next move?"

I didn't want to answer that, so I gave a politician's answer. "The question should be, what's *our* next move, Jonathan."

Okay, what's our next move, Jonathan, Hayley said. Jonathan heard her and smiled. The fact that she couldn't see that smile was probably a good thing. Even I wasn't sure what to make of it.

Our next move is to hide. We're going where Drude can't hurt us. Any of us.

In the rear-view mirror, Hayley stared back at me. Her hate had gone; she was just a child watching me. I relaxed and she gazed at the rear of the car. Instant shock stained her face. I turned, expecting to see Jonathan making himself visible for some reason.

A bus was closing in on us at tremendous speed. Tracy saw Hayley turning and checked the mirror. She screamed once, yanked on the wheel and we veered across the road. The bus moved with us. The driver hammered his fist on the window hard enough to crack it. The glass splintered but didn't break. The jagged lines obscured much of his face, but left enough visible; he was no longer solely human. He couldn't be and possess such a level of hatred.

"What's this?" Jonathan shouted.

Drude, I said, unaware I was only half right.

Hayley's cries filled the car; Tracy echoed them, even as she looked from the road ahead to the bus behind. It was almost on top of us. Drivers were doing their best to keep out of its way, most struck their horns hard, creating a horrible noise. A woman in the passenger seat of a car beside us filmed the bus on her mobile while the woman driving attempted to turn the car further to the left. The grass median blocked her, as did the other traffic. The bus wasn't backing off and there was little space anywhere near us. The bus drew even closer.

No more than ten seconds had passed since I'd seen the bus, and the thought occurred that my adventure might be finished within another ten.

I threw Hayley's hand out to clamp it on Tracy's wrist. Tracy let out a sharp cry and I spoke to Hayley as fast as I could.

I'll tell you what to Do - you tell your mother.

Okay.

Faster.

"Faster, Mum. He says so, he says go faster."

Tracy slammed her foot down and the car sped forward as if pushed. The roaring of the bus followed. Tracy took us between a van and a car without instruction; the bus couldn't keep up. She'd given us a few seconds' grace.

"Who is it?" She gripped the wheel hard enough for me to fear it might break. "What's going on?"

Hayley was asking me the same question and I spoke as quickly as I had a moment before.

I don't know exactly what this is. We need to get away. Make sure she knows that and she's to do exactly what you tell her.

Hayley repeated this to Tracy while I looked behind us again. Jonathan did the same, and as if it had seen us, the bus lunged forward. It clipped the van, sending it crashing into a car near the median. Car and van overturned, and the noise of splintering metal and breaking grass almost drowned out Tracy's noise.

The rest of the traffic was doing its best to get away from the bus. Everybody saw it coming for our car and they were only too happy to get away from us.

"What is it? What the hell's going on?!" Tracy screamed.

Jonathan reached from the back to place a hand on her shoulder. She calmed instantly and Jonathan nodded when he saw my silent thanks.

The road ahead was clear. The bus was coming to us again, the lunatic driver shaking his fist, and other faces—passengers, I presumed—a blur behind him.

Faster.

"Faster, Mum," Hayley said.

The fields and trees were a blur of greens and browns and the bus was still coming for us.

I said my next words to Hayley and hoped Tracy would react as quickly as I wanted her to.

She did.

She spun the wheel; we slalomed and she braked.

The tyres squealed, and for a moment, it seemed we would lose control. The car slowed as the bus overtook us, faces pressed against windows. Its own tyres howled as it slowed a fair distance ahead. Behind, the traffic stopped as drivers blocked the road to stare at us and the bus.

Are you ready, Jonathan?

"Of course."

I spoke to Hayley. She told Tracy and we sped forward again. Far ahead, the bus had slowed to a stop and was now reversing. It grew bigger the closer we drew to it and I was aware of nothing but its growing bulk. If I'd still been alive, my heart would have been thunder in my chest.

Inside Hayley, I grinned and she felt it.

The roar of our car was swallowed by the growl of the bus. We were aimed exactly in the middle of its rear and the only things I heard were the two vehicles.

And then the world in front was nothing but the bus.

Now.

Jonathan streaked between Hayley and Tracy, through the windshield and out to the back of the bus.

At the same time, Hayley screamed, *"Now, Mum, now."*

She didn't finish the second word before Tracy yanked the wheel and we flew to the grassy bank and came to a shaking stop halfway down the embankment.

The bus had also stopped. I craned Hayley's head around and caught a glimpse of something leaving the bus, some indistinct shape. I didn't have time to make a guess as to what it could be.

It dropped to the ground and vanished. Immediately after, every window on the bus exploded with hollow bangs. Glass rained. The doors blew apart and people ran from the vehicle. None appeared to be injured; all ran under their own power, all raced from the bus as if it was on fire, each person sobbing or screaming.

Jonathan appeared. He dropped through the roof of the bus and surveyed the fleeing people. I hadn't seen him so happy in years.

I called his name and he returned to our car.

"The driver wasn't acting alone. I didn't see who, but someone was definitely with him," he said.

Drude?

"No. I don't doubt he would have come for me. It was someone working for him."

Another demon?

"I don't know."

Hayley caught my half of this conversation. She didn't ask for clarification and I liked that. All through it, she'd kept her hand on her mother's wrist while Tracy tried to start the car. The engine coughed but wouldn't start. The bus remained in the middle of the road as if someone had forgotten it and the first line of vehicles crept behind it. Drivers on the other side of the carriageway were passing the scene and I was grateful for that. On the other hand, there were only a few moments before one of the drivers approached our car – and what would they make of a mother and her daughter who couldn't leave the vehicle?

Perhaps Tracy thought the same. She turned the key again and swore. The engine still didn't start.

"Start, you bastard!" she shrieked.

"Mum, it's okay," Hayley said.

She needs to start the car, Hayley. She needs to get us away from here.

I know that. Do you think I'm stupid?

The engine kicking into life swallowed any possible answer I could give. Tracy whooped her joy and reversed up the embankment, crushing grass. We hit the road, the car driving as if it was drunk, but at least we were moving.

People exited their vehicles close to the bus, a few waved in our direction, clearly doing their best to attract our attention. A man in a Transit van drove carefully past the growing crowd, coming straight towards us.

Go.

"Drive, Mum. Get us out of here."

Tracy drove like her life depended on it. Which was funny because it didn't. Neither did mine.

My death did.

Chapter Sixty-Four

The events on the road with the bus fell behind us. And I knew what that meant. As each moment passed, Dalry dropped further into my past. My future was a deep hole and I couldn't imagine what was down there.

At that thought, the memory of those moments above Hell hit me again, and shaking the images off was difficult.

"Melancholy isn't like you, Benjamin," Jonathan said.

Agreed, but this has been a difficult day.

He laughed with no humour in the sound at all, and stared at me, his face unreadable.

"I'd say so. Sally, Jim, Christopher all gone. Even the shades, Ben. What do you think of that?" He wouldn't take his eyes from mine. "What do you make of it? The forgotten ghosts, the Lost? All gone and all because of one demon."

What can I make of it? They knew what they were a part of.

"That's not what I mean."

Hayley listened to my side of our conversation with hungry interest while Tracy kept her eyes moving from the road to her daughter and back again.

Then what do you mean, Jonathan?

"I mean you've forgotten about the shades and what they did for us in the Square as if they never mattered. I know you didn't want to be a leader, but you became one. Now they're gone, now they've done their bit for you, you *could* care about that. You could care that those who managed to avoid Heaven and Hell for so long that they became almost nothing ended up losing everything for you."

Jonathan wasn't shouting. Maybe it would have been better if he had been. Instead, he spoke as if his words were the last he would ever utter and he wanted me to remember them for always.

Before this is over, I will do everything I can to punish Drude for what he did.

Jonathan appraised the traffic. "Of course you will."

Don't forget what I said. This hasn't been about running from Drude. This has always been about planning for him, getting ready for a fight. Always.

Jonathan said nothing.

Conversation was minimal for the rest of our journey. I think Hayley and her mother were too shocked at what had occurred to have any words. Jonathan was lost in his thoughts and I was planning for the next stage of my escape from Drude.

I directed Hayley to tell her mother which way to go. We reached the parkway that ran alongside the Meadows about ten minutes after the attack from the bus and joined Thistlemoor Road soon afterwards. The area was deserted, which was ideal. Tracy craned her head around. Her eyes were as dull as a dirty pond. It wouldn't be long before she was too mentally and physically exhausted to continue—a thought Hayley caught and I cursed myself for being so clumsy.

What do you mean, she won't be able to continue? You better not do anything to her.

I won't. Trust me, child.

Of course. Why wouldn't I?

Inside Hayley, I smiled, appreciating her sarcasm. *Tell her to park as close to the trees as she can.*

Hayley did so and Tracy pulled over further on. Shade from the trees fell over the car; birds sung, their voices still loud through the closed windows. There were no people anywhere in sight and I took an odd comfort in knowing the only living people anywhere near me were a teenage girl and her frightened mother. For the first time in years, I didn't want to have to hurt the living. All I wanted was to get into the woods and hide in the deep shadows at its middle for long enough to come up with a way of dealing with Drude permanently.

"That's your plan?" Jonathan said. "To hide?"

Do you have a better one?

He sighed. "Not really. Just doesn't seem like the sort of thing you'd do."

It's not. But what else can I do?

"There's one other option."

I stared at him and he stared back.

"The sea," he said.

Not a chance. Thistlemoor is our refuge. It always has been.

"It's a hiding place, Benjamin."

And what is the sea? I will not be chased there like a dog. We'll stay here, safe for as long as we need to be.

"As you wish."

Hayley listened to my half of this conversation without speaking, while Tracy watched for any signs of my actions. Birds sang again and I glanced at the trees. The shade between them could not have looked more welcoming.

I should have come here before now, I thought and knew why I hadn't. Jonathan was right, hiding wasn't in my nature. My nature was to do what I'd done. The big joke was, doing that had led me right here, ready to hide.

Gathering myself, I spoke to Hayley. *Listen. We get out of the car. All of us. We walk to the trees and I leave you there. So does Jonathan.*

What about the other one? Cooke?

I'd forgotten about Cooke, if only briefly. He hadn't spoken in hours. It was certainly possible that Drude's actions in the Square had been too much for Cooke to take and he was now powerless and lost deep inside Hayley.

He'll leave when we do. He can't stay with you, I said and felt the girl's doubt. She'd picked up on my feelings concerning Cooke's mental state.

If you say so, she said.

I do.

She gave a mental laugh. A decidedly bleak laugh, it must be said. *What about the sea? What does that mean?*

Forget about it.

Why?

I ignored her questions. *Let's go. Tell your mother.*

Hayley let her questions go, leaving me grateful. "Come on, Mum," she said. "We have to go to the trees. He said they'll go from there."

Dumb gratitude filled Tracy's face and a few tears dropped. She shoved her door open and ran around to Hayley's side as the girl jumped from the car. Jonathan stood close to us, standing straight instead of floating, as keen as I to conserve energy. The early morning was free from human noise. Even Tracy's tears were silent. The trees were right in front of us and all the hiding places I'd ever need were beyond them.

I didn't think it would end like this, I said to Jonathan who kept his counsel and held his gaze on the trees.

"Why are we here?" Tracy said in a croak.

I told Hayley, who spoke as soon as I finished. "He says this is a refuge for ghosts. He can hide here and leave us. He'll have to stay here forever, but he says he'll do that."

Tracy wept. She reached for Hayley's hand and I let her take it.

We took slow steps towards the trees. Without warning, the shadows ahead changed.

A white flash of light bloomed, followed by an instant of bellowed noise. Negation, argument—the noise was both and more.

We froze, all staring ahead.

"What is it?" Tracy whispered.

Birds sang prettily.

"Listen," Jonathan said.

I did so; I listened with my ears, not Hayley's. The secret sound in the bellow was still there, only it was now a whisper from countless voices. All those voices said *no* over and over from now until the end of time.

"What's happening?!" Tracy yelled and her voice cracked on the second word. Whether this was because she so desperately wanted me away from her daughter or because she'd picked up on some of the negation in front of us, I don't know.

Jonathan drifted ahead and extended a slow arm to touch the nearest tree. He didn't make it before other forms slipped from between the trees. Dozens of ghosts faced us. I recognised some; others were much older than Jonathan or I. They stared at me and me alone.

Not welcome here.

There was no way of knowing which of them had spoken and it probably wasn't important. Whoever did speak did so for each soul in Thistlemoor Wood. More than that, they spoke for Thistlemoor Wood itself. The last refuge for the dead within hundreds of miles was sealed to me.

This isn't right. The Wood is open to all of us. It doesn't judge us, it doesn't block us, I yelled.

You brought Hell to the world. The Wood is closed to you.

Drude brought Hell, you bastard, and you know it. All I'm doing is trying to get away from him.

You're not welcome here.

I caught a new scent, and while I might have expected the myriad aromas of Hell, it was a secret odour, something in the trees, something older than the bark and leaves. Before I had chance to name it, the smell vanished, leaving indistinct images; a sunset of thick, bloody red, a mouth open in a huge triumphant grin, the sea below, all foaming waves and currents deep under the surface.

It was gone, as were the whispering dead. Dozens of vague shapes and other well-defined faces had returned to the shadows and refuge of Thistlemoor Wood.

Jonathan floated to my side. "We could try it," he said.

No, we couldn't. I doubt even you would get through. And God knows what would happen if I tried it.

"What's happening? Aren't you going in?" Hayley said.

Tracy stared at her daughter and saw me far below Hayley's skin. Nobody moved.

Tracy screamed once, a harsh, broken sound that silenced all the birdsong.

Chapter Sixty-Five

Five minutes later, we were back in the car. We drove on, heading east.

Chapter Sixty-Six

We closed in on our destination about an hour after leaving Thistlemoor Wood: a town called Milton. I told Hayley to tell her mother to head towards the businesses and shops that filled the middle of the town and left it at that. I wanted to think.

Doing so was impossible. Hayley said nothing in reply, and she had no need to. Her sickened fury blocked my thought processes as easily as her raging at me would have. The girl didn't just want me gone, she wanted me *destroyed*, and that constant heartbeat of loathing jutted like a prison wall in the middle of my head.

By eleven on that long morning, we were sixty miles from Dalry. The coast was forty miles further on and I felt a brief yet strong urge to walk beside the sea, to see the water flowing to the rest of the world. Disturbed, I shoved the urge away. Despite Jonathan's words at Thistlemoor Wood, the sea was the last place I should head.

"Where are we going?" Tracy asked without looking at Hayley. Perhaps she was worried she'd see me in her daughter's face.

Keep going. Head for the shops, the businesses.

Hayley repeated this and Jonathan leaned closer to us.

"What makes you think this will work? You tried the same in Dalry, and remember what that cost us."

The words he didn't say were there all the same; it almost cost me him, too.

I'm not doing the same. We're going to use people as a shield between us and Drude, but not like before, I said.

"Meaning?"

Just wait for it. Please, Jonathan. And while you're at it, do me a favour.

"Yes?"

Don't mention the sea. I know you're thinking it, but don't say it. We shouldn't think of it.

He fell silent, although I doubted he'd remain so for long.

We were stuck in the traffic on the road that emerged from the suburbs and I, through Hayley's eyes, tried to look everywhere at once.

Will you stop that? You're giving me neck ache.

Your neck is the least of my concerns, child.

She laughed, full of bitterness.

I'd have thought I was top of your list. If I get hurt or if I die, doesn't that make things difficult for you?

I stopped searching the traffic. She'd hit a truth I'd hoped she would miss. And there was nothing I could do about it.

You won't get hurt if you do as I tell you. I'll keep you safe.

She laughed again and it was miles beyond hate. *Why don't I believe you?*

You don't have a choice, I answered and shut off her next comment by lifting her arm and pointing.

The shopping centre was practically identical to the one in Dalry, and not for the first time, I wondered about the living and their desire to build such monstrosities.

"There?" Tracy said. I welcomed her doubt. Logic— admittedly of the panicked kind—said if she wasn't expecting this, then neither was Drude.

We joined the line of slow vehicles heading to the centre and reached the underground parking area as the first drops of rain fell. The entrance swallowed us and those drops of rain fell harder.

The centre wasn't as busy as I would have liked. The car park was only halfway full and we saw no more than ten people on our scurried walk from the shadows and cars to the stairs and then shops. As soon as we were up on the first level, Jonathan floated beside Tracy, who was quite obviously exhausted. She didn't believe what was happening, not all the way down. Jonathan saw my concern and stayed as close to her as he could.

We walked between the shops and businesses; people paid us no obvious attention, despite it being a weekday and Hayley being out of school. They had their own business to consider, their own plans and worries. That was fine. I wanted their protection. What I didn't need was their attention.

We took the escalator down to the ground floor and stopped beside a large seating area.

"What next?" Tracy said.

Enjoy the peace while you can.

Hayley repeated this quietly and the lower corner of Tracy's mouth twitched. Later, I had time to wish I hadn't replied with such a flippant answer. It was a bald invitation to the events that immediately followed.

Those events started with a shadow over our heads.

Chapter Sixty-Seven

All of us tilted our heads to look up.

There was a massive skylight directly above. Thick raindrops coated it while heavy clouds filled what little was visible of the sky. Those clouds exhaled; there was no other word for it. The sky breathed and a ball of black speared down towards the skylight.

Jonathan and I flew at the same moment. He slammed a hand down on Tracy's shoulder; she yelped and he pushed her. Inside Hayley, I shoved her as hard as I could. The four of us leaped from our spot below the skylight as the glass exploded.

Giant chunks of glass streaked down to shatter on the ground. Deafened by the breaking windows, we raced into the shoe shop opposite, crashed into a display and sent shoes and boots spinning over the floor. Behind us, people screamed – and they'd become screams of pain. We turned.

The breaking glass lay scattered in pieces of all sizes, and those not fast enough had been caught by the flying chunks. Blood spatters sprayed across the floor and the sides of the escalators. A few bodies lay where the glass cut them down. A long chunk of glass had almost severed a woman's head, leaving it jutting from her neck on a few strands of bloody flesh. Beside her, an elderly man had fallen and held himself. He was also dead, which was probably a mercy; two giant shards jutted high from his stomach like bizarre growths.

Many of the injured crawled from the mess of blood and glass as if their injuries could be reversed by distance. Those who couldn't move called out for help, or just got quietly on with bleeding to death.

Tracy held Hayley as tightly as she could; she made no sound, and I briefly wondered how much of her sanity remained.

Come on, I said.

We took hesitant steps out of the shop; a few of the staff followed us, but most didn't want to get too close to the injured. Someone behind us was on the phone to the police. In front, people ran from other shops and from the floor above, shoving past one another on the escalators. Telling them to run for their lives would have done no good. They weren't going to listen to a fifteen-year-old girl.

What's happening? What is this? Hayley said.

Trouble.

What?

Be ready to tell your mother to run.

That shut her up. Her questions and panic fought to spill out, but she held them back, and for no obvious reason, I thought of Cooke, Cooke far below, Cooke silent for days – or so it seemed.

The ball that had crashed into the skylight appeared in the hole above. As it descended, we weren't the only ones looking at it. All around us, people saw the thing. Some ran blindly; others stayed with the injured.

"They see him, Ben," Jonathan whispered. I hadn't felt such strong fear come from Jonathan in years. "They see him."

Yes. So be ready to run.

The ball hit the ground and a dizzying tremor ran through it. People screamed, perhaps fearing an earthquake and more falling glass. That didn't happen. Instead, the black dissipated like smoke and Drude stood before us. He smiled and the wails reached new levels of terror.

People bolted. They didn't run; they actually *bolted.* None of them could have known exactly what Drude was, which made no difference. With their old instinct, the one that still knew irrational fear of lonely nights, the one that told them to avoid empty moors and old woods, they *knew*.

And they bolted.

The injured couldn't, of course. They lay or sat where they'd fallen, and they screamed. Pain was forgotten. Fear wasn't. They saw Drude and they begged for their lives.

"Such horrible noise." He glanced around at the glass and blood. "Such a mess."

Go away, I said, and he eyed Hayley as if she was some interesting new animal.

"Do you like him inside? Do you like him deep inside you?" His smile was bigger than anything; it would swallow us if it grew any more. "A little young to appreciate such things, aren't you? Having him penetrating you in such a thorough manner, having him all over you, having him shoving into you, having him in your body?"

"Shut up. Shut your mouth," Tracy said tonelessly.

"And if I don't?"

"I'll kill you." Tracy said this with the same lack of tone. There was no need for anger or even aggression. It was a flat promise.

Hayley shook and did her best to control it. At first, I believed the trembling was due to fear, before realising hatred was the cause. I couldn't say who she detested more—me or the demon. At that point, I think she would have been happy to see us both burning.

"I tell you what, Benjamin. Come with me, and the girl and the woman will be safe. How about that?"

Xaphan, Jonathan whispered.

"What was that?" Drude said sharply. I didn't react and I didn't follow Jonathan's gaze. He was looking up to the hole in the roof and I mentally screamed at him to turn away. Drude whipped his head around and up; I did the same and saw only low sky and rain.

My glance was only for a second, which was all I could risk. Before Drude could face us again, I was looking at him and him and alone.

"Do we have a deal?" he said, and I gave the only answer I could.

No.

He laughed. "I planned on you saying that. Which is why I have to do this."

He remained still. Behind him, shadows spread their discolouration, while blurred faces swam through the swirling muck and eyes peered out.

"A few old friends," Drude said.

You have friends? Since when?

"They're not *my* friends," he said. "They're yours."

Chapter Sixty-Eight

We faced each other, two spirits and a mother and daughter on one side, a demon with a wall of the dead behind him on the other.

"You saw them," Drude said in an oddly gentle manner. "On the road. They were in the bus."

Realisation bloomed as if I'd woken from a deep sleep.

"Your victims, Benjamin. The people you killed."

One of the swimming faces lunged out of the shadows, mouth open in a soundless howl. It twisted and lunged, seeking to free itself and doubtless bury me in its fury.

"Your first, I believe." Drude was telling the truth. The face caught in the hell of Drude's shadows belonged to the man I'd killed in the woods, the homosexual from my pub.

"They've come to say hello," Drude said, and I loathed him with a passion and a depth I'd never known.

You bastard. I gave them to you. They're just as much yours as mine.

"You *did* give them to me; I kept you out of the Pit. I kept you free from punishment for your wickedness. And now here we are, all together again after so long. But the thing is, Harwood, who do you think they blame for their deaths? Their murderer, perhaps? Or the demon they're powerless against?"

Not for the first time in recent weeks, I remembered the old days, of stabbing, of beating and giving the dying to Drude, each one to guarantee me a little longer out of Hell.

"So, will you come with me?" Drude asked.

If I don't, I take it you open Hell again and kill everyone here?

"No." He gestured to the seething ghosts around him. Each face stretched as if made of tar and my name was on countless silent mouths, countless screams of my name. "I let them loose."

From the gaping hole in the ceiling, rain poured. Around us, the injured and dying pleaded for help which didn't come. Drude stared at me while I hid inside a child. Sound faded. The noise, the rain, even Hayley's quick, frightened breaths—all of it vanished, leaving me alone with only Drude staring at me from somewhere else.

Xaphan spoke from somewhere close. *Thistlemoor Wood didn't work, Benny. This isn't working. There's one place left. You know what to do.*

Inside Hayley, I nodded. Inside her, I reached for Jonathan. His hand met mine, and in the darkness, we held one another.

For the last time.

Without a word, we sprinted from the mess and the bodies. Drude made no sound as we fled because he had no need to. The bastard had known all along what I would I do.

We ran past shops and the injured, took a sharp corner and the screeches of all the ghosts chased after us. Ahead, a crowd of shoppers and staff covered the floors from one side to the other. They saw us, a few screamed. Others, seeing a running girl and her mother, shouted for us to run faster. Then the dead streaked over us in a massive cloud to land in the middle of the people.

The cloud vanished. We stopped and faced a wall of the living possessed by the dead.

From behind, still surrounded by the mess he'd made and the people he'd injured, Drude's voice was a tremendous bellow that made the windows of shop fronts crack.

"I'm giving you one more chance, Benjamin. The only way you're staying out of the Pit is to see how fast you can run."

And I understood what needed to be done.

We ran for the nearest shop, as the possessed people sprinted at us. The ghosts inside them howled. Some managed to call my name. Most of them just voiced horrible, wordless noises.

Hayley and Tracy sprinted into a branch of Boots, both crying; I yelled at Hayley to run faster, and Jonathan herded Tracy forward. The few customers and staff in the shop saw us and a few advanced, as if wanting to help. They heard the howling coming at our backs and backed away fast. We passed wide displays of perfumes, then make-up and stopped at the rear of the store.

"Harwood."

My name sounded as if it was a cross between a bark and a shout—the sort of noise a dog would make if it learned to speak.

The dead were still coming, knocking others out of their way, bashing over the stands and smashing bottles to the ground. At once, there was a barrage of smells, all cloying, all horrible.

Hayley screamed at me, wanting to know what was happening, wanting it all to stop.

We have to go out the back, I said and Jonathan heard me.

"Destroy them. We can do it."

We do that and we'll be in the Pit a second later. I can't leave the girl.

They were still coming; we could do nothing but run. We made it to doors that led to the staff areas, and a security guard appeared from nowhere. He smacked into Tracy and both fell.

"You're not going in there," he shouted and pulled her up. She was too dazed to protest. I snapped Hayley's head around. The ghosts were almost on us, so I ran as Jonathan yanked Tracy from the guard's hold and shoved the man to the floor.

The doors flew open, exposing a short corridor with a fire exit at the end. As I took Hayley inside, Jonathan yelled my name.

He was still in the shop, blocked from the doors by a dozen or more people. Alone, they were no threat to him. The dead inside them, however, changed everything. These were not the newly dead we'd faced back in Dalry. These were the dead set free in the world that had long since forgotten them. They were the raging spirits with centuries of experience behind them. That experience that made them strong. If they reached Jonathan, they'd take him down to the Pit before he had time to do a thing.

Tracy ran from him, calling Hayley's name and the living ghosts let her pass. Several moved towards

Jonathan. He retreated and streaked high. Grasping hands strained to reach him. Inside the living, the insane dead advanced.

"Benjamin," he shouted. *"Help me."*

He saw me, then, saw me inside Hayley. As it had with Drude, everything went away until all sound disappeared, leaving me deaf inside a teenage girl, me hiding, me staring at my last friend. For an instant, I floated in the obsidian silence.

Jonathan shrieked. All the horror, all the betrayal and all the fury in the world was contained within that shriek.

I ran with Hayley and Tracy for the fire exit as the ghosts raced towards us in a melee of arms and legs and teeth, and as Jonathan's terror echoed along the corridor.

We bashed into the door and spilled outside to a car park; the rain had stopped and sunlight was a dazzling sparkle. I took her forward and couldn't stop her looking back.

"Mum!" she screamed.

Tracy was at the fire exit, pushing all her weight against it. On the other side, the dead hammered at the metal but their sheer numbers prevented them from gaining any hold on the door. The thunder of their fists and feet bashing against it drowned out almost everything else.

"Go," Tracy cried and spoke directly to me. She didn't see her daughter; she saw only me. "Keep her safe, you bastard."

Hayley wept and couldn't run to her mother. There was no time for me to speak. I took the girl at a mad dash across the car park while she wept for her mother who could do nothing but block the ghosts at the fire exit.

Chapter Sixty-Nine

ields, again.

We were a few miles away from the town. Early afternoon had arrived by then, and I'd made Hayley walk without a break since running from the car park and her mother. Neither of us knew Milton; instinct took me in the right direction, though. That instinct said to get away from people, so I'd pushed Hayley from the roads and buildings to a narrow side street which eventually ended at a cycleway. Following that for a mile took us to woods and beyond them, we reached farmland.

Hayley wanted to rest. She kept repeating this, thinking it in a fading mutter. She was unable to lift her head for long and the only thing that kept her going was my will.

As my interior clock estimated the time at close to one, I let her stop and fall into a tangle of hedges bordering the fields. She crawled into the shade, dropped her face into the earth and cried the tears of a young child.

Hayley, you need to listen to me.

I don't have to do anything. Fuck off.

Yes, you do. For your safety, you need to listen. You should know what happened and why I did what I did.

I was silent, thoughts of Jonathan taking away my words. I'd betrayed him again. There was no getting away from that. I couldn't even take consolation in knowing doing so was for the last time. He'd given me a second chance and I'd paid him back by damning him.

Those people who came after us, they weren't themselves. Drude sent ghosts into them and it was the ghosts coming after us. They won't have hurt your mother; it's me they want. Once they got through the door, I imagine they just ran past her.

She stopped weeping and lifted her head. Dirt stuck to the wetness on her cheeks. *Are you telling me the truth?*

I can't lie to you, Hayley. You can't lie to me. I don't know for definite, but I do think they would have ignored her.

She dared to hope and that was good. It made her stronger. *Who were they? The ghosts?*

I'd been expecting the question and wished I could lie to her. *They were people I killed. The demon sent them because he knew they'd make the living come for me. I couldn't stop them because killing people, killing the living in your body means you're damned with me. I do that and we'll both go to Hell. Letting them kill you so they can get to me means I'm damned. Leaving you means Drude has me in a second and I'm damned.*

So whatever you do, she said, *you're going to Hell?*

Not exactly. I'm going to the Pit.

What's that?

Inside her, I sighed. *Hell isn't exactly what you think it is. It's not all punishment and fire and brimstone. It's about atonement and work, about making up for mistakes in life. But part of it is different. The Pit.*

I stopped there, desperate to not think of the glimpse I'd got of the Pit that day early on in my quest or of Drude's promise to keep me out of there if I gave him bodies.

What's the Pit? Hayley asked with a child's innocence.

The Pit is all *punishment. It's the part of Hell reserved for people like me.*

And that's where Drude wants to take you?

So it seems.

She considered that and then said: *If this demon wants to kill people, why use you? Why not just do it himself?*

He can't. Demons aren't all evil, but when they are like Drude, they go for it in a big way. He loves to kill but he's unable to do it directly. He can do indirect things and get away with them without the rest of Hell finding out. That's why he came to me when I was alive and told me to kill for him and he'd keep me out of Hell.

What about the other one? Your mate? Where is he?

Inside her, I closed my eyes. *Running. He'll be running forever. Jonathan's in the same position as me. If he kills those chasing him, he's damned to the Pit immediately, and if he lets them kill him. . .you get the idea.*

God, she whispered.

They'll never stop. They'll always be after him, which means he can never stop running.

And you did that to your friend?

There was no way I could say any different. In the shade of the hedge where we sat miles from anyone, I said: *Yes. He was my friend and I betrayed him. Once to Drude and once forever.*

Screams rushed up from far below, screams that were nowhere near sane.

Richard Cooke had been listening and he was pure outrage, pure horror. He flew at me and I turned to face below, to stare all the way down as Cooke streaked upwards.

Chapter Seventy

The fields were gone. So was daylight. For the first time in long centuries, I had the sensation of a solid body, of flesh and bone.

There wasn't time for panic or fear. I was falling, dropping from an immeasurable distance, racing down to the ground as Drude had raced down to the skylight in the shopping centre.

Hayley, I thought and hit the ground.

Light exploded from the sky and from the ground. I couldn't shut my eyes against it; I couldn't even blink. It was as if I'd landed on the sun. More illumination than I'd ever known streamed from high above and directly below and I fought against it. It made no difference to the light. It pierced my skull and set my brain on fire.

See.

Unlike the light, the voice spoke only from below. Whoever it was, I didn't care at that point. It made the light fade to the light of twilight or early morning and I *saw.*

I was on a rocky, barren section of land, a charmless place brooded over by a low sky. I squatted and touched the rocks. They were damp, which made me wonder if rain had recently fallen. More likely, no sun ever shone here, and the dampness was down to the moist air.

I began to turn in a circle and stopped before I'd made it halfway. The craggy rocks ended in the distance. A thin blue line inked the horizon. The sky that way was lighter than directly above, and although I couldn't be certain, I had the idea that the few tiny dots in the sky over the blue were birds.

The area was unlike anywhere I'd seen before. To stand on a ruined land of ugly, barren rocks and see sea and beach however many miles away made absolutely no sense. In my long experiences of travel and seeing all the environments the world could offer, I'd never seen such a place.

As I turned in another circle, something above fell at a tremendous speed and my only thought was of Drude.

Cooke hit me like a furious bullet and we both flew to sprawl on the rocks. He kicked out and missed my stomach only because of luck.

He stood, gazing at me as I did the same. There was no doubt that he would close the distance between us any second.

"You," he spat. "Worse than I thought. Worse than—"

"I get the idea," I said. He rocked on his feet and held his stomach.

Without looking away from him, I said, "Where are we? Where have you brought us?"

He made an odd noise that was somewhere between a laugh and a snort of disbelief. "The girl."

"Hayley?"

He nodded frantically.

"She's here?"

He shook his head. Then nodded.

"Cooke, make sense, damn you. Where are we?"

"The girl."

"So you said."

Without knowing where we were or how to leave meant I couldn't afford to get too far away from the rocks or Cooke. I had a deep suspicion that he was my exit. Without him, I'd never get away from this odd, empty place.

"Looks like a war." He waved at the rocks between us. There was no need to ask for clarification. The land did resemble the site of a long-ago battle, a great fire, perhaps, or a violent movement below the earth resulting from an explosion in the distance. Whatever the cause, it had left the land as lifeless as mouldering bones in their grave.

"The girl," Cooke said. His eyes flicked from mine to the rocks between us and back again. I understood. All of it was nothing one second and everything the next.

"This is Hayley, isn't it, Cooke? We're *inside* her."

He nodded.

Somehow Cooke had brought us further into Hayley than I'd thought possible. As Drude had so indelicately put it, I'd invaded her, *penetrated* her. Cooke had gone beyond simple penetration. We weren't inside her mind as I'd entered it after the battle in Memorial Square; Cooke had brought us to her soul.

We were standing on her spirit.

Chapter Seventy-One

Cooke saw my understanding and his grin split his face in two. Snarling white teeth gleamed in the dusky light, and then he was upon me.

We crashed backward and struck the rocks. We were wrapped like lovers around one another; his fists pummelled at me and smacked my head back to bounce off the rocks. Jagged fingers plunged into my back, I groaned and headbutted Cooke. His grip fell from my form; I punched him in his throat and scrambled away. Cursing and trying not to pass out, I staggered upright and aimed a kick at Cooke's stomach. It missed and struck him in the upper thigh. He grabbed at my leg, I overbalanced and went down again. He launched at me, and spitting in each other's faces, we kicked and punched over the rocks before we hit a shallow crevasse and fell apart, gasping as blood poured from dozens of wounds.

I managed to stand before he did, but didn't have the strength to attack him. He lifted his head, one eye sealed shut with blood, and did his best to focus on me.

"Your friend," he wheezed.

"Yes, my friend," I replied. "I betrayed him again, and it wasn't even a betrayal to the death. It was betrayal for the rest of time. I know that; he knows that and the last thing I need is *you judging me.*"

I screamed my last few words with as much strength as I could, screamed them to Cooke and the sky and the rocks.

The ground split in long lines, spilling rock and gravel. I jumped out of the way of a growing crack, ran a short distance and turned back. Cooke was a prone shape on the uneven ground staring at me, although I doubted he could see me clearly.

"Cooke!" I bellowed. Two of the splits raced towards him. They met, the ground opened and Cooke fell into the spaces below the rocks.

"Cooke."

The splitting earth chased after me. I ran as if I was on stilts, convinced the ground would open below me at any second. When it seemed I could do nothing but drop to my knees and let the rents take me, the rumbling behind faded, and then stopped.

I continued until it was safe enough to stop. Choking clouds of dust had risen from the shifting earth, making it almost impossible to see. There was no wind, not even a breeze to shift the dust. I waved a hand in front, which did little good, before staggering further on. I'd lost any sense of direction and could only guess I was heading towards the faraway sea and away from the ruined wasteland of Hayley's soul.

You ruined her soul.

The words roared out of nowhere to fill my head and I froze, wishing I could find some argument against them, aware I didn't have a thing to say.

This ruined land was the girl's soul.

I had created it.

Movement was impossible. So was speech, for that matter. I simply stood on the rocks, surrounded by thick dust and let that realisation sink all the way in. Cooke brought us to Hayley's soul to show me what I'd done to it, and by showing me the ruin I'd brought to a teenage girl, he hoped I would be undone.

My left leg moved first, then my right. Movement was difficult due to the layout of the land but I kept going, determined not to be hurt in any way by what another dead person thought of me. The rocks became smoother the further I went; the dust fell and the blue line of the sea, while still faraway, was more defined the further I went.

I'm leaving it. I'm leaving all the grief I've given her.

At that thought, the blue flashed and more birds appeared over the water. I giggled. Here I was, walking on the battered part of Hayley's soul while the goodness, the purity and innocence that made much of her spirit was within reach. I ran in pained, lurching steps. Skidding on the damp, I dropped to my knees more than once. Just as I was sure the beach could be no more than a quarter of a mile away, I slipped again.

My head hit a jagged finger of rock and there was time for me to wonder if the rock was the last jagged piece between here and the sand. Then the tremor from my impact shook the earth to all directions. Again, the rocks split. Thin lines raced away and I made it up despite wanting to simply collapse.

"Harwood."

Cooke stood where I fell, arms extended, fingers clenching and unclenching as if he was eating me with his hands.

"Couldn't stay away?" I croaked.

His answer came from the land below. It didn't split. It *roared.*

Chunks of rock as big as houses flew upwards. I held Cooke's mad gaze for a heartbeat and ran.

Pieces of rock no bigger than my arm rained on all sides; a larger section hit the earth not far off, scattering smaller chunks. I ran as fast as possible, not looking back or up, not daring to. The earth was a downpour and I heard nothing but the explosions as it struck the rocks and broke into more and more pieces.

There was a moment of the blue and the now distinct yellow of the beach before a shadow bigger than the world buried me. I looked up, unable to move, and saw a rock dropping, bearing down to crush me into Hayley's soul.

A hand gripped my arm. And pulled.

I flew; my feet left the earth and there was nothing but the mighty crash of land colliding with earth.

Chapter Seventy-Two

"You rescued me."

The words tasted like a foreign language in my mouth. I repeated them, which didn't make any difference. Had I ever said those words before? A loose memory attempted to come; I reached for it and held nothing more substantial than smoke.

"I did," she said.

We eyed one another. She was prettier than I'd first thought. Of course, that was because I wasn't facing a terrified fifteen-year-old girl. I was facing her soul.

"May I call you Hayley?" I asked.

"That's my name."

She sounded coolly amused, as if I was the frightened child and she was the ghost with centuries of experience.

"Why did you rescue me, Hayley?"

She glanced over my shoulder. I turned. Cooke was a staggering shape in the distance. He aimed for us but the pits in the land made his movement slow. He'd reach us eventually. There was no doubt of it. The mad bastard would keep coming after me, no matter what.

"Cooke," she said and sighed. "He's a good man. He has a good soul."

"Which is half the reason he hates me so much."

We stared at one another again. Understanding passed between us, gentle as a sorrowful lover's kiss.

"He'd grow to hate me if he had time," she said.

"Why?"

"I'm human." She waved a hand to encompass what was left of the rocks. "Do you think this is *all* down to you? Don't you think my soul has its own damaged parts that are nothing to do with you?"

"I. . ." There wasn't anything I could add to that so I said nothing.

"I'm human. So are you, despite the things you've done. So is Cooke, although I think he's forgotten that." Her unblinking eyes filled mine. "He wanted to undo you. He wanted your deeds undone. But he forgot that evil has its place, just as good does. He forgot you can't have one without the other."

"Which means?"

She smiled and the smile was not a happy one. "Which means he can never beat you. He might know that, deep down. Maybe that's what drove him insane, not the level of your evil or your betrayals or your lack of repentance."

I took another look back. Cooke was closer. He saw me and howled. The educated, rational man I'd met on Azalea Drive was long gone. Hayley was right. Cooke was mad. Despite that issue, another one pressed on me.

"After what I did to Hayley's family, you still save me?" I said.

She spoke with a solid finality that said the conversation would be done as soon as she liked – and that would be within seconds. I had no choice but to accept it.

"I don't *want* to save you. Neither does Hayley. This is more important than us. It's more important than Hayley's family."

"Where does that leave us?" I asked her.

She walked to me, stood beside me and gazed at Cooke.

"Drude won't stop. All you have to do is decide where to face him." She glanced at me. "Don't forget what the other one told you. Don't forget Xaphan."

"I won't."

"You will eventually. You'll throw him away like you did the others." Her voice changed and I could do nothing but stare at her in dread as Cooke advanced.

"Jim. Jonathan. Sally. Christopher. Philip."

Each name belonged to a different voice, each one was the voice of the person she'd named. Their faces weren't with us, but the voices were enough. My damned friends were with me again, hidden in the face of a teenage girl. Hayley's soul, come to me in the shape of a teenaged girl, smiled and there was nothing forgiving about her smile.

"You threw them away. That's what you do. And you accept what you are in a way Cooke never would." She studied me with an awareness years beyond her. Something far older than me, something ancient looked at me in those last few moments. "In your own way, you're more balanced than Cooke. How about that?"

Neither of us spoke again until Cooke closed in. He stopped on a section of rock that resembled a pointing finger and stared at me. Dirt marked his face like a brand.

"Harwood," he said in a grunt.

"Cooke," I replied and bowed.

He made a noise which I eventually realised was a laugh.

"Cooke," I said again. A new feeling arrived. I picked over it for a moment before realising it was an odd kind of regret. Despite everything he'd done and all the trouble he'd caused me, I didn't dislike Cooke. Under different circumstances, he and I might have got on. We were both men of our word; we both stood by what we believed in. And another oddity: he'd been part of my life for a few weeks but it felt much longer—as if I'd known him as long as I'd known Jonathan and the others. Picturing the future, however much of it might remain, was as strange as picturing time ahead without the small collective of my dead companions.

Hayley walked from my side, arms outstretched. Cooke's face twitched and that twitch eventually became a smile. Man and girl held one another and Cooke stared at me over her shoulder.

"Harwood," he whispered.

I raised my hand in a gentle wave and Hayley's words were a soft and soothing whisper.

"You're free."

Cooke's expression remained the same, for which I was grateful. I didn't want to see his fear or confusion. The grey light in his eyes faded and in the end, he didn't know what was happening. He was solid one moment, a gradually disappearing shadow the next. After that, Hayley held a simple light-shape, still fading as I watched.

Cooke went from Hayley's soul in easy and welcome silence.

She turned to me. "He's free."

"So it's just us."

"End this soon." It wasn't a request.

I met her eyes. "As soon as I can."

She turned again and walked across the rocks towards the sunlight on the beach. I followed without once wanting to look back.

Chapter Seventy-Three

We walked for a time I couldn't measure. The sea did come closer, but paradoxically always stayed out of reach. With almost all my attention on the distant water, I left Hayley's soul and returned to the world of fields and trees. One step took me over the rocks, and the next brought me back to seeing the world through her eyes.

She shook me mentally, the way you might do so physically to wake an unconscious person.

What happened? Where did you go? Where's the other one?

Her questions continued in a speeding run and I struggled to think past her noise.

She didn't remember any of it, which made sense. The Hayley who'd come to Cooke and I hadn't been the girl sitting on the grass. She'd been some much deeper and far older part of the girl. Whatever claim to eternity the living can make, I'd met Hayley's piece of forever.

Listen, I said and by some miracle, she was quiet. *He's gone. He's free. It's just us now. I'll keep you safe.*

As soon as we get somewhere, I'll leave you and you'll never hear from me again.

Where's he gone?

She didn't believe me which was perfectly understandable.

He's gone. That's all you need to know. He couldn't carry on the way he was, so he's left us. There's just you and me now.

Silence for a moment. Then she spoke in a firm tone, a girl ready to take charge now we were near the end.

Where are we going?

I paused before replying. An idea, Jonathan's idea, had been circling my head since fleeing from Thistlemoor Wood. The ghosts Drude brought back would still be looking for us; they'd never give up. If it took them an eternity of jumping from person to person in order to track me, they'd do it as a few were doing at that moment with poor Jonathan. Even as Hayley and I sat below the sun, members of the public were under the control of the dead and while they were doubtless screaming to be left alone, they had no choice but to go wherever the dead took them, which was straight at me.

Which of course meant I had to go where the dead couldn't harm me.

We're going to the end of the country. Deep inside Hayley, I smiled. *We're going to the seaside.*

Chapter Seventy-Four

A walk of half an hour took us to a narrow road and I directed Hayley on to it after consulting my interior map. As we walked, I talked to her and she listened without comment or argument, simply because she'd realised that was the quickest way to force me out of her.

The dead will follow us wherever we go. We could go all over the country, hide in the hills or mountains and it wouldn't make any difference. They'll keep coming. All Drude needs to do is wait for them to catch us. Once they kill you, I'm exposed and he'll have me. If I leave you to fight them, you're safe but I'll be taken immediately. But if we can make it to the sea, they'll panic. They'll leave the living and come straight for me.

Hayley crossed into a wide area of shade cast by overhanging trees and lowered her head. The day was warmer than normal and she'd been exposed to the elements for several hours. It wouldn't be long before she would need food and rest.

As soon as they do, I'll do what I have to and this will be over, I said.

Why will they panic?

I didn't want to tell her because hearing my plan spoken made it feel much too weak and too open to attack. There was no way I couldn't tell her, though. We couldn't lie to one another as much as I might have wanted to.

It's a ghost thing. The sea, the water, it's alive in its own way. I'll be a part of it like I'm part of you.

Mentally, she frowned. *Part of it? What does that mean?*

It means my essence or soul or whatever you want to call it, it'll be part of the sea, separated into God knows how many drops of water. It's as close as I can get to having any physical shape.

Apart from being inside me, you mean?

Hayley realised immediately how her words could be taken and I spoke over her embarrassment.

As I said, the sea goes everywhere. I'll go with it. The water will take me wherever it wants for as long as it wants. The ghosts coming after us will leave the living rather than let me escape.

And what will you do then?

Best not to think of that, I replied and whispered: *Someone might be listening.*

I didn't truly believe that. If Drude was anywhere near us, he'd make a move. Still, I'd be wise to be careful.

That's what you meant back at the woods, isn't it?

Yes. Now be quiet, girl.

Eventually, the narrow road reached a wider one. It clearly wasn't well travelled, but as there were no others in sight, we had no choice. We walked on the wild grass which grew beside it. The sun shone. On the other side of the road, a steep embankment eventually met level grass. Birds sang. We were probably five miles from the town and our surroundings made it feel much further. We could have been on a country road a hundred or a hundred and fifty years before. The thought cheered me. Hayley sensed my uplifted mood.

What's made you so happy? she asked.

Thinking about the old days.

I waited for her next question. The road dipped in a small groove, forcing Hayley to steady her feet.

Why are you. . .what you are?

Do you mean, why have I killed people? Why am I a monster who's happy to walk with a child on a nice day and think about times gone past?

Yeah.

I am what I am. I am what I've always been. I know what's right and what's wrong. Morality or ethics or whatever you want to call it. We all know what we should and shouldn't do, but I don't care. What always mattered to me was the power of what I did, not whether it was right or wrong. I don't apologise for that. If there is a God, then He made me what I am. I don't argue with that.

Hayley didn't reply.

Cooke asked me why I killed and I told him the truth. The consequences of it, the power it gave me and the long-term effects stretching through time. I wanted all those things. I told him that. It was the truth, but when it comes down to the basics, I killed people because I felt I was worth more than they were and because I could and because I wanted to change the world. I stopped and considered something I'd often thought but never spoken.

What? Hayley said.

The thing about killing is, once you start, it's hard to stop.

She was silent. I went on. *I don't argue with what I am or what God made me, if He did. If there is anything decent in me, I don't argue with that either. I've killed people and I have ruined lives and I can walk with a child and I'll keep her safe for as long as I can. That's who I am. Maybe there is good in me. Cooke didn't understand that. I don't think he could.*

Keep me safe? Hayley said.

Yes. I'm not here to hurt you. I'll keep you safe.

Then I guess I have to say thank you. Sort of.

I smiled. It was strange to think I'd smiled more in the last few hours than any point in the last few months.

Speak, I said.

What?

You have your voice. Speak. I only ask that you keep your voice down even out here.

"What can I say?" she said aloud and laughed. It was the sound of a delighted child.

It's your voice. This is your body. I'm using you for protection.

"I don't like you," she said and the laughter vanished from her voice. "Actually, I definitely don't. I hate you for what you did in my house, with my dad. I hate you because you hurt people. But I think. . .I think I understand. Is that weird?"

No. Not really.

We walked for another few minutes. Her strength was gradually fading but she kept going, and not purely through my influence. She wanted to keep moving if only to get closer to the time I would leave her.

"The others. Your mates," she whispered.

Yes?

"Why did they join you? They must have known what you're like."

Indeed they knew. We all knew each other as well as could be known. They knew I betrayed Dennis before coming to them. Even when Jonathan beat me for it, he knew he would have done the same to survive. We were all the same. We were all killers and bastards, but even so we couldn't put up with Cooke trying to punish us for it. It wasn't his place. And despite my betrayal of Dennis, the others felt the same as me. Part of the reason they joined me was simply being scared Drude would come after them once he finished with Me; but if truth be told, most of the reason they followed me was because they would no more be judged than I would.

We walked on. The sun shone. The world of the living, of petty wars between countries, of shallow fame and fleeting joy seemed very far away.

"Being dead," Hayley said suddenly. "I mean. . .you're dead. . .and you. . .you could be in Heaven, right?"

Not likely.

"Okay, not likely. What I mean is you're still here. How did you do it?"

I told you. Drude kept me out of the Pit after I promised to kill for him. He can't hurt people directly and he couldn't risk alerting anyone else in Hell what he was up to, so I had to do his work for him.

"That's not what I mean."

Inside the girl, I sighed. *I know. You want to know how a dead man has managed to avoid Heaven and Hell for so long. What makes me special enough to have done that.*

"Yeah."

A bit of luck, a bit of Drude's influence. There's no one thing that's kept me here. Remember those ghosts I told you about? The shades? That would be me eventually. They stayed here for so long that they forgot who they were. The chances are I'd become like them one day.

"And you want that?"

No. And it looks as if I don't need to worry about it now. Not with Drude coming after me for the rest of time.

I laughed, suddenly exhausted.

She didn't say anything to that. Maybe there wasn't anything she could say.

Chapter Seventy-Five

I heard the car before Hayley did, which wasn't surprising. She was upright almost completely under my influence. Her physical energy was vastly depleted and the day's warmth wasn't helping. I guided her from the grass to nearer the road, stuck her arm out and told her to be ready to wave or run. She understood. The car was drawing closer; I estimated it to be a minute away, closing in on the curve of the road a short distance behind. Hayley faced the way we'd come and kept her legs tensed, ready to run should I say so.

Let me do the talking, all right? Let me have your voice.

She wasn't happy about it and her dislike of the idea radiated like heat.

"Okay," she muttered and the car drove into view at the curve.

The vehicle was a family car, that much was obvious immediately. A woman drove with a man beside her.

There were no children visible and I was grateful for that.

The car slowed, Hayley mentally pulled back a fraction and I came forward. The car stopped directly in front of us and the woman leaned past the man.

"Are you all right?" she said.

"I need help," I said and put a note of panic in my voice. "I need to get home."

The couple exchanged a look. They were in their early thirties, childless at least for today and probably on their way home. Here was a teenage girl in what they saw as they middle of nowhere, alone, asking for help.

Their decision was made before they stopped.

"Do you need a lift somewhere?" the man asked.

"I need to get home. My mum. . .we had a fight about my boyfriend. He lives that way." I gestured vaguely the way we'd come. "He kicked me out of his house and I've been walking for hours."

Sounding as if tears were close was easy. Hayley's physical exhaustion helped a fair bit – and I wasn't a bad actor.

The woman opened the back door and waved me forward. "Come on. We'll take you home."

"Are you sure?"

"There's no way you're staying out by yourself. It's miles from anywhere. Your boyfriend is a complete idiot to leave you alone here."

"Thanks."

We walked to the car. Hayley had been silent throughout this conversation. As I took her into the car, she said, *Food. I need food.*

"I'm Karen and this is Will," the woman said.

"Hayley," I said. "Thanks for stopping. I didn't know what else to do."

Food. I'm starving.

"So where do you live?" Will said. While Karen was, without question, attractive, he was not as similarly blessed. He made up for it with kind eyes and genuine concern in his voice. Coming from him was only a genuine desire to help a young girl.

"Dalry. It's a city—"

"Dalry?" Karen said and I knew what was coming. All at once, I knew the couple stopping hadn't been an accident. They'd been sent by someone. My mind whispered Drude's name but that didn't feel right. A vision of the sea filled my head, high waves hammering at each other, white foam spilling back into the water to spread all the way across the world.

"We're from there. We grew up there. Left a few years ago," Will said.

He smiled as people do in such situations and began to talk about the city as Karen pulled away from the grass. I let him talk and answered his questions without much consideration. Behind me, Hayley asked for food in a worn-out voice. Her energy and spirit were almost gone which would soon have a knock-on effect on me. When Will paused in his recollections, I said:

"Sorry. I know it's rude but could we stop for food somewhere? I haven't eaten since last night. And I'd like to call my mum. Tell her I'm okay."

"Sure," Will said and held out his phone. "We'll stop when we get to the next services. You can call her now, though."

I hadn't thought of mobile phones and cursed my luck.

"Thanks," I said and took the phone. I only had a vague idea how such things worked and called for Hayley to come forward. She did so, but slowly.

Help me use this, I said.

You can't call anyone. She was thinking hard. If she'd been in control of her body, she would have been close to collapse. Will was gazing at me, smiling; Karen looked from the road ahead to the rear-view mirror and there was no time left before my lack of action appeared suspicious.

Hayley's fingers stabbed at the phone. She dialled numbers, held the phone to her ear and the line rang twice. Her voice replied, she'd dialled her own phone. I pictured it in her empty house, resting on her bed and ringing in the silence before cutting off.

The message stopped. I withdrew and Hayley spoke. "Mum, it's me."

Will and Karen faced forward again and Hayley pretended to tell her mother she missed her while the miles sped by us and the raging dead drew closer.

Twenty minutes later, we reached a services stop and Will pulled in. Thankfully, Hayley had money in her jacket pocket so I was at least able to offer to pay. Will didn't have any of it, of course, and bought us burgers, chips and sweet cold drinks. We sat outside; Hayley ate with relish while I remained inside her and listened to her answer Will and Karen's questions about her pretend boyfriend and her life in Dalry. They in turn spoke about the city with obvious fondness, about their lives there before they'd moved away. It transpired that they'd gone to the same school Hayley attended. Again, I wondered who'd sent the couple to me and why. Believing they'd just happened to be on the road at the same time as I needed to escape the dead was far too much of a coincidence.

I shook that thought off, knowing it would get me nowhere. I was in enough trouble without thinking about who, if anyone, was influencing me as I was influencing Hayley.

Still, on hearing that Will and Karen knew Dalry as Hayley did and knowing all our lives were connected to the same small city, apprehension that wasn't far off fear filled me.

You're near the end now, Benny. Don't lose it.

The demon Xaphan spoke from what might as well have been miles away, and I chewed on the idea that he'd been the one to send the couple. Such a thing was possible, certainly, although there was no obvious reason why.

I let it all go as much as I could. Welcoming Hayley's growing strength, I focused on the conversation with Will and Karen. Despite my fears, those few minutes were a strangely pleasurable time. For the best part of four centuries, happiness for me had come from the dead, never the living. And yet, here I was enjoying time with breathing people.

This is very strange, I thought in a pause in the conversation. It timed with a pause in Hayley's eating. She heard me and replied.

What's strange?

Being here with no urge to ruin the lives of these people.

Mentally, she laughed although I doubted she genuinely thought I was joking.

I smiled with her lips and her teeth. And with her eyes, I saw the ghosts.

Chapter Seventy-Six

They came from the carriageway, making no attempt at cover as they drifted from road to grass, then to the road that formed a circle around the services stop. Karen was talking and I answered through Hayley's mouth but doing so was purely automatic. All my conscious attention was on the five ghosts who hadn't yet seen me.

"Back in a minute. Just going to the toilet," I said.

"Do you want me to come with you?" Karen asked, already rising.

"No, it's okay. I won't be long."

I tried to smile in a way that said I was a teenage girl and I didn't want company from a relative stranger in a public toilet. Perhaps understanding, Karen sat again.

"We'll get going in a few minutes. Get you home to your mum," Will said.

"I'd like that," I said, forcing a smile before walking to the doors behind us. Despite wanting to, I didn't run or even walk fast. I kept my head up and my focus on the doors. At any second, I expected the dead to give a howl of joy that only I would hear before they descended on Hayley's body. They did not; I made it to the doors and inside to the blasting air-conditioning. Hayley had picked up on a problem even if she didn't know what it was.

The ghosts are here, I told her. *Not all of them but enough to hurt us. We have to hide.*

The toilets. Get to the toilets, she replied immediately.

We were in the middle of the open floor by then. On all sides, people ate fast food or browsed in the bookshop or stood against the windows, talking on their phones.

Let me take over, Hayley said and I did so without a second thought. She took us diagonally across the floor to a spot I hadn't noticed. We passed several public phones, turned a corner and the toilets were directly ahead. We squeezed past a mother and her two noisy toddlers as the ghosts entered the building.

Hayley picked up on my surge of panic and ran the last few steps to the toilet door. It slammed behind us; we ran to the far end and stood below a window.

They'll find us in here, I said. *This is the only way out.*

What about Will and Karen?

They'll be fine. It's me the ghosts want.

I was going to add more but screams from somewhere outside the toilet cut me off. Hayley retreated inside again; I ran to the door and stopped with her hand on the handle.

What are you doing? Hayley shouted.

I have to see. I have to know what they're doing.

My instincts said otherwise. I knew the best course of action was to turn, run back to the window and climb through it. But I *had* to know. The living couldn't see the dead, so why were they making such a racket?

Before I could think any more, I yanked open the door, ran through the hallway and stopped where it met the phones.

Chaos filled the shops and the walkways. People were running for the exits or attempting to hide in the shops, spilling their phones and bags as they fled.

Exactly where I had been only a minute before, dozens of bodies stood tightly together.

They were dead.

They were *the* dead, come for me. It didn't matter that they were living on the outside. The genuine living people knew these fifteen or twenty people were dead and they ran from them.

I didn't give them time to see me before running back to the toilet and ignoring the people who were desperately attempting to hide in the cubicles. Hayley buried herself inside further and didn't react when I clambered up on to the ledge, shoved the window open and braced her body to jump the short distance to the pavement.

The toilet door banged open and a noise echoed throughout, bouncing back and forth off the tiles and sinks – my name said through a dead man's throat.

I jumped, hit the ground and the jolt thudded through Hayley's legs. The impact winded me, despite Hayley's healthy body and I ran in a lurch back to the front of the centre. A crowd were between the doors and my view of the interior. All of them were trying to see inside, but none would actually enter the building.

I pushed through them, calling for Will and Karen. Arms and fingers poked me. I couldn't see; the sun was too bright, and behind, the ghosts advanced rapidly.

"Hayley."

The name came from somewhere off to my side. I peered that way and saw someone's silhouette. It was Will, the sun at his back. I ran to him.

"Are you okay?" he shouted over the noise.

"Yes. Quick. We need to go."

Karen ran to join us. They'd obviously split up to search for me and again I wondered what it meant that I'd met this couple from Dalry.

She held my arm and pulled me close. "Are you hurt?"

"No. I'm okay. We need to go."

I broke free from her grip and ran for the car, a few seconds ahead of them. Will didn't reach me until I was beside the vehicle.

"What's wrong?" he said. The din from the building wasn't as loud, although there was extra noise from the cars pulling away.

I checked for the dead and saw none. Even so, they would be on me any second.

"Something's wrong here. We have to go," I shouted and Karen touched Will's hand.

"She's right. Let's get back on to the road. The police will be here soon. We can wait for them away from this."

Will glanced at me, then back to his wife. He nodded and opened the car doors.

"Quick," he said and I wondered if he'd picked up on more than simply normal fear.

Karen and I slid into the car; Hayley whispered to me that she should take over her body. As soon as I let her, she brought her legs up and hugged her knees. Her head darted from side to side which wasn't down to acting. My panic had terrified her.

Will slammed the door shut and turned the key. Staring past him revealed a man and a woman dressed in contemporary clothes, both possessed by two of my victims. The woman threw her head back and screamed. She raced to us over the car park, briefly drowning out all other sounds, an animal cry. Then she and the man ran straight at us.

I didn't need to say a word. Will saw and his fear took over.

He reversed the car fast, checking behind us, then the front as he steered to the road and drove much too quickly for the space. Karen told him to slow; he didn't. The man and woman were still running toward us, now both spitting, raging. People turned to watch them and when they realised we were the target, their fear eased. They watched. Some filmed on their phones. They watched the man and woman come much too close to us before Will took a sharp corner, hit the middle of the road and struggled to keep control. Karen was screaming by then. I let Hayley take over and she added her noise to Karen's. We drove from the circular road and took the road back to the parkway. Behind us, the running couple still ran but much too slowly. For the first time in what felt like weeks, I relaxed.

Will glanced at me in the rear-view mirror. "What the hell was that all about?"

And Hayley answered before I could. "Get us a few miles away and I'll tell you everything."

What? I shouted at her.

I know what I'm doing.

We drove away from the ghosts and didn't stop even when the first of the police cars sped past us on their way to the madness we'd left behind.

Chapter Seventy-Seven

Will parked in a layby a couple of miles from the services—and the dead, I hoped. None of us spoke during the brief journey. Will and Karen kept glancing at Hayley in the mirror and even though their eyes asked questions, their mouths said nothing.

We stopped beside a small group of old trees. Traffic drove by, and there was no sign on that piece of road of what had happened only a short way behind.

Will turned around. Taking a deep breath, Karen did the same.

"You didn't have a fight with your boyfriend, did you?" he said.

Hayley didn't answer him. She spoke to me. *Are you going to let me talk?*

A week ago, I would not, but if you think it will do some good, then feel free. Just don't be surprised if they take us straight to the police.

They won't.

I sat back inside her. She cleared her throat. "My name's Hayley. That's true. The thing is. . ." She cleared her throat again. "The thing is there's a ghost inside me.

His name's Benjamin Harwood. He's old. Like centuries old. And he's bad. I mean, *really* bad. He's inside me because he's hiding from a demon. He needs to get somewhere the demon can't get him. And the demon is sending people after him. He keeps sending loads of people. If they catch us, they'll kill me, which means they can get to him, so that's why we had to run back there."

She said almost all of it in one breath. When she was finished, she leaned back and inhaled massively.

Happy? I asked her.

Shut up.

Will and Karen hadn't spoken during Hayley's speech. Instead, Will gazed out of the rear window and Karen chewed on her thumbnail.

"Are you going to say something?" Hayley said and Karen finally looked at her.

"Hayley, listen. . ."

Hayley lifted a hand. "Are you going to tell me I'm a nutcase?"

"No," Karen said, but she looked away.

"I'm not. I know it sounds crazy, but I'm not. There's a ghost inside me."

"Have you had a fight with someone recently?" Will said. "Your parents? A bloke?"

"No," Hayley said evenly. She was losing patience, which made me smile. She'd accepted my presence without much difficulty despite having little choice not to, so why couldn't they?

"Trouble at school?"

"No."

"Have you been taking something?" Karen said and Hayley's patience broke. It snapped and I laughed again.

"No." She clenched her fists. "Listen to me. This is real. You're sitting right next to a dead man, okay? He

kills people and he won't leave me until he knows he's safe from this demon. He attacked my family weeks ago and *he won't go until he's safe."*

Karen and Will glanced at one another and in my imagination, Karen climbed into the back seat and restrained Hayley in a death grip while Will drove us as fast as he could back to the police behind us.

I whispered to Hayley and her reply was quick.

You sure? she said.

Yes.

All right, then. Do it.

She withdrew and I went forward. There was no physical change to Hayley but still, Karen and Will drew away as far as they could. Will's mouth trembled and I thought what a nice man he was to help a young girl.

"Hello," I said through Hayley's mouth. "My name is Benjamin Harwood."

It was impossible to say which one of them screamed the loudest.

Chapter Seventy-Eight

Will punched his hand against the door and I stopped him by speaking again. An old man's voice coming from a young girl's throat made him scream again. Thankfully, it wasn't anywhere near as loud as his first shriek.

"Please don't do that. We have to talk and we can't do that if you're panicking," I said.

Their heads were almost touching as they strained to get further away from Hayley speaking in my voice. Their backs pressed into the front of the car and they both stared at Hayley with the eyes of a terrified child unsure if their nightmare was a dream or reality.

"Everything Hayley told you is true. I am a ghost and I'm not a nice person. That doesn't need to concern you. I think my days of ruining lives are over. My priority now is survival, which is where you come in."

I stopped there deliberately. They needed a moment to absorb everything.

"Is this real?" Karen whispered.

"Yes."

"Jesus Christ."

"Never met him," I said.

Will blew out a long note which sounded as if he'd been holding it for a long time. Karen rubbed a hand over her mouth repeatedly. It looked as if she was attempting to rub away a stain.

"When were you born?" she said.

"1611. In Dalry; hometown to all of us, which might be coincidence but probably isn't. What else do you want to know? What life was like then? I could tell you; it would take a while, though."

"When did you die?"

I smiled and she recoiled. Chances were she'd never seen a teenage girl smile that way.

"1666. I missed the fire in London by a few months, although I still saw it. A lot of us did."

She mewled. There was no other word for the sound she made. She made the noise of a scared kitten.

"Hold each other's hands. It'll help," I said.

They did so and relaxed if only a little.

"Now listen to me. Like I said, everything Hayley told you is true. I have to get away from here. Drude, the demon, he'll never stop until he gets me. Neither will the ghosts coming after me. They're inside people the same way I am, and if they find Hayley, they'll tear her apart. Once she's dead, there'll be nothing between them and me."

"Sounds like you deserve to be caught," Will said and winced, probably expecting me to do something horrible.

"Doubtless I deserve that, but while I can, I intend to keep going. Which is the part that involves you."

"Us?" Karen said.

"You. I need you to drive us to the coast. I can't threaten you; you have all the advantages over me, but bear in mind that if you take Hayley to the police, she's as good as dead."

Traffic was still streaming past. For Karen and Will, it must have seemed insane to be parked between road and grass, to sit below the afternoon sun and listen to a dead man speak from a teenage girl's mouth. As long as they did what I needed them to, their mental state was the least of my concerns.

You're a real bastard, aren't you? Hayley said.

Yes. Have you only just realised?

"Can't the police keep her safe?" Will said. "And if they do, doesn't that mean you'll be safe."

I shook Hayley's head. "The police won't believe her. They'll keep hold of her until her mother comes. The dead will find her first."

"And they'll hurt her?" Will said.

"Yes," I said simply.

"But if they want you, why would they—?"

"To get to me," I said and held up a hand to silence Will.

"These things have a way of working out. I have no doubt once I'm gone, Hayley will be safe from the police or demons or the dead or anyone else I've brought into her life."

"Can we talk to Hayley again?" Will asked.

I withdrew and Hayley took over.

"It's me," she said in her own voice and Will shivered.

"This is real, isn't it? I mean, it's happening, isn't it?"

"Yes," Hayley said, and she sounded more like an adult than Will did.

Karen and Will held one another for a long moment, not talking. They didn't accept me, not totally. They wanted to, I was sure of it, but despite hearing my voice come from Hayley's mouth, asking them to believe in me was still too much. It went against everything they understood to be real. Putting my existence alongside their relationship, their jobs, their memories meant they could not yet accept me as real. Talking to me and hearing me speak from Hayley's mouth changed nothing. I was something out of fiction or madness for them.

That could be a problem, I told myself. Hayley did not ask me to elaborate.

We sat, the four of us, in their car by the side of the road and I let Will and Karen hold one another, knowing I had to if I wanted to trust them with my safety.

Karen spoke first. While I knew it was partly down to wanting me out of their lives in the way Hayley wanted me gone, I still liked that. She had strength in the same way that Hayley did.

"So. Where are we going?"

Hayley listened to me for a moment, and then replied. "East. And don't stop."

Chapter Seventy-Nine

We drove for several miles before anyone spoke. Will asked me the question I'd been expecting for a while. He did so without turning, clearly afraid to look at Hayley. Maybe he feared he'd see me peering out of her eyes.

"How did you die?"

He asked it as we passed under weighty shade cast by trees. For a second or two, shadows buried the car, and being out of the bright sun was nothing but relief.

"Who do you want to answer that?" Hayley asked.

Will struggled for a moment before replying. "He can."

He didn't want me to speak at all, and at the same time, he did. He wanted to hear the ghost speak from the mouth of a living girl just as he wanted to stop the car, throw us out and drive away as fast as he could.

Hayley withdrew and I came forward. "My heart gave up. I had a comfortable life and I didn't take care of my body. It was bound to happen." I glanced out of the window. The landscape was changing, becoming flatter and less populated. The fields were brown, tired while the sky edged closer to grey with each passing minute. We would be there soon.

"I died in my bed like a man much older than I was."

That was almost the truth. What I kept to secret was that I'd been in bed with a woman thirty years my junior at the time. Hayley had no need to hear of such things and there was no need to be coarse. Even so, she picked up on some of it, anyway.

What was her name? she asked.

Never mind.

That's a funny name.

It took me a second to realise she was gently mocking me. I surprised myself by laughing.

Her name was Kate. Satisfied?

I suppose so.

"So, you died and then what? You were a ghost looking down on your body?" Karen said and I came forward again.

Something like that, I replied and thought of that time after my death, time I couldn't measure because I wasn't part of the living world anymore. I thought of Kate wailing when she saw my corpse, of the evening sunlight sitting on my face and the motes of dust floating in that light; I thought of my sparsely furnished bedroom, the window open wide and the mostly good-natured voices from the street rising with the sunlight.

Sudden nostalgia pricked me. I hadn't pictured my home in many years. Lost for centuries, it was now unrecognisable as a suburban road of expensive houses perhaps five miles from Hayley's home. The four or five-bedroom buildings that held the ghost of my much more modest abode would have been palaces during my life. Thinking of it then brought a strange feeling, which I grudgingly admitted was simple homesickness.

If the others knew this.

But of course, they never would. Jim, Jonathan, Christopher and Sally were gone to whatever eternal nightmare Drude had planned. All at once, it seemed terribly unfair I would never see them again.

You will if Drude catches you, Hayley told me with no trace of humour.

True.

And it's not that you really care about them, do you?

I paused before replying. She felt me reaching for the reason behind her words and blocked me which was a surprise. We shouldn't have been able to hide anything from one another; yet Hayley still managed it. She waited for me to speak. Karen and Will watched us silently.

Meaning? I said as calmly as I could.

I mean you don't care what happened to your friends. You threw them away. They did what you wanted them to and you threw them away.

Again, I was silent. The deeper, older part of Hayley had said much the same after Cooke's departure from her soul. It was possible that part of her was speaking to me again, even if the Hayley that had known nothing of the world outside her life until I came had no understanding of it.

Of course I care what happens to them. Do you think I would still want to hurt Drude if I didn't care what he did?

You threw them away. Her reply was implacable. *They helped you out and you let them go. At least admit that.*

"Something up?" Will said, studying Hayley briefly.

"Nothing," I replied in my own voice and that was enough to silence any more questions.

We drove further east. Clouds formed the closer we drew to the coast and the wind grew into moody gusts.

Rain was probably falling far out to sea. I pictured the unstoppable waves that would take me wherever they wanted to, of the silent depths below while I was swept from one end of the world to another. There was no way of knowing how long I would be part of the world's waters, and I didn't know where I would end up. Neither bothered me. All I needed to do was get away from Drude and his vengeful spirits. All I had to do was run.

So much for all that time you spent getting ready for Drude, right? All that time you weren't running from him, Hayley said.

Shut up.

Why should I? You're lying to yourself. You were running from him the whole time. All that stuff you said about getting an army ready and about wanting to fight him, it was all lies. You were running and you're running now.

I said nothing.

How much further? Hayley asked and it was horrible to feel like a scolded child.

Ask them, I said, hating my petulant reply.

"How long 'til we get there?" Hayley said.

"Not long," Karen muttered and kept her eyes on the road.

Hayley and I understood at the same time: Will and Karen didn't want her with them. As much as they wanted to help her, it was too much to ask to deal with a ghost and demons and the angry dead. It was all too much.

Let me speak, I said to Hayley.

She pulled back without a word and I spoke. "Listen to me. I know this is almost impossible for you to accept, but you have to. I don't expect you to care about me, but you have to care about the girl. The three of us are the only things stopping the dead getting to her.

They don't care about her; they don't care if she's hurt –
so you have to. Understood?"

"Yeah," Will said, and was able to look at Hayley
only for a second or two.

He still doesn't believe, I said, partly to myself, and
partly to Hayley. *My God, are the living really so
stupid?*

*I didn't believe in you until you decided to ruin my
life!* Hayley shouted. *So just deal with it,* okay?

Inside her, I laughed gently. *All right, I will.*

Karen was looking at me, not Hayley.

"What are the chances you can do this? Get away
from the demon? Can you do it?" she asked.

I smiled, although I was almost too tired to do so. "If
I can't, I'm damned."

We drove on. The clouds were growing heavier.
They promised rain probably within minutes. Will
attempted a smile, which didn't quite work.

"Should have brought a brolly," he said. He glanced
at Karen and she gave him a reassuring smile.

"And a bucket and spade," she muttered.

I stayed silent. If they wanted to comfort one another,
that was up to them. All that mattered to me was getting
away from Drude.

Hayley gave a mental laugh. *You're the most selfish
person in the world.*

Probably, but it keeps me going.

She laughed and again it held no trace of humour.
There was a moment of regret that she'd become so
much older than she was. This wasn't a fair experience
for a fifteen-year-old girl. But on the other hand, since
when did *fair* matter?

That thought spoke as we passed under a bridge.
Shade enveloped us for several seconds. The gloom

lasted long enough for Drude's whispers to come to my ear, as if he was there with us in the car.

So like you, Benjamin. So like you to justify everything you do if it keeps you going. Hayley gave no reaction. Drude was speaking to me and me alone. *Leave them, Harwood. Do it now or they'll die when I come for you.*

It was a flat promise. Drude's theatrics were gone, leaving the naked truth. We passed the bridge and Drude was gone. His words remained like a stubborn stain.

I opened Hayley's mouth. "Will."

He looked at Hayley in the rear-view mirror and saw me in her face.

"Drive faster."

Chapter Eighty

So like you, Benjamin. So like you to justify everything you do if it keeps you going.

And.

All right, I will.

The words echoed in my head for the long minutes since Drude's whispers. We'd driven in silence since then and that was fine with me. It gave me chance to think.

Hayley knew I was up to something but she didn't ask questions. Not through trusting me, but through knowing I couldn't do anything that would hurt her. She was my ultimate shield from Drude and she knew that.

So I listened as I'd listened to the approaching shades on my journey around the country.

I listened.

And I heard them.

They were close, following the scent of me for miles and drawing in over the last half an hour. Their hate was behind us, calling my name. All the years I'd stolen from them, all the time they'd not known was closing in on me, propelled by their fury that I still walked the world while their time had been stolen.

So like you, Benjamin. So like you to justify everything you do if it keeps you going.

Right. Exactly right.

Tell them to stop, I said to Hayley. *Tell them you need the toilet.*

Why? I don't.

Do you trust me?

No.

Yes, you do. They *don't, but you do.*

She considered. *In a really weird way, yeah. Maybe. A bit.*

Good. Now tell them to stop.

I withdrew and Hayley said: "Can we stop somewhere? I need the loo."

Karen's and Will's eyes met; Will kept us moving fast.

"What does he say about it?" Karen said.

"He said it's fine."

Will still didn't slow. Karen laid a gentle hand on his forearm and he gave silent agreement, although he kept his gaze fixed firmly to the road.

We'd come off the carriageway two miles behind. The road we were on then wasn't busy, but even so, Will drove for another few miles before he said it was all right to stop.

We pulled over in a layby that bordered high hedgerows and farmland beyond it. Will stopped the car and turned to Hayley.

"Best be quick, hey?"

"I'll come with you," Karen said, unbuckling her seatbelt. Hayley listened to me and nodded.

She and Karen got out of the car and both stretched and almost immediately shivered; the temperature was a lot cooler there than a few hours before.

"Definitely looks like rain," Karen said, examining the sky.

I wasn't completely sure that was true, even though the clouds were obviously pregnant with potential rain. A downpour wasn't quite it, though. Through Hayley's eyes, I stared up and a slight memory tickled me. I'd seen the sky the same ugly colour before. Not during a sudden storm. This was something else.

Wind pushed at us as if we'd gone forward a month to the middle of October, and Karen gestured to the hedges.

"You're okay to go in there?" she asked.

"Yeah, fine," Hayley said and trotted to the short line of stunted grass that grew between road and hedge.

They're close, I told her.

If you know what you're doing, then what's the problem? she shot back.

No problem, I told her and couldn't help but grin inside her.

We slid down the short embankment and Hayley went behind the hedges after giving Karen a quick wave. Once out of sight, I directed her further along the hedges for another minute.

In there, I said and we slipped into a tiny gap in the greenery.

Now what? Hayley said.

Wait a minute.

She was silent. Her questions were there but kept below and I admired that.

Karen called Hayley's name. Hayley tried to stand and I didn't let her.

What are you doing?

Trust me.

What? We have to go.

Trust me.

Fuck you.

She shoved at me with her strongest effort and her body stumbled before I could overpower her. The movement was enough to tip her forward and out of the hedges. Karen saw her from the end of the green and shouted her name again before turning and calling for Will.

Trust me, damn you, I yelled at Hayley and all of us heard the approaching vehicles at the same time.

Chapter Eighty-One

Karen reached us and pulled Hayley. "What are you doing? Why are you hiding?"

I spoke through Hayley's mouth while Hayley swore at me. "You didn't believe me, did you? You don't believe in me. You will when you see who's coming after us."

Karen stared at me, mouth open, and her face as white as a dead fish. She yanked Hayley's arm and we ran back along the side of the hedgerows while a few drops of rain struck the ground, and the murmur of approaching cars grew into a storm.

We hit the embankment, lunged up and ran to the car. Will was halfway out, staring at us.

"What's happening?"

"Drive," Karen said and shoved Hayley towards the car.

I took control just as Hayley hit the car door and turned back to Karen.

"You have to see them. And you have to trust me if you, your husband and this child want to get out of this alive."

"Get in the fucking car," Karen screamed.

"Not until you see."

I turned to the road, facing the way we'd come, and saw the first few cars coming fast.

There were four of them, all speeding and all too close together. They were too distant for me to see the drivers – I wouldn't have known the faces of the living in any case for it was the faces below that were important; the dead people come for me.

One of the vehicles increased its speed. As Karen shouted at Hayley to get moving, a BMW passed us on the other side of the road. I caught a glimpse of the passenger looking out at us. Then they were driving towards the approaching cars and those cars were coming much too fast. The driver of the BMW hit his horn as the dead shot past him, too close and too fast.

He overcompensated for their speeding and slid across the road. We all heard the squeal of his brakes before he spun around to drop down the embankment to the fields. And still the dead were coming.

Karen screamed without any words; Will pulled on Hayley. I faced him, seeing he wanted to shriek like his wife.

"Now we can go," I said.

All of us flew into the car; the dead were almost close enough to see their faces, almost close enough to see the living held by the dead.

We accelerated, hit the middle of the road and raced on with the dead coming behind.

"Why the hell did you do that? Why did you hide?" Karen screamed.

"To make you see who's coming for us," I said and Hayley bellowed at me in an adult's voice. The child was gone.

No, you didn't. At least tell them the truth. You want to see all those ghosts chasing you. You want to look at them when you get away from them. You want to feel like you're in control of this and you want one last chance to fuck us up. You hate us because we're still alive and you're jealous of that. All that crap you came out with about being better than people, it's lies. You're angry that you're dead. And all that shit about why you kill people. Crap, all of it. You kill people because you like it. That's it. Nothing else. And now you're dead, you're jealous of living people and so you want to feel like you can still do whatever you want, right? Nothing else matters, does it? Not me or Will or Karen or my mum or your friends or anything. The only thing that matters to you is you.

I didn't answer her for one good reason.

She was right. About every single thing, the girl was right and I itched to have my hands around her throat, to see her face grow purple as I squeezed all the air out of her lungs before I tore her head from her neck.

Do it, she said dully. *Do it if you're going to. I've had enough of you.*

A mix of shame, rage and confusion burst through my core. Before I had chance to react to the ghastly sensation, Drude's whispers returned and it felt like thin fingers scratching at my head.

One last chance, Benjamin.

I yelled my reply at him without hesitation. *I think my point has been proved, demon.*

He was gone like a dream or a faint memory.

Will increased our speed, gripping the wheel as tightly as Hayley's mother had during the first part of my escape. His eyes darted from the road in front of us to the road behind and I looked back.

The nearest car was close behind. A woman drove it and her face shook and twisted as she fought against the dead person inside her. It was stronger than her and kept her car coming at us. Another two cars drew level with its side and filled the road. All three lunged at us.

"Oh, shit," Will whispered.

He'd seen the three vehicles blocking the road behind and he'd seen the cars coming the other way.

"They'll move," Karen shouted and I wondered if she meant the dead or the living. "They'll have to move, they'll have to."

Horns blared. The cars in front were straight ahead; a quick break in the clouds sent sunlight on to them. Then the clouds blocked the sun, rain spat against our windows and the horns blared again.

With seconds to spare, the first car in front veered off the road and into the fields. Perhaps thinking the other would move, cars driven by the living hit the ones driven by the dead almost full on.

The noise was mammoth. Cries from Will, Karen and Hayley were nothing compared to the ear-splitting crunch of metal and glass behind us. An explosion coughed up and out; our car shook. Two of the cars driven by the dead were flaming wrecks, as were the living, and the other car driven by the dead had crashed off the road.

That's why I let them find us, I said to Hayley. *Get it? This is what I am, child. This is what I do. No matter what it costs, I won't be beaten by a demon, by the dead or by the living.*

All I got in reply was her furious need to see me gone from her life and her soul.

Chapter Eighty-Two

We drove without much conversation and without further attack for fifteen minutes. Above, the clouds continued to amass and threaten much more rain than the few drops which fell without any strength. I kept my eyes on the sky, sure I'd seen such an ugly cast before and sure it meant something. We passed a few vehicles all going the other way. None travelled behind us, which Will commented on. I told Hayley to tell him it didn't mean anything and I don't think any of them believed me.

We reached a long section of straight road which ran through woods and I pictured Thistlemoor Wood, pictured its centre and felt no sadness I couldn't be a part of what was once a refuge for ghosts like me. Thistlemoor Wood was the past; this was my future, and not even Drude would get in the way of that.

We drove under overhanging branches, shielded from the spatters of rain by leaves, and shadows ran alongside the car. The road bent before levelling again. We cleared the trees. And there it was.

The sea.

The water was a wide line of sapphire beyond the land. Our road narrowed ahead; the fields closed in on it and a few houses were dotted around. We'd come away from the towns and here was green, our road, small houses, a long stone wall and sheep; here was one road snaking through the green to come to nothing half a mile from the cliffs.

Again, I thought of the sea, picturing it from my visions; the huge sheet of foaming water, white horses crashing into one another, and below, nothing but currents eager to take me wherever they wanted.

I leaned forward. "Just keep driving. Don't stop when the road does."

Karen glanced at Hayley. There was no fear, only a demand to keep Hayley safe. It had taken an attack from the dead to convince but here it was – she believed in me.

"Just keep driving," I said again. "We're almost there."

There was an echoing scream from below and behind. Dozens, hundreds of voices, all cried as one.

The car shook. The road shook.

"Drive faster," I said.

"What's happening?" Will shouted, spinning around.

They came from nowhere. The shadows in the woods were alive. They amassed into one giant pool and swept upwards. Much of the day's dim light vanished.

"They're coming for us," I said. "Drive."

"How do you know—?" Will said.

"Drive!" I roared.

Karen let out a tiny shriek; Will's face was the colour of old milk. Our speed increased as the great shadow swooped back down to the road. Behind it and coming in fast, a massive convoy of vehicles blocked the road. Two cars at the front broke from the ranks and bore down on us. The drivers were vague shapes, leaning forward. The ghosts weren't visible. They were there, though. They were coming for me.

Will took us to eighty miles an hour, eighty-five, and held the wheel as if afraid it might shake loose. We were on a long straight line of road, thankfully, and the fields streaked by in a blur.

"How far?" I said. The first of the two cars was almost on us.

"A couple of miles," Will yelled.

Karen's window was down an inch; the smell of the sea was like welcoming a friend I had not seen in many lifetimes. Then the car roared down on us. Karen shrieked again. Will spun the wheel and we streaked across the road. The car behind tried to follow and overdid it. It came close to veering off into the fields before righting itself. The road curved, forcing Will to slow. As soon as we passed it, he accelerated. Behind, the vehicles were rapidly advancing. The shadow raced over them.

"They won't stop. Keep going," I said.

The roar of the traffic closing in was huge. Men and women were coming for me, powerless to stop the ghosts controlling them. I pitied the living, briefly. They weren't part of my battle, they'd simply been unlucky to be caught up in it. It didn't matter to the dead how much the living begged to be left alone; they never would be until I was gone from the world.

Will swerved to avoid a car closing in on us. We hit the grass and jumped in our seats as we drove over uneven ground. Will swerved again, mud and grass spun away from the wheels. He straightened our course. The cars were still coming, although many of the drivers had stopped on the road, unable to cross the grass. Others came on foot, lumbering apace over the field.

"Stop here!" I yelled.

Will did so. He and Karen turned, and I was out of the car before they drew breath to speak. The clouds erupted and a wall of rain fell, blinding Hayley. Winter wind bellowed at us. September sunlight was forgotten, and all that remained was nature raging on all sides.

On the road, the huge shadow slammed down into the ground, sending mud, earth and rock to scatter in all directions. The black broke apart into dozens of separate shapes and those shapes screamed my name.

The shades were back, come for the one who'd led them to Hell. In echo of the shades' noise, the spirits inside the living shrieked for me. Inside the teenage girl's body, I ran over the grass, jumping and sprinting with all the strength Hayley possessed. Wind, heavy with the smell of salty water, pushed at me; I ran faster, young legs pumping, arms tight against Hayley's side while she shouted at me to *move it, to run*. I risked a look back and, in a glance through the rain, saw Karen and Will emerge from the car and sprint after me; the living ghosts rose behind them in an ever growing wall of flesh and the dead.

The cliffs were straight ahead, beyond a low fence; I used the last of Hayley's strength, clambered over the fence and sprinted to the edge.

The tips of her trainers poked over the side. Earth fell in tiny patters. Far below, rocks and sand gazed up at me through the sheets of rain lashing on Hayley's neck and head. She screamed in a steady breath. I pulled back, turned and spoke to her as Will and Karen closed in with the ancient dead closing in fast. The shades were flying to me, their mouths of smoke calling my name.

When I go, they'll follow. Run to them. Run to Karen and Will. Run, child.

She was trying to speak, trying to tell me something. There was no time for it.

Thank you, Hayley.

I flew from Hayley's body and her mental scream became a physical sound. There was the faintest tug as we parted; the ghosts saw me and as one, they abandoned their hosts. The wall of the living ceased their mad dash. Some fell, others screamed and a few ran for those nearest them to hold each other. The ghosts of my victims, of Jonathan, Christopher and Jim's victims, and those whose lives I'd hurt during my death floated and stared at me in their hatred and their judgement.

Then they were coming for me.

Chapter Eighty-Three

The water raced upwards, the rocks and sand were no longer far below; they were rushing up to welcome me.

I streaked downwards, turning to see them all for the last time. The scene at the top of the cliff changed everything.

My descent to the sea stopped and I floated a hundred feet over the water and half that from the cliffs. Up on the land, a long line of the dead stared down. Despite the years, I still recognised a few faces. People I'd killed stared down at me, faces and bodies still bearing the wounds I'd given them. Then the living were there, all curious to look at the water through the steadily decreasing rain.

A section of crowd parted and three more stumbled through, were *pushed* through.

Will, Karen and Hayley stood surrounded by the living who saw nothing and the ghosts who saw everything.

My plan hadn't worked. The dead hadn't followed, and I was left with the three people who'd helped me, the three *living* people who'd helped me, surrounded by ghosts.

Without a sound, without any pretence, Drude was there. He didn't come from the crowd of living or appear in the air with the dead. He just was.

The rain stopped. Instead of sunlight, murky clouds took their place, followed by gusting wind.

"Nice view," Drude shouted, deep voice carrying with ease through the air while I hung over the water. Jagged rocks loomed over the sea; coves and beaches untouched by only birds and crabs spread below, and the tide soaked the sand and countless stones.

Drude had appeared beside Karen, Will and Hayley. They hadn't heard his arrival; they heard him now, though, and whirled around. Hayley attempted to run. She got no further than two steps before Drude's huge arm blocked her and pulled her close to him.

He held her directly in front, blocking his massive grin from sight, then pushed her to one side.

"Nice view," he said again. I floated over the sea and stared at him, cursing him with all my strength. He knew what I was doing, and his ugly smile grew.

"An interesting plan. I suspected this would be your final move from the beginning. I'm happy you didn't disappoint me," he bellowed.

"Always a pleasure," I called and his laughter roared down at me. The image we gave was of two friendly rivals at the end of a long argument. That was miles from the truth and it was easy to imagine that pleasing him.

"If I'm honest, I knew it would come to this. Everything you've done, Benjamin, I knew we would end up here just like this." He stared at me, no longer smiling. "What do you think of that?"

"Whatever you want me to think, Drude. I really couldn't care."

That wasn't far from the truth. Physical tiredness didn't come into it, I had nothing left to give and Drude knew it.

"What comes next is up to you, Harwood," he replied, and I risked a glance down. The sea was a vast blanket below; too far below. I'd never reach it before he could make his move. And even if I could, it was a gamble that he'd leave Will, Karen and Hayley and choose to come after me. The other half of that gamble would mean their deaths.

Gamble? You know what he'll do. He told you.

There was no way I could argue with myself. Drude had told me he'd kill them and so what if he couldn't do it directly? The shades would be more than eager to do so.

"Jonathan is still cursing you," Drude said. "I imagine he will do so for the rest of time. And your other friends, they curse you, too. Even now, while they spend eternity in the Pit, they're cursing you for bringing them into our quarrel and for betraying them to me."

"I didn't betray them," I argued.

"You did. As soon as you involved them, you betrayed them."

Drude was calm, smooth. His voice was the surface of the sea. But below that surface, there was emptiness. "So, now it's all up to you, again. You betrayed your friends, you gave them to me and the dead. What will you do for these three?"

Will, Karen and Hayley weren't struggling to free themselves. Doubtless, they knew there was no point.

Even if Drude hadn't held them as if they were no more substantial than tissue paper, they were surrounded by ghosts. There was no doubt that, should they manage to escape from Drude, the dead would be on top of them immediately.

"What about you, demon? Exiled from Hell for all time? Is that what you wanted? To get to me, you damned yourself."

He shrugged. "You can't go home again, Benjamin. You know that."

"See," said a new voice, "that's where you're wrong."

The smile vanished from Drude's face. Below, Xaphan rose from the sea to float beside me.

"Afternoon," he said.

"Didn't expect to see you here," I replied.

"Just passing through." He smiled, revealing all his teeth, and I couldn't do anything but smile back.

"Xaphan," Drude called, "this isn't your argument."

"You're right. It's not." He shrugged. "But I'm still here. What are you going to do about it?"

Above and around Drude, the dead shifted restlessly. Most gazed down at me with flat hate; at the same time, there was a definite movement pulsing in and out. The faces of the living were still blank, although I picked up on the movement behind their eyes. Whatever control Drude had, it was slipping.

He pulled Will, Karen and Hayley closer; Karen was crying and Will was shouting at the demon. Only Hayley was still. She hadn't looked from me since Drude grabbed her; her expression was unreadable.

"Leave us, Xaphan. The ghost is mine," Drude yelled.

"I can't argue with that. What I can argue with is *you*, Drude. I can argue with you opening Below as if you had any right to do, I can argue with you using the dead as if you have any right to do so, and I can argue with you threatening the living when you know the rules." Xaphan's face suddenly grew dark and I was briefly grateful that he was at least partly on my side.

"How dare you? Who are you to use the living and the dead in such ways, demon? Who are you to open the Bottom? Who are you to judge yourself fit to have that right?"

Drude's reply was immediate and deafening. *"I am Drude and he is mine."*

Xaphan spoke to me. "It's on you, ghost. Leave and he kills the people who helped you. Go to him and he destroys you but they're safe."

"Is there a third option?" I said.

"Actually, yes."

I stared at him and struggled to speak.

"Your third choice," Xaphan said. "Come with me."

"Where to?"

"Back. Come back and undo your deeds. This is your second chance, ghost. This is your chance to make everything right."

There was no struggle to speak then because there were no words left in the world.

"My patience is running out. Your choice, Harwood," Drude shouted.

"That's right," Xaphan whispered, "your choice, Benny."

Chapter Eighty-Four

Below, the sea. Above, black sky. In the middle, me; in the middle, a ghost, two demons and the decision of a lifetime. Or a death.

Hayley was still staring straight at me. Will and Karen had ceased their struggles and even Drude's horrible ranting had fallen silent. He gazed at me, ready to order the deaths of the living people who'd helped me and ready to damn me to the Pit.

"What happens to them?" I whispered.

"They'll be safe," Xaphan replied in a low voice. "The second you move, Drude will come for you. The second he does that, I've got a few friends up there who will take the people."

"And I can undo my actions? My murders?"

"Yes."

The past exploded into life before I could speak. I saw the bodies belonging to the flesh and blood up on the cliffs. I saw my knife, my gun and my hands killing, ending lives, changing the world. To undo all that, to change the world again wasn't simply a second chance.

It was a life.

And it was a betrayal of myself.

What choice is there? You want Drude to lose, yes? You want to beat him. This is the only way you can do that.

I faced Drude for the last time and spoke to Xaphan. "Take me back."

I sensed, rather than saw Xaphan's smile. "The first decent thing you have ever done, Benjamin."

"Just do it," I muttered, inhaled and bellowed to Drude. "Do you want me, demon?"

His answer came back immediately. "More than you could imagine."

"Then what are you waiting for?"

Several things happened at the same time, just as nothing at all changed.

The world turned over, turned inside out. A tremendous squealing, grating rumble burst out of the sea and the land. Darkness, then light, then the world turned over again and Drude was streaking down from the cliffs, coming for me faster than light, coming for me as slow as an old man's breath.

Pulsing red crashed over the people, over the living and the dead. Will and Karen were looking up, both screaming as Hayley looked at me, our eyes locked together, a dead old man and a living teenage girl linked across space, across time. A burning light spilled over the ghosts, drowning their howls, drowning their names and faces. The red illumination winked away, taking the dead with it and Drude was still coming, still flying like a spear with his mouth yawning open into a cavern full of forever, a forever of no memories.

Xaphan floated beside me, making no move as I faced the demon hurling down, eyes locked with Hayley's, eyes never to see her again, to see her always with the world turning over, turning inside out. And

Xaphan's voice fell from the furthest edges of space, fell from centuries ahead as the world fell apart, as time and space are opening before me, Drude's final cursing cry of my name is falling from the sky, falling from the long years ahead, coming while Xaphan's place in my death is all around, Xaphan sealing Thistlemoor Wood, Xaphan sending Karen and Will to me, sending me here again and again and again and—

It's coming, giant arms reaching from the hole in the floor of the world, stretching across everything as it howls my name and reaches for me. And it is. And it is.

It is.

Hell opens.

The Pit opens.

"Go back," Xaphan says. And the world is gone. The world is white space. Drude is gone. Hayley is gone. Coming in their place, coming in the place of everything is the smell of water, people arguing, laughing, talking, the touch of market day and my feet on the ground, walking, carrying me beside the river, carrying me from my pub and the young man is just a few steps ahead, my first back again, my first murder here again, my hands pulling into fists as the white space is all gone and I'm left with the first to undo, the first to stop, and all the while, Drude is stuck outside Hell, stuck in the Void, stuck forever cursing my name.

And it.

It.

Dear God please oh please get me.

Forever.

Stuck in the black.

The Pit.

It is me.

Xaphan's voice for the last time, crashing on to me from four hundred years ahead in one word of judgement and punishment.
Forget.

Life.

Chapter Eighty-Five

Hayley, Will and Karen stand in a row on the crumbling cliffs. Behind them, people weep as they walk towards the road. Nobody speaks and nobody meets anybody else's eye. They don't want to think of what has happened, of the invading dead or the horrific thing that had been with them on the cliffs. They think the word *demon* but they don't say it.

It doesn't take more than a few minutes to reach the road. Some go in one direction, others go the other way. All continue to weep and none talk.

Hayley is the first to step forward as the figure floating over the sea drifts toward them. Karen reaches a shaking hand to pull her back and drops it when Will murmurs something that isn't quite a word.

The three watch the figure come to them and drop to the grass where it ends at the cliffs.

"Hi," he says. "My name's Xaphan."

"Hello." Hayley smiles. Xaphan returns it.

"Hayley. Will. Karen. How's it going?"

"You. . ." Will begins and closes his mouth. He holds Karen tightly and somehow manages to keep his head upright when Xaphan studies him.

"Relax. I'm your friend. Just be glad I'm here and Drude isn't."

"Where is he?" Hayley asks.

"Drude?" Xaphan shrugs. "Away. In an empty place." He smiles. "Well, *empty* isn't the right word. He'll wish it was, though. Anyway, that's all you need to know. And that you'll never see him again."

The wind has warmed and the last of the rain has gone. The clouds are still heavy, though; summer is done and autumn has come to this middle of September. Xaphan gestures to the grass away from the cliff edge and they walk to it. Far below, the sea pounds against the land, retreats and the water goes everywhere in the world and it goes there untouched.

"What about him?" Hayley asks.

"Was he real?" Karen murmurs.

"He was as real as you, me, the grass, the sky, the sea," Xaphan tells her.

"Where is he?" Hayley whispers and all three of them involuntarily take a step back from Xaphan when he smiles again. It is like seeing winter come to life: endless snows, endless nights and all the wailing winds of the world blowing from sea to sea. Inside the smile, night slinks ahead forever and forever.

"Back at his start. Back where he made his choices. Back trying to undo those choices." He shrugs again and the smile is gone. "He'll get it right one day. Might take him a while, though."

"What happened? I mean. . .he thought you were helping him, didn't he?" Hayley says.

"I never told him that. I gave him the odd push in the right direction, that's all."

"By doing what?" Hayley asks and Xaphan laughs.

"Don't let anyone ever tell you ask too many questions, will you?"

"Aren't questions allowed?" Will whispers, and Xaphan glances at him.

"Always." He looks back to Hayley. "I gave him a chance to atone. He saw Hell and had the chance of giving up then. He didn't and never told his friends what he saw. If he had, he wouldn't be stuck where is now, and if he had made it into Thistlemoor Wood, he'd be safe from Drude – and what kind of justice would that be? What would he learn from that?"

"Why us?" Karen asks, and Xaphan sees the rest of her question.

"I sent you to him and Hayley for one reason."

"Which was?" Karen nearly shouts this and Xaphan replies easily.

"You were in the right place at the right time."

"That's it? That's the extent of it?" Will asks.

"More or less."

Xaphan glances at Hayley again and in the second that Will and Karen are not looking at him, he winks. She has no idea what to make of that wink and doesn't care to. The horrors of the last couple of days are slipping from her. Everything she knows is returning to take their place and that is the best thing in the world.

Xaphan sets out towards the road. After a moment's silent conferring, they follow; Hayley trotting to keep up with the demon. Will and Karen are happy to walk behind her, arms around one another.

"What now?" Hayley says and Xaphan glances back at her.

"Now you go home. Your mother will be glad to see you. So will your father."

"Is that all we get?" Will mutters.

Xaphan halts and it's obvious by Will's face that he surprised himself by asking the question. Even so, he does not drop his gaze.

"Is that all we get?" he says again. "The things we've seen, the things this kid has gone through. . .I mean. . .how do we deal with it?"

Xaphan's final smile is gentle. The coldness is gone. "You'll forget. People always do."

"What?" Will says and Xaphan ignores the question.

"In the meantime, why don't you visit Dalry sometime? It's a nice place."

Xaphan falls into the ground. His coat billows out on the grass, then that is also gone. Will, Karen and Hayley are left with each other, with the grass and the cliffs and the sea. For long minutes, they stand over the spot where Xaphan vanished and they don't speak. The wind touches them, and the scent of salty water is fiercely strong. Below, waves strike land in regular beats and there is nothing in the world of demons or the vengeful dead. There is only the land, the sea, the air.

Hayley is the first to walk away. She heads to the road and the car, moving in slow steps; Karen takes Will's hand and they leave the grass and the cliffs and the sea. They leave the dead spaces and anything there might be in the worlds beyond the sea and land and air.

With each step, life welcomes them back again and again.

Epilogue

The young man turns just as the older man behind him knows he will. They face one another this evening in the dying sunlight, surrounded by people; drunken people, people going home, people walking into dank alleys with prostitutes. This is Dalry. This is beside the river and all life and death is here.

"Leaving my pub so soon?" the older man asks as if it is still daylight, and not gone nine o'clock.

"I apologise, sir," the other replies. "I have an early start and need my wits."

"I understand. You must be a conscientious young man. Your wife or sweetheart expects you?"

The younger man drops his gaze to his feet and it is clear why he has no wife. "No, not this night," he says.

"Then let us walk. It is warm and it will do an older soul such as I good to see the sights and hear the sounds of our city after dark."

They walk side by side and talk of the city, of the younger man's home life and the older man's public house beside the river and before long, they have left the streets and the people behind; they are a few minutes' walk from a woodland popular with men of their persuasion, a secret woodland, a mutual secret.

They walk towards it, not hand in hand, not out here where angry eyes might see and judge them for who they are. They walk towards the darkening woods and the older man has never felt so solid or alive or powerful, so ready to change the world with the simple action of knife to flesh.

My first, he thinks as they near the woodland.

And if there is a voice screaming from far below, a voice calling at him to stop, to turn around and leave this murder undone, to make everything right, a voice a tiny fraction louder than last time and the time before and the time before and back to the very first, then that voice is once again too far below for him to hear.

Lost in the light blazing like white fire in the pit.

About Your Author

Luke Walker has been writing horror, fantasy and dark thrillers for most of his life.

The dark fantasy Dead Sun is now available as are the horror Hometown and the short story collection Die Laughing. Upcoming novels include The Unredeemed, Ascent, The Dead Room and The Day Of The New Gods along with the novella The Mirror Of The Nameless. Several of his short stories have been published online and in magazines/books.

Luke welcomes comments at his blog which can be read at www.lukewalkerwriter.com

…and his Twitter page is @lukewalkerbooks.

Sign up to his newsletter at www.tinyletter.com/LukeWalkerWriter

While working on his tales, Luke has worked as a hospital orderly, in a record shop and in a library.

He is forty and lives in England with his wife and two cats.

Other HellBound Books Titles
Available at: www.hellboundbookspublishing.com

Them

Ray Sanders returns home from Florida to bury his mother.

Soon, the supernatural evidence behind his mother's demise begins to surface in the form of dreams and mysterious happenings.

During all of the madness, Sanders must face his destiny and vanquish the generations-old evil that has plagued his family since the 1800's...

In 1854, Louis Sanders, with the help of Elias Atkins, dug a well to provide water to the family farm. What they did not anticipate was the water to be infested with Odomulites - ancient sins. These malevolent beings - were trapped in our world on their way to the spirit world - formed a pact of protection with both Sanders and Atkins; the families would serve as guardians of the Odomulite nests and in return, a blind eye would be cast when the Odomulites took host bodies to inhabit and feed upon. It was this pact, which in 2016 would propel Sanders and Julie Fontaine - a young woman with a special connection to the Spirit World - into the heart of the last active nest to rid the town of its insidious Odomulite population.

Blood in The Woods

Based upon true events...

For Jody, growing up in the late eighties and early nineties in the small Louisiana town of Hammond with his best friend Jack was filled with wonderful childhood memories.

Time spent playing in the woods, shooting pellet guns, blowing up mailboxes, fighting at school and upon the dawning of interest in the fairer sex, their carefree lives typical of children with few responsibilities and no worries beyond the next pop-quiz or getting to second base. As they grow older together and experience the joys and pains of life, love, family and friendship, they uncover a grim secret that their home town has kept, and through little more than an innocent, idle curiosity, Jody and Jack stumble upon something horrific in the woods and their lives quickly take a most sinister and dangerous turn as they find themselves hunted by an unspeakable evil...

Southern House

"Move over Slenderman, there's a whole new reason to be afraid of the dark!"

There are some places that lie where the barrier between worlds is thin and growing thinner. These corridors are as old as the Earth itself, hidden in dark and forgotten places, waiting to be found. There is a being who stalks these places and travels between those worlds. He was given the name Mr. Shift by generations of children and madmen. Just as Hickory Grimble hits rock bottom, he inherits his grandparents' farm and believes his luck is changing. He soon finds he inherited more than money and land. Haunted by his own inner demons, now he has new problems. He begins to see strange creatures on the dark, sprawling acreage, animals that have no business living in middle Tennessee. He also discovers a decrepit, abandoned house in the forest that never seems to be in the same place twice. Balanced on a razor's edge between, addiction and fate, Hick is now face to face with an ancient evil that has returned once more to claim more of the town's children.

Worship Me

Something is listening to the prayers of St. Paul's United Church, but it's not the god they asked for; it's something much, much older.

A quiet Sunday service turns into a living hell when this ancient entity descends upon the house of worship and claims the congregation for its own.

The terrified churchgoers must now prove their loyalty to their new god by giving it one of their children or in two days time it will return and destroy them all.

As fear rips the congregation apart, it becomes clear that if they're to survive this untold horror, the faithful must become the faithless and enter into a battle against God itself.

But as time runs out, they discover that true monsters come not from heaven or hell…
…they come from within.

Demons, Devils and Denizens of Hell: Vol, 2

The second volume in HellBound Books' outstanding horror anthology fair teems with tales of Hades' finest citizens – both resident and vacationing in our earthly realm…

Compiled by the inimitable P. Mattern and featuring: Savannah Morgan, Andrew MacKay, Jaap Boekestein, James H Longmore, Stephanie Kelley, Ryan Woods, James Nichols, P. Mattern, Marcus Mattern, Gerri R Gray, and legion more…

Flanagan

From the author of *Tenebrion* and *'Pede...*

"Straw Dogs meets Fifty Shades - heart pounding, gut-wrenching, sexy as all hell and with a twist you'll never see coming!"

Meet the Sewells, your typical, all-American couple; happily married for ten years, respected high school teachers, still crazy about one another and with a secret, shared dark side.

During their annual Spring Break vacation to recharge their batteries and reconnect as a couple, they are waylaid by a perverse gang of misfits in the one horse, North Texas town of Flanagan.

Taken hostage as the focus of the gang's twisted games, the Sewells are brutalized into performing increasingly vicious physical, sexual and emotional acts upon one another, until events take an unexpected turn - triggered by an unintentional death.

As their circumstance descends into the worse nightmare imaginable, the Sewells find themselves involved in an altogether different situation...

Luke Walker

A HellBound Books LLC Publication

http://www.hellboundbookspublishing.com

Printed in the United States of America

www.ingramcontent.com/pod-product-compliance
Lightning Source LLC
Chambersburg PA
CBHW050613170726

48283CB00001B/221